The Seventh Child of Nod

The Seventh Child of Nod

by
Eula Youngblood

codex

Quartz Hill, California

Codex is the Fiction Imprint of Quartz Hill Publishing House
which is the publishing arm of Quartz Hill School of Theology,
a ministry of Quartz Hill Community Church
43543 51st Street West · Quartz Hill, CA 93536
www.theology.edu
info@theology.edu

CHAPTER I

At five in the morning fifteen year old Esmeralda awakened, chilled and trembling in the apartment of her sister Leticia and brother-in-law Leroy, on Woodcrest Ave in Los Angeles. She slept in one of those pop-up hanging beds that swung around on the back of a closet door in the dining room. The weather was fairly nice for early November, but the nights could cast a chill that caused a sleeper to snuggle comfortably beneath the blanket.

There wasn't much that Esmeralda could see in the darkened room except the hutch and folded table that had been pushed to one side so that the bed could flip down easily. She breathed deeply and trembled trying to shake off the fall chill, and she wrapped the blanket tightly around her shoulders.

She had awakened halfway between dream and reality and not yet able to shake off the horror of her nightmare. She groped for the small lamp near the bed, making sweeping movements with her arm to find the cord which would banish the darkness. But her hand clutched empty air and her panic rose.

Half paralyzed with fright, she called out to her brother: "Clarence!" It was the sound of her own cries that awakened her and brought her back to reality only a little less a horror than the world of nightmare. She had just lain back on the bed when her sister and brother-in-law ran into the room and turned on the light. Her trembling slowly subsided and she felt the wetness of a tear on her face.

"What the hell is wrong with you?" Leticia asked with surprise and impatience, a loaded .38 pistol in her hand. "I thought someone had broken in."

1

"I'm..... I had a bad.... I thought I was with Clarence and someone had attacked him and me." Esmeralda felt embarrassed as she watched the way Leroy was eying her cleavage, and she wrapped the sheet about her chest.

"Well, you are not with Clarence any more; you're with me, and I don't want to hear your cock-a-mammy stories about God calling you to service, and everywhere you go, men are always trying to abuse you sexually. Just remember what I told you before!"

How can I forget a horrible threat like that? The yelling and the loaded gun in my face while she yelled that if I cause problems between her and her husband, I'd surely pay with my life.

Esmeralda knew she'd have to cope with her fears and nightmares alone, with the absence of her brother Clarence's gentle explanations.

"You've moved from pillar to post, always got yourself into trouble by seducing men. As you said they attacked you. I believe that like I believe this table is going to get up and run off. These lies won't stand up here," Leticia waved the gun around as Esmeralda cowered, and Leroy grinned boyishly.

"I'm going to work later, but Leroy doesn't have a Pullman Porter run until tomorrow. Since you have no classes today, I expect to find this apartment sparkling when I get home. There's a grocery list on the sink, and a roast thawing. Make that Yankee pot roast I like so much. Watch yourself, little tramp!" Leticia punched the child's shoulder hard with the barrel of the pistol.

What did I get myself into? I was better off staying with grandma and my uncles. All I had to do was stay out of the way when my uncles entertained. They were always so afraid their men friends would prefer me to them. Cinderella didn't have it any worse than I do. Oh, God, where is the end of this trouble? Help me find a safe place to live, and I can cope with the studies, and ministry you have de-

signed for me.

Esmeralda loved her sister and thought she was very pretty despite her bitter disposition. The girls were Negroid, but Leticia was fairer than Esmeralda, a pale pumpkin yellow color, with extremely curly hair, and light brown eyes. Although petite, she had shoulders that were too large for her tiny hips; she was shaped like a boy.

Esmeralda, on the other hand, was darker, silky black hair, and expressive green eyes. Her tiny waist was small which accented her figure. She did not have the typical looks that would win a beauty contest, but she didn't appear to be Negroid, and had the kind of physical development that caused women's heads to turn enviously, and men with dishonorable intentions to pursue her forcibly. Her father had labeled her when she was pre-teenage as being sinfully seductive.

It had been over six months since Leticia had threatened Esmeralda with the gun the first time, but she could still hear her voice angrily shouting at her and could feel the stirring indignation within as she remembered facing her sister again and the horrible smirk on Leroy's face.

Before long, everyone was dressed, and Leticia was off to work. Esmeralda had washed the breakfast dishes, swept, mopped, and waxed the floors. The pot roast that her sister had requested was already in the oven, and she had dusted the dining and living rooms, and sat down in the breakfast nook to work on math problems for school.

She was interrupted when she looked up into Leroy's eyes. Intently studying, she hadn't noticed him there. She was shocked at what she read in his make-up, and was speechless. Leroy stood before her nude, his private part stiffened, and a strange grin on his face.

Esmeralda looked around for an escape route, but there was none. She felt trapped. No way out of the breakfast nook. Leroy was all over her: his hands on her breast, and his Listerine over cat litter breath was heaving heavily upon

3

her face. He was trying to find her lips.

"Oh, my God," she yelled, and she imagined she heard her sister's threats. She knew that her only option was fight and flight. She reached down to his genitals, and with her finger nails ripped upwards, taking skin, hair, and blood with her. When Leroy fell back away from her, she kicked him as hard as she could in the same area he was trying to nurse, and he slumped helplessly to the floor.

Leroy's screams brought the landlord from the next apartment while the injured man lay grimacing on the floor in a pool of blood.

"What's the problem here, Mr. Shaw?" The landlord asked.

"This little tramp tried to tear my privates off!"

"What are you doing in here without your clothes?" He made a quick assessment of the situation, noticed the opened schoolbooks, and Esmeralda cowering against the wall.

"That witch attacked me."

"Yeah, right. Now you get dressed; I'll drive you to the doctor." Leroy ran off down the hall stooped over, as Esmeralda washed her hands in the kitchen sink.

"Are you all right, miss?" the landlord asked.

"Yes, sir; but I can't stay here. I'm turning the roast down to 250, packing my things, and getting out of here."

"Where will you go, child?"

"I haven't had enough time to think about that yet, but it can't be here.

*   *   *

Esmeralda searched apartment listings one after the other, only to have the door slammed in her face or was told lies that the place had been rented. Sometimes she faced dirty old men that looked at her the way her brother-in-law had. By the end of the third day, she was tired, de-

4

cided to rest at the Westwood Shopping Center, and maybe get a bite to eat, before curling up in her van for another night.

Weary from her search for lodging, Esmeralda sat on the white bench in front of Clifton's Cafeteria in the Westwood Shopping Center. Even though she had not eaten since early morning, the aroma of palatable foods permeating the air played no part in improving her mood or stimulating her appetite.

Night was only a whisper away, and the thought of sleeping in her van again was not an acceptable action she wanted to entertain. It wasn't from the lack of funds that had caused her to be homeless. It was the late forties, her fifteen year old status, belonging to the Negro race, and her need to escape sexual deviates like her brother-in-law.

Esmeralda's mind drifted to recall her beginning; she could not stop the rivers of tears and choking sounds from her throat. There were times when she thought that if she could gain a lot of weight, men would leave her alone for she always believed her sins had almost caused her brother Clarence's death.

At that moment of emotional breakdown, Phyllis and Ian Raven exited the Clifton Cafeteria, talking casually about the case they'd been working on. They were an attractive, white middle-aged couple, who appeared to be extremely educated. By the time they reached the bench where Esmeralda was seated, a slight disagreement had ensued between them about the outcome they felt should've been chosen.

Ian noticed that Phyllis was no longer following along with him but had trailed off towards the young girl seated on the bench, crying. Phyllis went over to embrace the girl hoping to console her. She found the child cold as ice and her teeth chattering. After all, it was November, and heaven only knew how long the girl had been sitting there alone, cold, and probably hungry. By this time, Ian had joined them with many questions on his mind.

"What is your name?" Phyllis asked

"My name is Esmeralda Wilkins," the young girl whispered, her voice jerking from the flood of convulsive tears and the upsurge of a late fall chilling wind.

Phyllis told Esmeralda that they were both lawyers and had stopped to grab a bite to eat before going home.

"Where do you live?" Ian asked.

"No place," Esmeralda quickly replied but thought that she should not have said that for she was just fifteen and this couple might think she was a run-away. They could force her to return home and submit to her sister's husband, she thought. *No way, I'll die first. I'll kill him if he puts his hands on me again,* she thought.

Ian put his hand on her shoulders, stating: "We want to help you, child. You can't stay here all night; they lock the mall up and will probably take you to jail."

"Besides, it's getting awfully cold," Phyllis said.

Esmeralda closed her eyes and leaned back as though she was trying to understand what she should do next. As she sat there with her eyes closed and tears streaming down her face, she thought she heard the angel that had always guided her when she felt that things were hopeless: *Trust in the Lord with all thine heart, and lean not unto thine own understanding. In all thy ways acknowledge Him, and He shall direct thy path.*

She opened her eyes and then wiped them with the back of her hands thinking out loud: "Can this be my guiding angel sending you folks to rescue me? Please don't play mean jokes on me."

"This is no joke; we want you to come home with us tonight. Tomorrow is Saturday; we need to be in the office briefly but will be home soon, and then we can figure out what to do with you," Ian told her.

Encouraged, Esmeralda stood up and smiled at her benefactors as they both hugged her, and led the way out of the Center. But they were not going in the direction where Esmeralda had her van parked, and she halted for a moment.

Phyllis was holding the child's hand and felt the tug when she stopped walking willingly. "What's the matter, Esmeralda?"

"The van where I've been sleeping is parked over this way," she said, pointing in the direction where she'd left the van.

Ian told Phyllis to go with the child after he'd inquired about the van's owner and was told that it belonged to Esmeralda. It was the way she was able to get around and take her important items and equipment with her. Even though the couple had many questions, they thought they'd better leave them for later for fear the girl would refuse to go with them.

Even though Phyllis held Esmeralda's hand as they walked through the Center parking lot and to the van, she thought it would be best not to say all the things she had in mind until she could gain the girl's confidence.

When they came to the van, Phyllis paused and embraced Esmeralda, kissing her cold cheeks tenderly. She noticed that the girl's muscles tightened from surprise and apprehensiveness, then pulled away.

"Please forgive me," Phyllis pleaded. "I've always had a secret desire to have a daughter, and you remind me of that fantasy."

"You don't have children?" Esmeralda inquired with surprise.

"Yes, we have one son," Phyllis answered. "I lost two babies; one was a girl. Please don't mention this to my husband; I'm supposed to be over this desire to have a daughter. I allowed my maternal instincts to control my reasoning."

"It's alright," Esmeralda said smiling and gently touched Phyllis's arm.

7

"Do you mind if I drive?" Phyllis asked. "From here, there are a lot of turns, and it will be easier for me to make them instead of trying to explain them to you."

Again, Esmeralda smiled as she handed the keys to Phyllis. She thought it was good to see the girl smile. She was so beautiful with those nature-painted lips and perfect teeth. Even little dimples spread open momentarily.

When the courtesy lights illuminated the late model Chevy van, Phyllis paused to observe the builders' tools and other supplies stored in the back, but thought she'd better not push her luck with questions. Esmeralda saw the puzzling look on Phyllis's face but decided it was too soon to explain. Besides, who'd believe her anyway?

It was indeed a lot of turns to travel the five miles to the Ravin's home, but their destination was finally accomplished. It was an area of Los Angeles close to Brentwood. The homes were upper middle class, neat but some badly in need of repair. Esmeralda's assessment of the area was a retirement community of aging Jewish families who'd lived here all of their lives, and the only other place for them to go would be a rest home environment.

Phyllis pulled the van into the overgrown driveway in a jerking motion when she came to a stop behind the Mercedes that her husband was standing behind, and then he leaped to safety into the flower bed. Phyllis climbed out of the van laughing.

"I thought I'd better run for safety," Ian said,

"I haven't driven a stick shift since we were courting. Are you all right, Esmeralda?"

"I'm sure I've lived through worse than that. The driving was OK; it was the stops that sort of shook us up."

"Get your bag, sweetheart. I'm sure you'll want to freshen up," Phyllis stated.

When the trio entered the house, Esmeralda noticed that it was not really dirty but just cluttered and dusty. Curtains and drapes were fading, and the tiled floors were badly in need of wax.

"You take her upstairs, Phyllis, and I'll make a pot of coffee," Ian said.

"Come with me, Esmeralda. I'll show you where to put your things and where you can freshen up."

Esmeralda was led upstairs to a room with pink ruffled bedspread and curtains and a set of white French provincial furniture with several stuffed animals on the bed. She noticed that Phyllis seemed embarrassed with the toys lying around, and she wanted to put her at ease. She picked up one of the stuffed animals and hugged it tightly. "I've always loved stuffed animals."

Phyllis seemed pleased with Esmeralda's acceptance of her 'little girl' fantasy and she moved quickly to show her the bathroom. "You'll have to share this bathroom with our son."

Esmeralda noticed that the door from her room opened into the co-ed bath and another door in the bathroom opened into her son's room. The bathroom was badly in need of cleaning care. The soap scum in the bathtub needed to be scraped off, and the toilet was also in need of serious cleaning. Even dirty underwear was still on the bathroom floor.

"I'm afraid my son is not too neat, but he goes to work so early and returns very late."

"What kind of work does he do?" Esmeralda asked.

"He's a doctor," Phyllis answered.

Esmeralda ran her fingers across her mouth as though she was trying to keep her thought from sounding out loud. *Good Lord! I hope he never doctors on me. I can't believe how sterile they are at the office or hospital but sloppy at home.*

"He's not married?" Esmeralda asked.

"He was married to a selfish bitch who nearly destroyed him," Phyllis snapped. "He spent three years in the navy trying to get his life together. Now he hates women. I guess I'll never be a grandmother," Phyllis said sadly.

"I'm so sorry," Esmeralda stated, squeezing Phyllis's hand sympathetically.

"It's not your fault, child. I hope you will find it in your heart to stay with us. Now, you make yourself pretty, and join us in the kitchen for coffee or tea. It's not like you could make yourself any prettier than you already are." She touched Esmeralda's golden brown cheek and left the room.

Despite the untidy bathroom, the warm shower was exactly what Esmeralda needed. The spraying water running through her hair and down her face and body, gave her new energy and vitality. Even the fog in her brain seemed to have left. She looked down at the swirling gray water running around her feet, then down the drain. Wiggling her toes, she wondered if she'd get some sort of fungus; but for now she accepted the good feeling of finally having a good bath after several days.

She turned the water to a cooler temperature and higher intensity, and she thought she saw a rainbow spraying against the walls of the ceramic tiles. A sense of peace flooded her soul.

CHAPTER II

The tired, overweight and aging doctor stood in the doorway of the private office where the name on the door read Philip I. Ravin, M.D. For a few moments, the old doctor watched the young doctor working, reading reports, looking at x-rays, and writing on charts. Young Dr. Ravin appeared tired for he rolled his head backwards, massaged his neck with his hand, and exercised his shoulders several times.

His crew cut hair, white long sleeved over starched shirt, black tie, black pants, and shinny Navy shoes made this young doctor appear older than his 28 years. He felt that someone was watching him, and he slowly lifted his red strained eyes to see his boss there. "Dr. Beckman, I didn't see you standing here. Is there something I can do for you?"

"Dr. Ravin, you do more than your share already. It's going to be my pleasure to turn my practice over to you. For now, son, you go home and get some rest for we have a big day tomorrow. Oh, oh. I am getting old, for tomorrow is Saturday, isn't it?' he laughed.

"I'll be going home in a moment, Dr. Beckman. I just wanted to take another look at the Kennedy child's x-rays."

"You will take rounds this weekend?" Dr. Beckman asked.

"Yes sir, I'll be happy to do it."

"Then, I'll be getting home now; Harriett always worry when I'm late for supper. Good night, Dr. Ravin."

"Good night, Dr. Beckman."

It felt good to hear Dr. Beckman call him doctor. He was such an excellent surgeon, so well liked, and respected. He watched the old doctor walk slowly out of the office.

The nurses and receptionist had long since left, and now it was quiet and peaceful, and he had time to think about his future. Would he ever be able to measure up to Dr. Beckman's reputation? Men, women and children alike seemed to glow when this man entered the room. He had such charisma and bedside manners. He knew he'd have a long way to go.

He was a bit worried about Dr. Beckman's health for he had only recently taken the State Board examination and felt that he was not fully ready to run a medical practice as lucrative and established as this one. He'd studied hard and sacrificed long, but most doctors have to wait for years to get what he'd accomplished is this short time. He was in no way ready to go home, either. His mother had a professional practice of her own, and the house would feel cold and empty.

What the hell is wrong with you, Philip? he thought. *You are no child, and your mother had the right to pursue her own career.* Besides, she had no choice now because his divorce from Annette had caused him all of the inheritance that Grandpa Ravin had set aside for him, and most of the fortune that his parents had accumulated.

How could he have been so naïve? Why couldn't he have seen what his friends saw in Annette. He wanted so badly to be married like Joe, and Marty. He could remember how alone he felt as a small boy. He was alone a lot while his mother worked. His parents did their best to give him what he needed, but as a picked-on child he needed more. Only his two best friends stood by him.

Dr. Martin Heller, who was now professor of clinical psychology at UCLA, and Dr. Joel Markowitz, now practicing at Cedars in OB/GYN, were both there for him. They were two years older and watched over him.

School was a snap for him, and he graduated at sixteen. But why not, he had nothing else to do but stay inside and study. If Joel or Marty wasn't around, the kids naturally would pick on him, beat him up, or call him hurtful names. Instead of Philip, they'd call him Phyllis the cream puff sissy, Christ killer, or "you clipped us" tree, instead of Eucalyptus tree. He hated being named after his mother, and he hated being Jewish.

He felt that a cup of coffee would give him the pickup that he needed now, so he got up and walked out to the coffee stand. What a disappointment it was to find the coffee pot empty, everything washed, and put away. He felt so all alone. He remembered how alone he felt as a small boy. He was alone a lot while his mother worked.

That pain was always swollen inside his chest and stomach as a child, and now he felt that same pain again. Was something about to happen? Why was he dreading to go home? Why was a man his age still living at home with his parents? he thought. His friends had their own homes and families. Oh, God, how he love to be a father with his own kids, but in order to be a father, he'd need a woman. How he hated a relationship with some selfish ass female. The thought made him shudder with disgust.

He looked at his desk clock that read 8:15 p.m. If nothing else, he needed to go home, take a shower, and get some sleep, for he did not feel hungry. Never having relied on prayer, he had only his instinct to guide him. Yes, he'd had a Bar Mitzvah, but he never understood what it was all about. In his home, he'd never really celebrated the high holy days or went to Temple other than a wedding.

*   *   *

Philip looked back at the three story building from which he'd just left, before entering his 1948 Fleet Master Business Coupe and began his drive home. As he drove along the empty streets, he felt a need to be close to God or some Divine Spirit that could help him deal with the pain he was feeling inside.

"Oh, God, help me," he whispered. Even though it was

warm inside the car, his fingers were cold, and his forehead was damp with perspiration. He reached to wipe his brow with his sleeve. "Maybe I'm corning down with a cold," he mumbled.

As he drove along the boulevard, he noticed several restaurants with the operation lights still on. "Oh, yes, it's malnutrition. I haven't eaten since early morning." He really didn't want to stop for food for he was much too tired to get out of his car.

"There must be canned soup or a frozen pie. That'll be enough," he thought. He remembered purchasing some frozen beef and chicken pot pies at the market sometime in the last few weeks. Surely he hadn't eaten them all. "Damn, what the hell is wrong with me?"

Finally reaching the driveway of his parents home, he wondered who the van belonged to. Maybe his folks had guests, but he didn't remember anyone who drove a van. He got out of his car, and thoroughly examined the van before turning off his headlamps. "No clue," he thought. Building tools. Maybe his parents were planning to do some remodeling.

Satisfied that he'd figured the puzzle out, he unlocked the front door and entered the house. Hearing voices in the kitchen, he stopped to thumb through the mail lying on the hall tree desk at the entrance. He wanted time to figure out who was there and why they were visiting. Without appearing to be prying.

He heard his mother call out to him: "Philip, is that you?"

"Yes, Mom," he answered.

"Come in here, please. I want you to meet someone," she yelled.

When Dr. Ravin reached the kitchen where his parents were entertaining Esmeralda, his bluish/gray intimidating eyes met and locked with her frightened green eyes; she felt the resentment penetrating her insights, and she trembled at

14

the sight of him and thought of running away. Phyllis noticed her apprehensiveness and reached out to take her hands.

"It's alright, child, this is our son Philip."

"Who is this?" Philip asked impatiently.

"This is Esmeralda. We found her in the shopping center crying and alone."

"Dad, did you go along with this insanity?"

"We couldn't leave her out there alone at night. Do you realize what could've happened to her?"

"She's only a child," Philip continued. "And a problem child. Did you stop to think of kidnapping laws, abduction, accusations of rape? For God sake, Dad, you and mom are lawyers; you're supposed to know all this. How old is she anyway?"

Phyllis spoke up in defense of the girl: "She's fifteen and will have a Master's degree in Architectural Engineering in June. She is the author of several novels, two teleplays and numerous songs."

"She's a dreamer, or a big liar," Philip said. "What school would issue a Master's Degree to someone 15 years old?" Philip asked doubtfully. "And whose van is that out there? She can't get a license to drive at 15—a learner's permit maybe."

"She said she's attending UCLA," Ian said with skepticism.

"That can be checked out easily. If that school had someone so astute attending there, Marty would surely know about it. Let's call him now." Philip said. He dialed the phone, waited for it to be answered, and when a woman's voice came over the wire, he asked to speak to Marty.

"Evelyn, this is Philip; let me speak to Marty please." He heard Marty's firm voice on the phone, and he began his inquiry. "Marty, we've got an unusual situation here. My parents brought home a stray, runaway girl who said

15

she is a 15 year old graduate student at UCLA." He paused while Marty asked several questions.

"Yeah, she said that she's fifteen... I guess so. Yes... she's very pretty and has green eyes.... OK, her name just happens to be Esmeralda, he replied. What do you mean Negro? East Indian, Mexican, or something else, but she doesn't look Negroid. OK, I'll see you shortly." He hung up the phone, appearing sorry, but not apologizing.

"What did Marty say?" Phyllis asked.

"She's a student in one of his classes and also a patient due to the abuse she's suffered mainly by her own family."

For several moments, no one said anything, but watched as the tears rolled down the cheeks of the frightened young girl sitting across the table. Philip apologized to his parents by pouring them another cup of coffee, before pouring his own as well. He offered to pour Esmeralda a cup but she turned it down. He noticed that she had an empty potpie dish in front of her, and he stared at it hungrily.

Realizing that Philip must be hungry by the way he looked at the food tray, Phyllis told him that there were two more pies in the oven.

Eating the food as though he'd not eaten for a week, Philip gobbled down every crumb, paying little attention to the three other people sitting at the table. Esmeralda noticed the crude way he ate, and the way he held his fork. Not only was he rude and impolite, but he had absolutely no table manners. He reminded her of the beast in the fable "Beauty and the Beast," and he looked older than his father, she thought.

The family made small talk, trying not to ask the many questions they had for Esmeralda, for fear of upsetting her even more than she already was. Except for occasional shoptalk, most of their wait was in uneasy silence.

Ian turned to Philip and asked: "How was your day, son?"

"Busy as usual, but I worry about Dr. Beckman. He has a minor heart problem and is getting on in age.

Esmeralda couldn't imagine Dr. Ravin worrying about anyone. He didn't have a sympathetic drop of blood in his veins. She noticed that Philip was taking quick glances at her. He wanted to apologize but felt that if he did, he'd let his guard down, the barrier that he'd set up between himself and all women.

Finally the doorbell rang, and Philip went to answer it. Momentarily, he returned with Dr. Heller following close behind. He was a 30 year old, with brown eyes and hair, and he appeared to be extremely mature and self assured. When Esmeralda saw him, she ran into his arms, crying. "I couldn't take any more. I'd rather die first," she said.

Taking her gently in his arms, Dr. Heller pleaded for her to stay calm: "Calm down, child, just tell me what happened."

Crying convulsively, she began her story: "He was all over me with no clothes on, pawing, and trying to kiss me, with his...er...you know...he had...."

"Are you trying to tell me he had an erection?" Dr. Heller asked, finishing the sentence that Esmeralda had trouble saying.

"Yes he did," Esmeralda said. "The last time I told my sister about him, she threatened me with a gun and called me dirty names. She also said that mama and daddy didn't want another girl, and I should've died at birth, or better still, should never been born for I'm nothing but trouble."

Trouble, how true that is, Philip thought.

Dr. Heller asked the girl to sit down, and Philip brought another chair from the dining room as he tried to put the girl's mind at ease. "It is not true that you are a problem, a mystery perhaps, but certainly not a problem. Your parents just couldn't understand how they could've had such a precocious child. You have a gift that is far too advanced for even men in my profession to truly understand. You've mastered four years of college and almost two years of Grad. School at fifteen. That is why we have assigned you to Para-psychology. We want to find out what makes brains like yours tick. Your engineering professor told me that the house you designed and built has gained national acclaim in Architectural Digest."

"Doctor, I just want the pain inside to go away. My father said that it was my fault that white man was dead in Georgia, and my brother almost got killed. He said if I was not so sinfully seductive it wouldn't have happened."

"You can't go through life blaming yourself because sick grown men with children of their own decide to violate someone else's child. That idiot tried to rape you when you were just a baby. Your brother did the right thing. That bastard deserved to die," Dr. Heller said with determination.

"I have no place to go. What's going to become of me now?"

Dr. Heller patted her hand gently to reassure her. "The Ravins will take good care of you. I'll vouch for that."

"But their son said they could get in trouble for kidnapping a minor. I don't want to cause anyone problems," Esmeralda cried.

Dr. Heller searched the eyes of the Ravins for confirmation before speaking. "I'll see that the county awards custody to them. As my patient, I have records of child abuse by your family members that I will give to the social services department. Now don't you worry; I'll take care of everything. Yes, even your new foster brother, here." He gently punched Philip in the midriff, smiling.

Shaking hands with three adults and hugging Esmeralda, Dr. Heller said good night, leaving Esmeralda alone with her apprehensions and fears, and so was Philip.

CHAPTER III

E smeralda had read many books. A good many of them were about prayer and Bible lessons. Often, she returned to some of these books when she needed guidance about how best to pray for a certain person or a troubling situation.

The long night reading and awaken hours had left her more tired than she could remember ever feeling before. Naturally, she wanted to make a good impression on her new family, so she was dressed early. She wanted to be out of the unity bathroom before Dr. Ravin awakened so she tiptoed quietly to the bathroom and around her room.

This morning she concluded her devotional time early, but remembered family, friends and social concerns. She was suddenly stopped by a voice that spoke aloud: "Pray for the deepening of this relationship with your new family."

Esmeralda had been reminded by this inner voice that she had been planted there by God Himself. What did he have in store for her? She was also reminded that Jesus had promised the Holy Spirit would continue to be present and active in our lives, communicating to us messages meant specifically for us from God. He had spoken, and she needed to understand all that this voice was telling her. She knew too well that it is good to both hope and wait on the Lord, for He will not cast off forever.

Walking quietly down the stairs and into the kitchen, she searched for items to prepare for breakfast. The coffee pot needed washing from last night's usage so she washed it, found the coffee, and started the coffee brewing. In the refrigerator chiller drawer, she found a pound of bacon. *Hum, bacon? I thought they didn't eat pork. Oh well, what*

19

do I know?

She placed the bacon in a pan with a half cup of water to boil out some of the salt and fats. There were no eggs, but she did find oatmeal, milk, a half loaf of rye bread and a can of sliced peaches.

Washing the kitchen table, she set four places, opened the peaches, and carefully divided them into four small dishes. Next, she placed four cereal bowls, spoons, sugar, milk, and napkins on the table. She found some small juice glasses and poured four glasses of orange juice at each place setting. Rinsing and drying the bacon, she started it frying. She removed and set aside the ready oatmeal and placed four slices of bread on the toaster rack.

The aroma of the bacon and coffee took Ian and Phyllis by surprise. With their robed-clad bodies, they took the stairs about the same time. "That sure smells good," Ian said.

"I hope Esmeralda doesn't plan on spoiling us," Phyllis teased, as she followed Ian into the kitchen.

As the senior Ravins raced for the kitchen, Dr. Ravin was in close pursuit, but fully dressed. They were all surprised to see the good looking fixings prepared for them.

"Can I help?" Phyllis asked eager to assist.

"It's ready; please, sit," Esmeralda said, then finished with a friendly "Good morning."

Phyllis and Ian both spoke in unison: "Good morning." As Esmeralda dished up the oatmeal, she served the toast and bacon, and set the milk close. Dr. Ravin began to eat before Esmeralda could finish serving. She finally sat down, bowed her head, and closed her eyes reverently. The family stopped to stare at her and then continued eating only after she'd poured milk on her oatmeal.

"This bacon is so good. Where'd you get it?" Phyllis asked.

"It was in the refrigerator," Esmeralda said.

"I don't remember buying bacon that taste this good."

"I par-boiled it to remove some of the preservatives," Esmeralda explained.

"An excellent idea. I'll have to remember that," Ian said.

Although timid, Esmeralda decided she'd ask about her share of the household load. "If you don't mind, I'd like to prepare the meals, so you don't have to stop out at a restaurant all the time. I know how to cook healthy foods, and I don't mind paying for it as my share of the expenses here."

Philip looked at Esmeralda and then at the faces of his parents to see what their answers would be. When they said they'd be delighted to have her prepare the meals, Philip pushed his empty bowl away from his setting, stood up, kissed his mother, and shook his father's hand, before strolling out without a single word.

Noticing the way Esmeralda stared at Dr. Ravin, Phyllis attempted to explain why he seemed so rude. "Esmeralda, Philip has been deeply hurt. Please don't let his attitude get the best of you."

Esmeralda watched Dr. Ravin leave and thought to herself. *Now there's a man who is hurting inside perhaps more than I am. He is one who needs my prayers.*

Ian felt a need to explain his son and put Esmeralda's mind at ease. "He doesn't mean to be rude. I'm sure that he will get used to you," he promised.

Emeralds knew she should keep quiet where Dr. Ravin was concerned. She could see in his parents' eyes how much they loved their son and how much he loved them. She didn't want to do anything to alienate her new family at this point.

Actually, Esmeralda was practicing what could be called benign neglect. Sometimes we ignore the cries of the poor and suffering, and those with emotional pain. They make us uncomfortable. But to ignore these people, is to do them harm, she thought.

21

God's word says that we should love others as we love ourselves. It was going to be difficult to love Philip, for the wedge that he'd driven deep beneath himself and women in general was going to be hard to remove. He wanted it there. He wanted nothing to stand in the way of his work. Nor did he want another relationship with a woman. These insecurities were revealed in his face, eyes, and even the way he dressed and ate.

The coming week was thanksgiving, and school was out for Esmeralda. There were faculty conferences on Monday and Tuesday, but naturally Wednesday through Saturday was holiday time.

Esmeralda thought that this time alone would give her the time to clean up the Ravin home in order. Jewish people celebrated Thanksgiving, so she'd prepare a festive dinner after she cleaned the house

Working diligently, Esmeralda cleaned the kitchen, the bathrooms, living room and dining room. She washed the crisscrossed curtains in the dining room, and the dull yellowish gray returned to a brilliant white. She washed windows that she could reach and then pulled out her portable sewing machine. Finding a piece of kitchen curtain fabric in her van, she sewed curtains to replace the greasy, torn ones that hung over the breakfast nook.

After washing the kitchen windows, she hung the freshly made kitchen curtains. She had already cleaned the stove and put the pot roast on more than an hour ago; she remembered that she needed floor wax and left the house by the kitchen door leaving it unlocked for she had no key.

One will never know why Dr. Ravin felt the urge to go home earlier than usual, and he arrived in the driveway only a few moments before his parents. They were all amazed when they unlocked the front door to behold the change in the downstairs rooms. Everything looked so fresh and clean, and the aroma coming from the kitchen was tantalizing. Turning around, they almost stumbled over each other when they realized they could finally see through the cleaned windows and freshened drapes. They all stopped to look at the unusual and beautiful place settings in the dining room for they hadn't eaten in there for years.

Esmeralda had prepared tender flaky biscuits, Yankee pot roast, a tossed salad and peach cobbler. She had found the wine cellar, chilled a Cabernet wine, and placed three crystal wine glasses on the table. "Dinner will be ready to serve as soon as you've washed," Esmeralda announced.

"Who can wait to wash?" Ian said, and he and Phyllis washed in the kitchen sink. Dr. Ravin washed in the guest bathroom near the entrance. Esmeralda brought out the chilled salad and dressing while Ian poured the wine in three glasses. The fourth glass had iced water with lemon.

"No wine for the chef?" Ian asked.

"No, thank you, sir," Esmeralda answered.

Phyllis gently punched Ian's shoulder, reminding him: "She's too young, Ian."

All during dinner, Esmeralda was quiet as Ian, and Phyllis complemented her on the work she'd done. "Where'd you get the curtains in the kitchen?" Phyllis asked.

"I made them. I design clothes sometimes, and the fabric was in my van."

"So you sewed them with your fingers?" Dr. Ravin asked condescendingly.

Aware of his skepticism, Esmeralda explained: "I made the curtains. I design clothes, and the fabric was in my van.

Dr. Ravin continued to torment Esmeralda by asking: "Did you make them by hand?"

"I have a portable sewing machine in the van would. Would you like me to go get it?" she asked with impatience.

"No, I don't want you to go get the machine, but explain how a fifteen year old can own and drive a new van?

You can't get a driver's license."

"I will not dignify your question with an answer."

Phyllis could tell that Esmeralda was growing tired of her son's inquiries and decided to take charge of the situation. "Why don't we sit and enjoy this delicious and delightful dinner that Esmeralda has worked so hard to make for us?"

Esmeralda took quick glances at the Dr. Ravin who was snorting his food down, shoving it into his mouth with both hands. She remembered a project she'd had in her psychology class that described a young boy who ate the way that Philip did.

This young boy was ten years old and had watched one of his brothers gunned down by gang violence, a teenage sister who died at home in childbirth, his parents arrested for drug usage, and another brother being hauled away in handcuffs for attempted murder.

She wanted to put her arms around Dr. Ravin, and hear him pour his hurt out to her. Maybe there would be something in their communication exchange that could open this door. Why hadn't Dr. Heller helped him? *I know it is unethical for friends, or families to practice medicine on their own, but if someone else did it, and the word got out, it could be the end of Dr. Ravin's career. People just don't understand that emotional or mental illness is no different than a breakdown of physical body. For now, we'll just have to wait and see.*

Ian noticed how deeply Esmeralda was in thought and decided to interrupt her thoughts: "What's for dinner tomorrow?"

"We are having leftovers. A vegetable beef soup made from the stew we are having today with cornbread, a tossed salad, and the rest of the dessert."

"Sounds good to me," Ian said. "By the way, how much did you spend on this meal?"

"It was not much. I got the roast from the Calorie

24

Counter; my uncle is head chef there. I want to contribute to the expenses. I have money; I'm just too young to live alone."

"You mean to tell me that Booker T. is your uncle?" Phyllis asked.

"Yes, ma'am. He is my father's youngest brother. I used to live with him, and my uncle Al and grandmother, but my staying there was not conducive to their life style. They always thought I was chasing after their male friends. I think my uncles are homosexuals."

"We now know what one uncle does, but what does Uncle Al do?" Phyllis asked?"

Uncle Alger is a musical arranger for Metro Goldwin Meyers and a private tutor for up and coming young musical personalities. He has trained some very established musicians.

"Why do you think your uncles are homosexuals?" Dr. Ravin asked.

"In life, we become whatever the choices we make earlier on, sometimes influenced by those family members or friends we emanate or hate. My grandfather was murdered when these uncles were not much more than toddlers. There were six sons, and my grandmother had to make a living for them the best she could on a farm. So she became an expensive prostitute and educated three of her six sons. They all hated her."

"So you think this might've been the reason for your uncle's life style?" Ian asked.

"Unequivocally. Pardon my grammar, but God don't make no junk! Homosexuality is a situation of the mind where someone is seeking some kind of band aid to cover the hurt or anger inside, not realizing that the choices they make are not correcting the problems, but intensifying them, and tearing down the mind and physical body. Many of our illnesses are caused by our psychosomatic determinations."

Phyllis looked at Esmeralda, shaking her head in disbelief. "Child, you amaze me. You sound so grown up."

"There, you've hit the nail on the head for one of my problems. I am a child with a grownup's mind and that makes me a misfit. I don't belong with the kids my age, and those who are my equal mentally are too old for me.

No one had anything to say after this presentation. They all needed time to absorb all that Esmeralda had just said. They wanted to sift it, categorize it, and try to think of a response that would be appropriate.

During the brief pensive pause, Esmeralda managed enough courage to as a question: "May I make a thanksgiving dinner?"

Dr. Ravin was first to respond: "Only if I can invite my boss and his wife. Their son was killed in the Korean conflict, and they are getting along in age and are alone."

Surprised that he'd spoken directly to her in a semi-pleasant tone; Esmeralda stared at him for a moment and then turn her attention to Phyllis for a final answer.

"A holiday dinner is a lot of work, and Thanksgiving is just a couple of days away," Phyllis said with reservations.

"I don't mind the work. My uncle Booker taught me how to prepare meals without it being laborious, and I can get everything I need from the restaurant. A prime rib roast, turkey, cornbread stuffing, mashed potatoes and gravy, candied yams, green bean casserole, Parker House rolls, pumpkin pie, apple pie and ice cream. Does it sound good so far?"

"There are two conditions. I'd like to invite Uncle Zech and Aunt Winnie and be able to help you," Phyllis said.

"Both invitations are fine. Dr. Berman and Uncle Zech, but the helper part, we'll have to think about.

Everyone pitched in. Dr. Ravin even helped take the heavy dishes in and out of the oven, while Phyllis and Ian dressed the dining room and table according to Esmeralda's instructions. There were cornucopias in the center of the table and china place settings with polished silverware. Cranberry jelly sat in two crystal dishes in the center of the table, and the main dishes were brought out by Dr. Ravin and Ian.

Thanksgiving Day was a true miracle to all parties. Phyllis and Ian appeared to be fulfilling a life long dream with all the joy that this festive dinner had to offer. Dr. and Mrs. Berman seemed to be so happy just being a part of a family again. Aunt Winnie and Uncle Zech had not eaten so royally since they moved into the retirement home. Dr. Ravin actually smiled, complemented the cook, and requested that Esmeralda say the blessing over the food. Esmeralda experienced a feeling of usefulness, acceptance, and belonging.

After dinner, Esmeralda turned on classical music in the living room and asked the family to please retire there for coffee and dessert. Phyllis pleaded to her to allow her to help but was told to entertain her guests. "There will be other times when we may work together in the kitchen and exchange girl talk, but today is your day to be a guest. Shoo," she waved her hands at Phyllis.

"I'm sure there will be," Phyllis said, and she gave Esmeralda a big hug before retiring to the living room.

Esmeralda brought out a silver tray filled with coffee cups, saucers, sugar, cream, and a coffee decanter. She sat this tray on the freshly polished Duncan Fife serving cart, and then quickly returned with a silver serving tray filled with dessert dishes, forks, napkins, and a variety of home made desserts which included baklava, halva, pumpkin pie, sliced pound cake, and apple pie. She sat this tray on the coffee table so that everyone could see and chose their favorites.

As she served the Berman's their choice and was handing Aunt Winnie her favorite, the fragile and soft wrinkled old lady took one of Esmeralda's hands. "Wait, child.

You're a Christian, aren't you?"

"Yes, ma'am," Esmeralda replied.

"Does that mean you believe that we Jews are not going to heaven?" Aunt Winnie asked.

Carefully thinking of the most appropriate response, Esmeralda examined each person's face before answering: "No, ma'am, not that at all. You are God's chosen people who have strayed away from his teachings, but with the help of a special messenger, you'll find grace again," she said.

The frail old lady with humped osteoporosis in her shoulders stared at the uneasy young girl before her. Her paper thin, velvet-appearing hands trembled as she held onto the coffee cup. Her light blue eyes stared piercingly at Esmeralda. Uncle Zechariah tried to stop his wife's questions by whispering to her to be quiet. He moved away from her, and it appeared that he had rubber bands on his legs the way his feet jerked up and down. His body shrunken with age, he appeared like a newborn bird.

"So you're saying that Judaism is not right?" Aunt Winnie asked sharply.

"The only thing that I find wrong with Judaism is its incompleteness. You don't believe that the Messiah has come, but He has. His coming is foretold in the Five Books of Moses, but you fail to accept the fact that you read in your own Torah. The fact that one of your own could not be him, you think. Excuse me ma'am, but I must clean the kitchen," Esmeralda said as she turned to leave.

Surprisingly, Uncle Zech spoke up for the first time without being prompted to talk. The white, frail old man stood up and took Esmeralda's hands in his, lifted his face, and tenderly kissed her forehead, his voice a gravel whisper: "Thank you for all that you've done. It is good to see life again. I was a Rabbi for forty years, you know, so I understand what you are talking about."

Esmeralda hugged the thin, old man and could feel the

bones in his back "I mean no harm, but feel compelled to speak the truth about the Bible or Torah. You'll see in Geneses Chapter 3, verse 15. God told the serpent that the seed of the woman would bruise his head. The woman has no seed; it is the man. God was speaking of the coming of Jesus the Christ, the Messiah who was developed in woman without the seed of man. Shall I get a Bible?"

"No need to get the book; it's in there," Uncle Zech said sharply.

After several question and answer sessions about the Bible and Esmeralda's astute answers, it made the old Rabbi begin to wonder where the child was from: "Where are you from, child?"

Esmeralda appeared apprehensive at first. She couldn't understand what uncle Zech was trying to understand about her, so she quickly responded: "I was born in Georgia, but my family moved to Pittsburgh, Pennsylvania when I was nine years old..."

Uncle Zech interrupted her in the middle of her statement: "Who are you?"

Suddenly aware that Uncle Zech was suspicious of her mission and covenant with God, Esmeralda backed away, trying not to show her nervousness. For she thought it was not yet time for her to reveal why she was there and where she'd come from. Phyllis noticed that the pressure was too much for the young girl and asked uncle Zech to back off: "Leave her alone, uncle Zech!"

Uncle Zech did leave the girl alone and slumped back into his docile attitude, but before he completely let go, he had one last thing to say to the group about Esmeralda, and his graveled, tenor voice spoke up again: "My gut feelings' tell me that this child has a spiritual agenda. I think she may be the one we old Rabbis were trying to tell our people about so many years ago. Her coming is foretold in the scriptures, and now that time is at hand. It won't be long before you will see what I am talking about. Keep your eyes open and on her."

CHAPTER IV

S everal days had passed since the Thanksgiving dinner. Esmeralda was already feeling like she was part of this family. However, there was still the estrangement between her and Dr. Ravin. She decided to turn it over to the Lord, and He'd let her know when it was time to reach out to him.

It was almost time for her to leave for school, and her new family hadn't come down for breakfast. When they finally arrived, Dr. Ravin was dressed in his usual dismal navy attire. And Phyllis' gray suit was a bit too tight. Ian was fairly well dressed, but his beige suit was thread worn in obvious places.

The three Ravin family members grabbed for bits and pieces of food without sitting, slurped down the orange juice, pausing only to breath, and took their coffee cups with them as they rushed out the door.

Esmeralda thought that there must be something she could do to make their lives easier. Her mind whirled most of the day and between each class. And then in mid-afternoon was a class cancellation, so the two hours free time was exactly what she needed to develop plans.

While she sat in the study hall sketching on the remodeling plans she had in mind, Bernard Bell, football star and a drafting classmate of hers, plopped down at the table where she worked and begun to talk: "Hey, pretty mama, what's got you so occupied?"

Esmeralda shrugged her shoulders, and covered the sketches with her hand: "Not much, just thinking of a term project that we can all work on..."

Bernard was a fairly attractive young man with the assurance of a one of a kind stud. He was tall and muscular, and his motives were clearly transparent. Esmeralda was definitely part of his planned scheme to satisfy his wanton desires.

"Are you going to the game Saturday?" he asked.

"I don't think so."

"Why don't I ever see you at any of the sport's functions? Don't you like sports?"

"It's OK," she answered.

"I'm going to be out there this weekend kicking butt just for you, my lady," Bernard bragged.

"Not for me, Bernie. I really don't understand football. A bunch of silly grown men running over each other, rolling in the dirt, and then ten more big tanks pile on top of the downed man and try to finish killing him.

Bernard laughed at her description: "For such a smart and pretty little mama, you really don't know much. Why don't you let me take you to the game; then afterwards we can relax at my place while I teach you about football and life," Bernard said, being very suggestive.

"No thanks," Esmeralda said. She was not only annoyed but angry. *Why was it that all of the black men wanted nothing more than to take me sexually?* She wondered if any of the black girls on campus were still virgins. If this is true, she thought, then why haven't they become aware of the Eve syndrome. The snake was beguiling, also.

When I get married...if I get married, I will definitely take a virgin to my husband's bedroom.

It was a pleasure to see Professor Thorne enter the study hall, and she quickly beckoned for him to join them. The man was a tired-looking, upper middle gent with salt and pepper hair, a wrinkled face that told a story of many disappointments, and problems... She remembered that he'd told the Engineering class early on that he once had his own very successful business, but due to divorce, he'd lost it. He was always so proud of Esmeralda's performances and told her once that he wished his sons bad her drive, and tenacity.

When Professor Thorne reached the table where Esmeralda and Bernard were seated, he shook their hands, greeting them pleasantly: "Bernard, are you working on that fill-in project you need to make up credits?" he asked.

Bernard was caught off guard and appeared somewhat embarrassed: "To tell you the truth, professor, I've been tied up in football practice."

"Son, you're a star now; but if you become a pro, you will need to be extremely frugal. The career of a pro football player is short lived. You should have a solid backup profession," the professor cautioned.

Bernard was annoyed with what he thought was meddling on Professor Thorn's part, and he snapped back impatiently: "I can only take one day... One step at a time!"

"You do that," Professor Thorn said sadly. "Esmeralda, you wanted to see me?"

"Yes, sir," Esmeralda responded. "I've made some remodeling plans that the entire Engineering class can work on. I'd like you to peruse them and see if we can finish them before Christmas. They may help all of us meet final exam requirements."

"You can drop them off in my office tonight, if you'd like."

"I have a few minor details to finalize, so if it's all the same to you, I'd like to bring them by early in the morning, if I may."

"Of course tomorrow will be fine," he said before turning to leave the room, but he stopped, stared at Bernard and Esmeralda for a moment: "Oh Esmeralda, keep both eyes wide open and on Bernard. I heard he's a lady's man."

Even though Professor Thorne laughed and pretended to be joking, Esmeralda knew he was giving her some very sound and concerned advice, for she had heard of the romps in the hay that Bernard had with his teammates and cheerleaders.

Jealousy flooded Bernard's face, and he attacked Professor Thorne's intentions unjustly: "That old man is just like all the other old white dudes around. They want to beat us black guys to our own women. Look baby, you're gonna give it up to someone, and it may as well be me. Nobody wants a pig in a poke. At least we're two of a kind."

"What kind is that, Bernie? I wouldn't be caught dead with an animal like you. You don't even have the ability to be serpent smooth with your approach. You're so sure every girl wants you, so you have no regards for her feelings at all. Do you know what Bernie? I wouldn't have you if you were the last man on earth. Now put that in your pipe and smoke it."

Bernard took hold of Esmeralda hands and pulled her closer to him, but was surprised with the maneuvers she made so quickly. He found himself on the floor, twisting in pain, with his arm folded behind his back as she squeezed it to induce more pain.

"You're a fraken little white folks' nigger. Martial Arts won't help you when we decide to gang rape your little tail."

"Get out of here and don't you ever come near me again," Esmeralda ordered, as she applied more painful maneuvers and Bernard pleaded to be released... When she finally released him, he left the room rubbing his arm, looking around to be sure no one had witnessed the submissive state that Esmeralda had caused him to be in.

* * *

During dinner, Esmeralda showed her remodeling plans to the Ravin family. She explained that the school would furnish the supplies needed, and the project would give the class grades required if they did a real professional job and finished it before the end of December.

Not yet understanding how the work will be paid for,

Ian said with reservations: "I don't know, child. We just can't afford it right now. Business hasn't been that good. Too many clients can't afford to pay, and those who do, pay not paying on time. Payments are always late..."

Esmeralda patted Ian's arm and told him to listen: "Wait, please, and listen to me. I don't think you heard me. The State has a budget that supplies all the supplies we need, if the project is accepted. That will include building material, drapes, windows, tiles, water fixtures, and the whole thing. All you have to do is say yes and sign the release forms. The school's administrators and Engineering staff will inspect the house, and the rest is up to the students—that's us," she points both index fingers back toward her chest.

"I'm looking at the house interior, but what are these other sheets?" Dr. Ravin asked.

"The second phase will be done in the spring. Merchants donate these supplies to the school, and use the donations as a tax write off. They will even deliver them to your house after we let them know what we need."

Dr. Ravin jerked the plans out of Esmeralda's hands and studied them carefully. "A Sauna, Spa, Pool exercise equipment, an elevated sun deck, flagstone patio. All this for nothing? Beware of Greeks bearing gifts," he quoted. "What is your gain in this project?" he asked.

"The second phase will be done in the spring. Merchants donate these supplies to the school, and use the donations as a tax write off. They will even deliver them to your house after we let them know what we need."

"My gain is experience in my chosen field and passing grades," she said with impatience, her gentle green eyes filling with tears of disappointment.

"Do it," Phyllis said. Giving permission without further thought, for she had become tired of her son playing the devil's advocate.

Realizing that his mother had deliberately defied his

decisions, Dr. Ravin slammed his fork down on his unfinished plate and stormed out of the room.

Esmeralda watched the doctor go and then she turned back to his parents: "I'm so sorry. I don't want to cause dissention within your family."

"It's alright, Esmeralda," Ian smiled at her. "If Phyllis hadn't approved the project, I would have. This house is old and badly in need of some repairs that we can't afford. I've often wished I could give my wife a brand new kitchen or living room."

"Please pay no attention to Philip's moods. He is suspicious of every thing. He thinks everyone is out to get him, I think. His closest friends seldom come around anymore," Phyllis said.

Approvals were made, County Permits issued, and more than fifteen young students sawed, hued, widened, tiled, partitioned, and tiled the Ravin home The place was hardly recognizable. The upstairs Sun Room still had the sheets draped over the door for Esmeralda was not yet ready to exhibit it to her new family.

The forty eight foot by twelve foot junky storage room had been partitioned into three separate sixteen foot by twelve foot rooms, decorated with appropriate wall paint, and French beige carpet on the floor. To the left of the three separate entrances was a sign that read Phyllis Ravin/Ian Ravin, Attorneys at Law. That office was decorated with two large executive desks, back to back with two leather chairs at each desk that caused the Ravins to face each other.

This first office also had four leather upholstered chairs that matched the fabric of the desk chairs, a wall to floor bookshelf housed a large volume of law reference books, and a vertical file was against a blank wall to hold client and other pertinent information.

In the center, was the office with a title that read Engineering office, but no name was listed in the allocated slot.

This office had a large drafting table, paper and protractors, a silver cup with several drafting pencils, a vertical file with extra wide drawers, and a high stool at the drafting board, with two upholstered chairs against the wall.

The third office had a sign that identified it as a Medical office. It bore the name of Dr. Philip I. Ravin. This office had a large executive desk and matching chair, with a matching love seat against one wall, and two chairs with low backs sat in front of the desk. A vertical file sat against another blank wall and above this was a large Norman Rockwell painting of a little boy with his bare gluteus maximus cheeks exposed, and an old gent with a hypodermic needle in his hand looming ominously nearby. All of the new offices had vertical blinds covering the windows facing the out doors area, and there was a matching drape that covered the top of the window and hung down the sides.

The office suites really looked like an upper Wilshire executive suite. They were perhaps the most impressive addition to the house. Esmeralda's classmates helped her move the Ravin's personal files into these offices. The hand written law transcript that lay on the dresser in the master suite had been typed, and placed carefully on top the new double backed desk. All other folders were labeled alphabetically and carefully filed away.

After her classmates had cleaned up from the two-week long project and left the house, the Inspectors and Professor Thorne had made their assessments, signed the release forms, and were gone. Esmeralda put a roast in the oven to bake, washed and wrapped Irish potatoes and put them on a cookie sheet to bake, washed and salted broccoli to be cooked later. She lay down on the dining room floor and from extreme exhaustion, fell fast asleep.

Esmeralda's nap was restless and disturbing, for she dreamed of loud voices shouting in disagreement, calling out to her in panic and anger. She dreamed that she saw a number of accusing fingers pointing at her, and she thought she was deep inside a hole. The voices had become baritone, and in slow motion, surrounded her. She tossed restlessly trying to get up, but her body was too heavy and her movements snail slow.

Just before she choked to death by the hands of her accusers, she awakened, and realized that the Ravin family had arrived home, missed important documents and were frantically trying to awaken her so that she could tell them where she'd put things.

Being so tired, Esmeralda couldn't determine where she was, and if the family was trying to tell her that something was burning, and she ran to the kitchen. Dazed, she asked fearfully: "Where am I? What is the matter?"

"The transcripts that were on the dresser in our bedroom, what did you do with them?" Phyllis asked. Esmeralda ran upstairs, with the Ravin family in close pursuit. She pulled down the taped sheets from the new offices, opened the door that read Law Office, and entered, pointing to the raw data and freshly typed transcripts lying on the large desk beside the new typewriter. She pulled open the low vertical file drawers to show that all of their other documents had been filed in order.

Phyllis sat at the desk that had the name plate with her name, and Ian took the side that displayed his name. Phyllis read the typed transcript and passed each sheet over to Ian who read with approval, apologies, and gratefulness written on both their faces.

Dr. Ravin hurried to the door that read Medical office, and found it as organized as his parent's law office. He searched through files and books and appeared satisfied that everything was in order, and he sat down to read the mail that he found on top his new desk.

"May I be excused?" Esmeralda asked, and with the smiles of her new parents, she took it to mean she could go, and she left them alone, admiring the imposing office area.

Together, the Ravin family inspected the Engineering office, and was amazed to see all of the drawings and planned shopping centers on drafting paper. Another drawing easel had an array of newly designed spring fashions. Ian was first to speak: "I am truly ashamed that we were so suspicious and treated Esmeralda with disrespect."

"What can we do to make this up to her?" Phyllis asked.

"Just let it be," Philip said. "We don't want her to feel she can just take charge."

"Must you always have an ulterior motive for everything?" Phyllis asked.

"Mom, when you know these women like I do, you'd understand that they will go to all means to get their way."

"I believe that child is as pure as spring's first rain," Phyllis said.

"You're right, but she's polluted by earth's contaminations, of course," Philip said.

"Look, you two, just cut it out. Time will tell, and I have a feeling it won't be long. So let's go downstairs, apologize and eat whatever it is that smells so good," Ian said.

"Time may be too late," Philip said.

*   *   *

Esmeralda didn't talk much after the encounter she'd had with the Ravin family. She was always very polite, did her part, kept the house looking nice, prepared the meals, but found a way to spend her spare time in her new office, or going to the park to run. She was always in a hurry to go someplace important.

Phyllis and Ian noticed that she cried a lot more than she'd done since she came to live with them. They even followed her to the park, after they'd noticed her dressed in a sweat suit, and tennis shoes. They were amazed to see her streaking around the park path like a gazelle, passing all other runners.

They were bothered by the fact that a man was watching Esmeralda, and checking his watch as he stared at her. He looked at the Ravins and asked: "Do you know that girl?"

"Of course we know her, she's our foster daughter," Ian said with authority. "What is your interest in her?"

"I've checked her speed each time I found her here. I'd sure like to enter her in the Olympics. She'd bring home a gold for sure," the man said. "Oh, excuse my rudeness. I'm Ernest Smalley, Olympic Scout," he extended his hand to Ian and Phyllis, who introduced themselves.

Ernest told the Ravins that he'd tried on several occasions to talk to Esmeralda, but she appeared troubled and afraid. "If she's your foster daughter, there must've been something painful in her relationship with her biological family; am I right?"

With firm determination, Phyllis told Mr. Smalley off: "I'm afraid our daughter is not for sale. Good day, Mr. Smalley." Seeing that Esmeralda had stopped to rest, Phyllis ordered Ian to go get the girl. "Go get her, Ian, now."

"What if she won't come with me?"

"Well, you put your foot down, be firm with her. After all, we are now her parents, and it's about time we started acting like it."

Ian walked across the path where Esmeralda was resting, and then an argument ensued, but she finally submitted to Ian's demands. They walked back to the car where Phyllis was waiting, and she put her arms around the girl, admiring her pony tail, and then kissed her cheek lovingly before they all climbed into the car and drove away.

CHAPTER V

Christmas decorations were glistening all over town. People had decorated their homes, and colorful lights blinked on all the streets except the one where the Ravin family lived. Esmeralda tuned in the radio in her van, and the typical sounds of Christmas flowed melodiously from the speaker. The music made her cry.

"God, I know the celebrations that we do are not the most sacred, but it is our Lord's birthday in a few days, or at least the day that Christians have set aside to celebrate the birthday. I realize that my new family doesn't accept you yet, but I'd still like to do something nice for them. Will this be wrong? Can you hear me, Lord?"

For several blocks, she drove in silence listening to the inspirational music sometimes singing along, as her moods led her, periodically thinking of something she could do for her new family. "Yes! Yes! That's it, I'll do it. Thank you, God."

She sped up the van a bit trying not to attract too much attention, for she was aware that she only owned a learner's permit to drive. She wouldn't be old enough to get a real license for six more months. She wanted to be sure she got home before her family, and before the sewing room closed for the day at Emerald Fashion Designs.

When she drove into the Ravin's driveway, the coast was clear. Dashing inside, she went straight for the telephone, dialed it hurriedly, and waited for an answer.

"Good afternoon, Emerald Fashions," the voice said.

"Marsha, this is Esmeralda; please let me speak to Juan."

When Juan's Spanish accented voice came over the receiver, she asked him to please wait for her for she had some samples she'd like him to duplicate, and she'd be there as soon as possible. Juan stated that he would be there until she came.

When Esmeralda hung up the phone receiver, she was in such a hurry that she missed the rack, and had to try it again. She ran to her foster parent's bedroom, pulled down a man's suit and shirt, a woman's two piece suit and a blouse. After rolling them up and tying them with the long sleeved shirt, she ran to Dr. Ravin' s room. She had to take measurement of waist, inseam, shoulder width and sleeve length, for there was only one suit hanging in the closet, and she knew it would be missed. She also took a shirt, and a pair of his navy shoes. After rolling them up in a ball, she rushed downstairs, and out to her van. Seemingly, because she was in a hurry, every car that was ever manufactured was on the streets, causing her to stop and crawl. She finally reached the sewing room and realized that she had forgotten to take her coat. After all, it was December, and the cold winds sent icy chills through her body.

Shivering, she rang the emergency bell and waited patiently for Juan to answer. Her watch read 5:00 o'clock. "Hurry Juan," she whispered as she shook off the cold.

After what seemed like an eternity, Juan finally answered the bell. The happy-appearing, middle-aged Hispanic gentleman with a heavy mustache practically pulled Esmeralda inside, taking the packages she was carrying.

"Senorita jefa, what is the big problem?" Juan asked.

"I want to surprise my new family for Christmas. Their clothes are so drab."

Juan spread the old fashioned clothes out on a table, turned up his nose, and shook his head. Drab is no good, pobre is better. I thought you said they were Arbogados de Judio," Juan asked.

"They are Jewish lawyers, and their son is a doctor, but they are struggling. People don't pay their bills, and they were sued some time ago."

42

Juan held the man's suit up with two fingers as though he felt he'd catch something contagious: "These are so old. Are you sure they still fit?" he asked.

"The man's suit still fits, but the woman's is a little tight around the nalgus. When she buttons it, she could use about two inches on the jacket and the same with the skirt. We'll alter them after they open their gifts at Christmas time. Can they all be done before that time?"

"You drive a hard bargain Chiquita Jefa, but most of the winter orders are filled. I believe it can be done."

Esmeralda hugged Juan and thanked him for his cooperation with her surprise for the new family that God had sent to her: "Juan, please don't call me little boss lady. I'm just Mera, and am not ready to tell anybody that I am the owner of this business."

Juan laughed and said: "If I was the big jefe, I'd want the world to know, but whatever you say... er...Mera." They smiled at each other as she left the building with a piece of cloth wrapped around her shoulders.

Esmeralda searched through the freezer for something to cook quickly. "Ah, ha," she said as she lifted out a two pound package of ground beef, unwrapped it, put it in a large Dutch oven, and covered it, after turning the gas on low. She prepared celery, bell peppers, and an onion. And then she took down four cans of tomato sauce, and other spices. Stirring the vegetables and meat periodically, she then washed lettuce and other salad greens, dried then on a towel, and began to break them for the salad. In another pot, she set water to boil for the spaghetti, and as soon as it began to bubble, she dropped in the pasta.

With the meat and vegetables finally done, she drained off the oils into a colander and an empty jar. She then added the tomato sauce, a cup full of the mushrooms she had washed for the salad, two cups of water, the spices, and returned the meat sauce to simmer. With jet-like speed, she worked to finish before her family arrived.

The next thing that she did was to put a tablecloth on the dining room table, and set four places with all the utensils necessary to accommodate an Italian dinner. She remembered seeing Italian sausages in the refrigerator's meat chiller drawer and rushed back to dump them into the simmering sauce. Remembering that she had to have bread, she took the thick sliced French bread out of the refrigerator, spread the slices onto a cookie sheet, melted butter, added garlic powder, and spread the mixture on the bread.

"Oh, my God, I forgot to turn on the oven." When she started for the oven, she remembered that the wine needed to be chilled, and she went to the dining room to get the wine. The phone rang, but she only looked at it, and continued doing what she had to accomplish. The phone was persistent so she thought she'd better answer it.

"Hello," she said sharply.

"Well, aren't we testy today!" It was Dr. Ravin's voice on the phone.

"I'm sorry, I didn't mean to sound impatient, but I was trying to accomplish too many things at once," she apologized.

"Are you cooking extras tonight?" Philip asked.

"It's just spaghetti and meat sauce, a salad, garlic toast. It won't be difficult to stretch. Are we having guest for dinner?"

"I called almost two hours ago but got no answer. Marty's wife wants to meet you. So do Joey and his wife."

"Is something wrong?" she asked with skepticism.

"Nothing is wrong, they are just curious. I should be there to help you within forty minutes, if you need help;, the rest will be arriving about seven thirty." And then he hung up. Esmeralda stood there for a moment, trying to think of what she should do to expand the dinner from four to eight and three little kids.

"Mera, use the rest of the sausage; get several cans of mushrooms down and add them, two more cans of tomato sauce, boil more pasta." She threw the mushrooms and sausages into the sauce, removing those that were done, added three cans of tomato sauce, with water, then she took out more salad greens, looked at her watch, and mumbled to herself: "Six forty five. It's too late to sauté more vegetables. She washed more salad vegetables and put them on the towel to drain, and then she sliced the cooked sausages, returning them to the sauce mixture. After she added two cans of mushrooms, the additional sausages, and tomato sauce with water, the mixture was about three inches from the top of the large pot. She put another bottle of wine in the freezer and removed the one she'd put there earlier, placing it on the refrigerator rack.

"What about dessert? There are bananas, but Dr. Ravin eats all the cookies he can find. Maybe he didn't find the vanilla wafers." She looked in the cupboard, found the box of wafers, and two instant pudding mixes. "This will only take five minutes, maybe ten at the most."

Esmeralda heard the first key in the door and familiar voices. She knew that this was Mom and Dad. With the aroma tantalizing them, they headed for the kitchen instead of their rooms to change. "What is going on?" Phyllis asked.

"Dr. Ravin called and told me that his friends, Marty, Joe and their families are coming to dinner."

Making an assessment of the area, Ian said: "You look like you can use some help."

Esmeralda laughed at herself: "I had to make a stop and was late getting home, so I've been working like a one armed paper hanger, even before Dr. Ravin called.

"There are two things you must remember; you don't take orders from Philip and you don't have to call him Doctor Ravin. Philip would be enough for the family."

Esmeralda knew better than to engage Philip in a lengthy conversation or debate, for without a doubt, his extemporaneous manner of speaking would cut her feelings to the quick. It was better to go along with him as long as it was not insulting.

"When I saw all the fixings, I thought it was my birthday. You have everything looking so festive," Ian complimented her efforts.

"I have a bottle of wine in the freezer and one in the refrigerator; the corks need to be broken, the salad greens needs to be broken also and mixed, and the garlic toast is ready to be put in the oven, the spaghetti needs to be lifted to a serving dish that is right here, and the sauce can be served from the pan it is in. Here's a hot pad. Oh, oh. Another key. That would have to be Dr... er... Philip." He's coming to help.

"If the guests will be arriving at seven thirty, we've got thirty minutes, I'll just wash my hands, break the lettuce and mix the salad," Phyllis said.

Ian examined the two bottles of wine before putting the corkscrews to them, and then he went to the dining room and filled the wine glasses. Philip came into the kitchen awaiting his task and was told by Esmeralda to dish the spaghetti into the large serving dish and take it and the sauce to the dining table. Phyllis tossed the salad in a large paper bag, put it into a salad bowl with lifting tongs and took it to the table. Esmeralda took the bread from the oven, and the doorbell rang. Philip went to answer it, and Esmeralda could hear her stomach growl from nervousness. Phyllis took a platter of bread to the table, and Esmeralda followed her with the crystal bowl of Banana Pudding.

She forced a smile as she was introduced to everyone, and they in turn complimented her on the things they'd heard about her. The young girl was somewhat embarrassed and wondered what good things Philip could possibly have told them about her. When she walked to the kitchen to get a picture of iced water, Phyllis and Ian followed her back there.

"Thank God for you, child. Those men are Philip's two

best friends coming back into his life," Phyllis said.

"Don't count the chickens before they're hatched," Ian said.

Since Philip was the host, Esmeralda had all of the serving dishes set in front of him; the salad was individually dished and the large bowl removed from the table.

Dr. Joel Markowitz was tall, slim and his semi curly red hair seemed to be bleeding onto his face, leaving it extra pink. His wife Pamela was also tall and blond, and her blue eyes offset the smooth chalky color of her face. Evelyn Heller was short and tiny. She appeared to be more Italian than Jewish. She was devilishly attractive, and her magnetic personality stuck in Esmeralda's mind.

"I like Evelyn," Esmeralda thought, and Evelyn smiled back at her—a pleasant acceptance that made Esmeralda feel good inside. She understood why Dr. Heller appeared to be so happy. Their two boys displayed the same personality as their parents and immediately took to Esmeralda like an equal playmate. Joey Jr. (J.J.) was kind of a stand-off shy child. His hair was between red and blond, a light auburn color, and he seldom talked, even though he played after dinner games with Esmeralda and the Heller boys.

When the guests were gone, Phyllis assisted Esmeralda with the cleanup in the kitchen and dining room, but Philip never took time to thank her for the unsuspected request he'd placed upon her. To him, she was just a servant anyway.

Only two days after the spaghetti dinner, Friday to be exact, the gentle tray turned and the storm that Esmeralda always feared hit without a warning. Since Philip's patient load was light, he decided to attend the conference that his boss had suggested.

He walked around his bedroom in his underwear, trying to find his blue dress shirt. He noticed that his shirts were all neatly stacked in the top drawer of the dresser. He opened another drawer and found his socks folded and coordinated by colors; his underwear was also the same way. Maybe he'd sent the blue shirt to the laundry.

Philip sat down on the bed with his head in his hands, wondering if he had sent the shirt to the laundry. No way, he thought, not so. For he hadn't worn the shirt since the last time it was laundered. He would know, for he considered this shirt a dress-up shirt. OK, why fret about a shirt; Esmeralda had everything so orderly, that maybe she had put it in another place without thinking...

"I'll just wear a white shirt," he thought. There were numerous white ones in the drawer; besides the time was passing fast for he heard his parents came in from work, and go to their room. "I must wear the new navy shoes. I haven't worn them since the last conference," he thought.

After searching the floor of the closet and not finding the shoes, he began to put his suspicious mind to work. The suit he'd planned to wear was not where it usually hung. He took it down and hung it in the center where it usually hung. He appeared puzzled and annoyed. He went back to the shirt drawer and flipped through his shirts. "Gone, the blue shirt is definitely gone, and so are my shoes."

He decided to re-inspect other drawers, but found everything ironed, matched according to color, and placed neatly in their place. Instead of just thrown into the drawer by piece, his socks were matched, folded together, and placed according to color. "Could this be some kind of satanic witch craft? Invasion. That's it, invasion of my privacy."

"This has to be her way of trying to get me to come on to her sexually. I knew there was something wrong with her when mom and dad brought her here and fell for her bull. She's just too perfect to be real." Anger and resentment began to boil over in his mind, and he called out to Esmeralda: "Esmeralda, get up here now," he shouted.

Stopping what she was doing, Esmeralda knew that this was the apprehensiveness she'd felt most of the day.

She took the stairs reluctantly, trying to imagine what was about to happen. As she reached the top, Philip met her in the hallway.

"Where are my navy shoes?" he demanded.

"They're at the designer's shop," she answered, trembling.

"I suppose my blue shirt is there, also, and did you move my things around in my closet too?" he snapped at her.

"No, I just cleaned up in there and freshened the closets so they would not smell like sweat."

Half dressed, Phyllis said to Ian in their bedroom: "I'd better go out there and referee."

Ian took her arm and told her: "This is a brother/sister quarrel; let them settle it. He'll get used to the orderly way she's put us all in."

Philip blocked Esmeralda's exit, took her shoulders, and shook her violently.

"I took down the suit only to measure it," she said. How did he know, she thought. Her head was hurting from the verbal accusations and shaking.

"I imagine you came on to your sister's husband, too, and when he decided to take you up on it, you ran." Philip accused her.

"I didn't do anything wrong. Why do you hate me so?" she cried.

"Shut up. From now on, you make the bed, clean in the middle of the room, and get the hell out of here!"

Esmeralda was crying uncontrollably and pulled herself free of Philip's grasp. "I won't even come into your room again at all, I promise. As far as my attempt to turn you on, don't flatter yourself. I doubt if any woman would want to turn you on. You're not very desirable. You look like a middle-aged Jewish Rabbi."

The insult hit Philip like a brick; his anger turned to defensive action, and he struck Esmeralda across the right

49

side of her face with his open hand, causing her to fall against the hall tree.

Neither of them had heard Ian and Phyllis rush from their room to investigate the commotion. Esmeralda pulled herself to a sitting position, blood oozed from her nostrils, and the three people standing there moved in and out in her mind, sometimes becoming six.

"What in God's name is wrong with you, Philip? There was no need to become so violent. I think you need help, son." Ian stated.

Phyllis stooped to assist Esmeralda. Get me a towel and some ice," she said. Ian went to get the towel, but Philip stood frozen as though he could not move. "Philip, I need ice. Didn't you hear me.?"

"This little gutter tramp was trying to come on to me," Philip stammered nervously.

Ian looked up at his son with disappointment. "Coming on to you how?" he asked.

"My clothes in the closet have been moved, and the pair of shoes I'd planned to wear tonight are missing. Some kind of African voodoo. These Negroes believe in that, you know," he said.

"She's done the same thing to our room, too. Do you suppose she was coming on to me too, Philip?"

"I've never seen you so irrational. I agree with your father, you do need help."

"So now you think I'm crazy. Don't be surprised if you find her in bed with dad," Philip shouted, and he rushed back into his room to finish getting dressed and shortly left in a huff.

Phyllis and Ian assisted Esmeralda to her room, and Ian brought cold, wet towels to apply to her face and nose. "Honey, we've got to find a way to help our son," Ian said.

Esmeralda strained to get up. "I'll leave. I think I'm the reason he's so angry; he probably thinks that I'm stealing his parents away."

"That is just not feasible," Ian said. "You are legally our foster daughter; we can't allow you to go out there alone again."

"What am I doing wrong? I only wanted to help."

"You are helping. There has not been so much liveliness in this house since Philip was a little boy, and you've brought it back in less than two months." Trying to calm the young girl, Phyllis took her in her arms and cradled her gently.

Both Ian and Phyllis were curious about the missing shoes and asked Esmeralda if she'd moved them. She agreed that she had taken the shoes and clothing measurements to a designer's shop to have copies made. "Philip's closet and room smelled so unclean from over wearing the same outfits, I thought that if I could make him look better, he wouldn't be so irritable," Esmeralda said.

Ian cautioned her with good advice: "Just stay away from him as much as possible. Let him request things of you. Maybe he'll loosen up.

"Have you eaten, child?" Phyllis asked.

"No, but you go ahead; I don't feel like it now.

Ian started for the door, rubbing his hands together with excitement: "The kitchen smells good, and I'm hungry."

"You need to eat, sweetheart," Phyllis coaxed.

"I'm afraid I'll throw up if I eat. Maybe later when I've calmed down." Esmeralda crawled beneath the covers fully dressed, and Phyllis fluffed her pillow and covered her with the blanket before going to join her husband for dinner.

*   *   *

Morning came and Esmeralda was up early. She felt the side of her face and noticed that it was very sore. She went to the bathroom to shower and found that she was somewhat unsteady. When she looked into the mirror, she verified her suspicions. Her face was swollen, and her left eye was badly blood shot. "God, he tried to kill me." Why did I allow it to go that far; I should've taken him out before his hand connected. Oh God, I would've exposed too much of myself too soon," she thought.

Esmeralda thought to herself that his parents loved him so much that she would be afraid to hurt him, and she knew she could seriously injure his hands which were the life of his practice. Besides, she thought, he was only going to shake her and yell.

Carefully, she managed to shower without falling, and after dressing, she went down to prepare breakfast, wearing sunglasses to hide her injuries. When the food was safely far enough along and the table was set, Esmeralda sat down to talk to the Lord.

In her prayers for Philip, she felt a warm compassionate embrace by the living arms of the Holy Spirit, trying to assure her that everything would eventually be alright.

"God, how can I bear this treatment? How can I help Philip?" she prayed. It seemed that a light brighter than she'd ever seen before lit up the kitchen and warmed her soul. At this moment, she knew that she alone was sent to help Philip face his demons and rid himself of them.

When she'd turned the other cheek instead of using Martial Arts, the shock of what he had done would finally make Philip reach out for help. She knew that even before she moved things around in Philip's closet, that God was speaking to her heart and setting the stage for the change to come. She knew that sometimes pain precedes a positive change, and it takes a crisis to open out eyes.

The Ravin family showed up to breakfast, but stood quietly with their heads bowed awaiting Esmeralda' s completion of prayers. When she was aware that she was no longer alone, she attempted to get up to serve coffee but staggered unsteadily, almost dropping the coffee pot. Philip rushed to assist her and set the pot down, assisting her to her seat. When Philip removed her sunglasses, he shuddered with remorse after realizing what he'd done to her. He picked her up in his arms and carried her to the living room sofa. Phyllis and Ian were in close pursuit. There, he examined her carefully, but found no ideology that would warrant further treatment.

"Rest; just rest and cold compresses to the face," Philip said.

Even though he never apologized to her, Esmeralda knew he was sorry by the expression on his face. His parents also knew that a change in their son was just on the horizon.

"I'll stay home with her," Phyllis stated.

"Remember that one of us needs to be in Van Nuys court, and the other needs to file a deposition down town. At eleven o'clock."

"Will she be alright alone, Philip?" she asked.

"She should be alright if she stays in bed. I'll check on her as soon as I can," his voice trembling.

The Ravin family had just driven around the bend when Esmeralda remembered that she had a calculus examination today. So she put on her coat and scarf and left for her van. She made it to school and took her test, but passed out only a few moments after she'd finished her examinations. She was rushed to the UCLA Medical Emergency Room where a diagnosis of concussion was made, and a recommendation to be hospitalized for a few days was made.

Dr. Martin Heller got word that Esmeralda had passed out from injuries and had been hospitalized. He rushed as fast as his legs could carry him to her room. When he saw her beautiful face so swollen and bruised, his anger boiled over.

"Did Bernard and his groupies do this to you?" he demanded.

"No. I fell at home."

"I'm going to call the Ravins, so you'd better give me the whole story. Do they know you were injured?"

"Yes."

"Why did they allow you to come to school?"

"They think I am at home where they told me to stay, but I had a test."

"Did Philip examine you?"

Esmeralda's nervousness was very noticeable, and Dr. Heller became suddenly alerted that this could be something that Philip would be capable of in his present state. He took Esmeralda's hand, squeezing firmly. "Did Philip do this to you?"

"I fell against the hall tree up stairs," she whimpered.

"What made you fall, Esmeralda?" he asked.

"I wasn't too careful," she said, her heartbeats pounding against her chest.

"I'm going to ask you again. Did Philip do this to you?" She began to cry hysterically. "No. Oh, God, no, please no."

"Why did he hit you?" Dr. Heller had changed his approach.

"He didn't mean to hit me."

"Then why did he hit you?"

"I cleaned his room and sent some of his musty old shoes and clothes out to be replaced." Esmeralda was crying floods by this time.

"Sick bastard," Dr. Heller whispered under his breath, as Esmeralda turned to see what he was saying. "You're going to be alright. I promise you that. I'll call your parents and let them know that you are here. Keep your spirits up."

Dr. Heller left the room and Esmeralda wanted to die. It seemed that she was more trouble than she was worth. She wanted to call her brother Clarence, but didn't want to be a problem for him either. "God," she whispered. "Please tell me what to do" And she soon cried herself to sleep. She dreamed she'd heard the voice of an angel, a beautiful golden spirit with bright light surrounding its head, silver wings protruding from the rear sides of its raiment that dazzled the eyes with brilliance.

The voice of this spirit that beamed and reverberated through the walls of the hospital room, stated: "It Is Time!" Esmeralda awaken and tried to understand the significance if the dream. She knew she had to get to Rabbi Terah, and he'd help her understand what it all meant.

*   *   *

Dr. Heller sat at his desk in his private office on the university campus, his teeth clinched and jaws taught. The party on the other end of the phone finally answered.

"Law offices," he heard the voice say.

"This is Marty Heller, Mrs. Ravin. I just wanted you to know that Esmeralda's in the hospital with a concussion. She passed out in class; she had a Calculus exam and didn't want to miss it." There was a long pause, and Dr. Heller responded: "Yes she told me he hit her after I wrung it out of her. She was trying to make me believe she fell accidentally."

"I am going to call him now.... You're right, he does need help, and I'm going to see that he gets it without hurting his practice.... I'll keep in touch... Good bye."

Dr. Heller dialed the phone again and waited for an answer. "This is Dr. Martin Heller. May I please speak to Dr. Ravin?" He waited several moments before Philip finally came on the phone. "This is Dr. Ravin."

"Philip, hear me out. I have made an appointment for you in my private office tomorrow at 6:30 p.m. I realize that it is not ethnical for friends or relatives to practice on their own, but I don't want the medical world to know that you are having psychiatric consultations. If you don't keep these appointments, you are out of medicine forever. Do you understand?"

"What the hell are you talking about?" Philip asked, disturbed.

"Esmeralda is in the hospital with a concussion and possible blood clot on the brain. Do I need to say more? You are one of my best friends, and I expect you to get your act together before it is too late." He hung up the phone abruptly.

And cold chills enshrouded Philip. His arms were temporarily paralyzed. He could feel the hair rise on them and the back of his neck, and he had a difficult time releasing the phone to re-rack it. His stomach growled loudly, and a tear formed in the corner of one eye as he stared down at the floor. Something was crawling there, he thought.

A bug, maybe. His head jerked around so his eyes fell on the recessed crease of the Berber rug on the floor. No bug there.

"Oh, my God," he whispered. "They're on my arms." He looked to see if the creatures he thought he saw were crawling on his arms. He slapped his arms and raked his hands over them as though he was clearing the creatures off and onto the floor; nothing could be seen.

"Nerves," he said; his voice shook as goose bumps rose over most of his exposed skin. He slipped into his hanging lab coat, trying to keep warm, but sweat was now dripping from his forehead, and his entire body was clammy and cold.

Philip tried to stand, but his legs would not support him; he plopped noisily back onto the chair. He thought that his heart would quit beating any moment now, for there seemed to be an instant shortage of oxygen in the room. He wanted to cry for help, but the only name he could remember at this moment was mama. How could he whine like a little boy? he thought.

A whimper came from his throat as he envisioned attending Esmeralda's funeral. She looked so fragile and helpless, so positively beautiful. More beautiful than any woman he'd ever known. His mind wandered to Snow White and the Dwarf's fable, and he compared himself to the wicked stepmother Queen... How he wished he had another chance. For the second time in his life, he cried out for God to help him. "God. If you are real, I need you now," he prayed.

"I truly didn't want to hurt that little girl. Please give me another chance. Don't let that child die."

His prayers must've been louder than he thought for his nurse rapped on the door. "Dr. Ravin, are you alright?" she asked. He grunted some sound that was not interpretable, and his nurse opened the door. Seeing him, she screamed: "Oh, my God!"

Several others rushed to the room to assist, and Dr. Berman was there in a flash. If ever a tortoise won a race, it was Philip's boss. "Get him on a gurney quick," Dr. Berman ordered.

"I just need to get to the hospital," Philip said.

"I'll drive you there," his nurse said.

"I'm able to drive myself. A family member had an accident. I'll be alright."

"Go on, boy, take care of it immediately. I'll manage here," Dr. Berman stated.

"The waiting room is about clear now," an assistant said.

Philip was already gathering his belongings and slipped into his top coat, one arm in and one out as he rushed out the side exit.

*   *   *

Esmeralda appeared to be sleeping when Philip arrived in her hospital room. She was lying on her side, facing away from the door, a large gauze bandage wrapped around her head, and ice packs were leaning against the bandages.

Philip was afraid to wake her. He just stared at the

swollen area on the side of her face. The color was a dark purple. He reached out his hand like a timid swimmer testing the water first. He tried to call her name, but his throat was so dry that no audible sound came forth, just a puff of air.

As slight as the puff of air was, Esmeralda felt his presence. His moldy, smelling clothing made it easy to assess who was there. She did not let on that she was awake. She groaned deliberately, and Philip withdrew his hand quickly, leaving it suspended in the air, his fingers spread wide apart as though he was shaking off the idea of touching her.

Finally mustering up enough courage, Philip gently called out her name. "Esmeralda, it's me, Philip."

Who else would smell like a sack of daddy long legs? she asked herself, still not letting him know that she was awake. She opened her eyes, but did not move as he went around the bed so he could face her. One of her eyes was swollen shut, and with the other, she stared at a fixed spot on the wall and appeared not to notice Philip's presence at all.

Again, he called out her name, but she did not move. He took out his stethoscope from the medical bag, pulled down the neck of her gown to place the listening device directly on her chest; but he exposed her cleavage, she quickly sunk a fingernail into his hand, and then pulled the gown securely around her neck.

"Esmeralda, I just wanted to check on your condition," Philip said apologetically.

"I have a doctor, thank you," she said as she rolled to the opposite side of the bed, covering her head with the sheet.

"Please, forgive me," Philip begged, but Esmeralda still would not talk to him. Philip wanted to move back to the door side of the bed to plead for her forgiveness, but as he made several steps, his parents entered the room, their faces drawn with fear.

"How is she?" Phyllis asked.

"She is not responding to me at all," he said.

Phyllis leaned over to kiss Esmeralda and was met with a loving, forgiving hug; she passed this warm greeting on to Ian as well.

Philip watched these greetings and froze in his spot. Had this girl stolen from him the last two friends he had in the world, or was he such a nerd that his parents had turned on him? he thought. I've got to make a change, or I'll be a street bum. But how? How can I do this? Can Marty really help me? I know you can if you will, God. Show me the way, please. He looked at his watch and told his parents he had an appointment.

CHAPTER VI

P hilip could hear his footsteps echoing on the tiled floor leading to Dr. Heller's office. He dreaded this appointment.

Martin Heller was a friend of his... Yeah, was a friend of his before he lost his grip, he thought. Maybe somehow, he could re-kindle this relationship. How could he, after being threatened with notifying the medical board if this appointment was not kept.

Joel Markovitz was his best friend, but they didn't see much of each other anymore. Besides, Joel and Pam were having marital problems, and he thought it would be better if he stayed out of their way.

Right now, this very moment, he could use any friend. He stopped outside the door that read Martin H Heller, Professor of Psychology. Philip drew in a deep breath and let it out slowly as he reached for the door knob. He stopped, opened his sweaty hands wide, and decided to knock. The voice from within, barely audible, said: "Come in, please."

Philip stepped inside, staring nervously at his friend who had now become his judge and jury. He felt the iciness, the estrangement in his old buddy as he heard him say without looking up from the papers he was signing. "Sit down, Philip. I'll be with you in just a moment."

Hesitant, Philip sat down, clasped his hands together on his lap, and noticed how numb and cold his finger tips were. He stared at his friend who seemed not to even notice him sitting there. The frigid temperature started to climb up his arms and penetrate his shoulders. He shuddered, shaking off the chill.

After what seemed like an endless time, Dr. Heller finally dropped his glasses low on his nose and stared at

Philip without saying anything. He then removed the glasses, placed them in the case, looking Philip squarely in the eyes, as he rocked backwards in his big office chair.

"Do you want to tell me what's going on with you and Esmeralda?" Dr. Heller asked.

"This horrible fear and hatred boiling inside me, seems to choke me to death," Philip began. He waited for Dr. Heller to say something, but he didn't, and both men sat staring at each other.

The waiting for the silence to end was tormenting for Philip. It hadn't occurred to him at the time that the psychiatrist role is to get the patient to talk.

"I don't... I just wanted... My shoes were missing... I was in a hurry to get to a meeting. I didn't mean to hurt the girl. I...er..."

Interrupting, Dr. Heller asked: "Do you want to sleep with her?"

Appearing shocked, Philip asked: "What?"

"You heard me! Do you want to make love to her?"

"I don't want to have sex with anyone at this point in my life," Philip declared defensively.

"Why not, Philip?"

"Why? You know what happened with Annette."

"What does your former wife have to do with your relationship with a woman now?" Dr. Heller asked.

"I'm afraid that I'll go through hell again if I open up to another woman. I can't afford it. My finances and my parent's finances suffered with that divorce."

"Do you want to sleep with Esmeralda?" Dr. Heller asked again.

"She's just a child, a very shrewd child invading our home and fooling my parents."

"Is that why you called her a prick teaser?"

"Did she tell you that?"

Without speaking, Dr. Heller nodded his head in an affirmative manner.

"It seemed appropriate at the time. Cleaning up our rooms, remodeling the house, matching socks, everything in order, smelly stuff in the drawers like perfume," Philip said.

"Did it ever occur to you that maybe she's just showing her appreciation for what your family is doing for her? She sure whipped up a mighty good meal on the spur of the moment when you snapped your fingers and invited all of us to dinner."

"What she does never occurs to me. She's like a servant. No matter what she looks like, she's still African descent, and they believe in voodoo. She's too seductive to be a child.

"So you've noticed how sexy she is?" Dr. Heller asked.

"I'm sure everyone's noticed. How could you not see that a fifteen-year-old is too shapely to be a child?" Philip shouted.

"So you admit you wanted to make love to her."

"I guess I thought about it. If I wasn't impotent... Yes, damn it, I thought about it," Philip declared. He bit his lip and clinched his fist, as he took a long and deep breath. "I don't think I would've though."

"You hit her, didn't you?" Dr. Heller asked. "How can you not mean to hurt someone when you hit her so hard that she sustained a concussion?" he asked. "Oh, yes, there is one more thing. Do you remember those racial names you were called when you were a child? Do you realize that you just slandered Esmeralda the same way. You called her an African Voodoo practitioner, and because she's Negroid, you called her a servant.

Philip put his hands over his face and cried out: "Oh, my God. She fell against the hall tree when I slapped her. I didn't mean to hurt her."

"Philip, you are not aware that Esmeralda has a Black Belt in Martial Arts. She could've intercepted your hand

and broken it off at the shoulder. She chose not to injure your surgical ability and to get hurt in order to teach you a lesson. She has a spiritual agenda, some kind of covenant with God. Your family must've been chosen to help her with this Godly mission," Dr. Heller said.

"Uncle Zech said that the first time he saw her. How can I help her?" Philip asked.

"You can't help her until you get help for yourself."

Philip paced around the office with his fist clinched. "I don't know where to begin, Marty. My life is such a mess. I pray and there's no answer. I know I'm hurting my parents, but I can't seem to overcome the pain. I sometimes wonder if God only hears the prayers of his favorite people."

Dr. Heller stood, took Philip by the shoulders, and then embraced him. "Esmeralda said that we Jews are His favorite people."

"Do you think she'll ever forgive me for what I did to her?" Philip asked. "It doesn't make sense that I behaved that way," he continued.

Dr. Heller squeezed Philip's arm understandingly. "No, it doesn't make sense, but she taught me that when God forgives, and He will if you ask Him sincerely, He doesn't remember the sin that He's forgiven."

"My God, Marty. I wish I could change this whole thing and start over again."

"You can't change what has happened in the past, but you can try for a better future."

*   *   *

Dr. Heller told Philip that Esmeralda's brother who helps her, lives in Chicago and refuses to take a family until he is sure she is going to be alright. "Philip, you can help him with her by protecting her from harm and giving her a safe home until she can manage without assistance. Be the big brother she needs. Do you think you can help me and her brother get her grown without a bunch of us dirty minded old men trying to violate her rights to marry as a virgin?" Marty asked.

"I don't know if I can be the brother she needs, but I'm willing to learn," Philip told Dr. Heller.

"You must let her lead, for she's fifteen, going on forty, already nearly finished with Graduate School and heading for a PhD before she leaves her teens. According to Professor Thorn, she's the best engineer he has in his class. She is a fashion designer, song writer, novelist, script writer, a damn good cook, and house keeper, and from what I understand, an excellent Bible teacher.

"She'll blaze the trails; you just be there when her race and age throw up a road block for her."

"I can do that," Philip said.

Dr. Heller pointed his finger and spoke very sternly: "No preferential treatment, mind you. It will appear phony, and she's too smart for that."

Philip noticed that Dr. Heller was writing something on the chart that he'd made up for him and wondered what it could be.

When Dr. Heller closed the folder, Philip jerked to attention as his name was called: "Philip, psychological problems don't develop in a day, and they don't heal in a short time either. I'd like to see you at least once every week for about three months."

"No problem," Philip said.

Both men stood and Dr. Heller extended his hand to Philip. They shook, and then he walked around his desk and embraced Philip: "This was a good session. See you next week, friend."

A faint smile cracked the corners of Philip's mouth as he started for the door, feeling better than he had for several days.

"Oh, Phil," Dr. Heller called out as Philip opened the door to leave, then turned to see what it was that Dr. Heller wanted.

"Mera is not with Evelyn and me because I found her to be too desirable sexually, and I, too, wanted to make love to her."

"Mera? You wanted her?" Philip asked.

"Mera is part of the spelling of her name, and she likes to be called that. And, yes, as much as I love my wife, the animal in me made me think what it would be like to make love to her. The young black men at school try to demoralize her verbally to make her submissive. But that little girl is fighting to stay alive in this masculine rat race. Thank God for Domani's Martial Arts Classes she's enrolled in. I've heard that Tai Qwan Do is the killer one, and she's the teacher's fastest learning pupil.

*   *   *

Phyllis and Ian drove in stop and go traffic on their way home from work. The streets were colorfully decorated and busy with holiday shoppers. They heard the sounds of Christmas bells being rung by numerous Santas and dressed up volunteers for various organizations, who were standing in front of large businesses.

Small children anxiously played 'tug-of-war' with their parents, trying to free themselves of their safety grip for a chance to talk to Santa or examine the latest toys on display in the store windows.

Determined that they'd be stuck in traffic for awhile, Ian looked at Phyllis: "You're awfully quiet, honey. What's on your mind?"

"Our children are on my mind. This seems to be such a happy time of the year, and our lives are in turmoil."

"I know, I thought about that, too."

"Esmeralda told us how to have an effective prayer life. So you suppose we are praying wrong, Ian?"

"I don't think there is a right or wrong, Phyllis; prayer

is prayer," Ian said impatiently. He was mainly upset with the traffic snarl. "I'm not sure you should put a right and wrong title on prayer. You pray sincerely from your heart, talk to God; if you're worthy, He'll answer." Ian found an opening in the traffic and shoved the pedal to the floor, forcing Phyllis to loose her balance and fall backwards.

"Did you just display an example of our worthiness, Ian? Maybe that's our problem, we're not worthy," she said reprimanding him.

The car came to a stop sign, and Ian turned to look at his wife to say that he agreed with her last statement. "We're good people. We mind out business, work hard, pay our taxes, and don't mistreat anybody. Many people are fairing splendidly and do half the good we do."

"So why do we struggle so much trying to survive?" Phyllis asked.

"I can't answer that, honey."

They drove on without speaking for awhile, just listening to car horns, brakes screeching, and the occasional tintinnabulation of Christmas bells. When they came to a stop at an intersection awaiting the light to turn green, Phyllis glanced to her right, staring at the shoppers in a Christmas tree lot.

"Wait, Ian! Turn into that lot."

Ian quickly angled the car for the lot, asking in amazement. "Why on earth are we going into a tree lot?"

"Esmeralda will be coming home from the hospital tomorrow, and since she's a Christian, wouldn't it be nice to surprise her with a tree?" Phyllis asked.

Parking the car, Ian became very annoyed: "Phyllis, we don't celebrate our own High Holy days. We don't go to Temple anymore. All of a sudden, we're going to put up a Christmas tree?"

"Why not?"

"It just won't be proper."

"Our office will be closed for Christmas; none of our

clients will be coming in; the banks and schools are closed; there's no mail delivery. There you see. We are celebrating in a way. So why don't we do it for our daughter?"

"Are you related to Gracie Allen? All right, already. But do you know how to decorate the tree?"

"Of course not, but I'm sure there are pictures in magazines we have at home. Maybe the salesperson can help us pick out something."

The Ravins walked around looking at trees, paying close attention to those other buyers were choosing. "How are we going to get the tree home?" Phyllis asked.

"We can come back in Esmeralda's van," Ian explained.

Momentarily, a salesman wandered up and asked how he could help them?

"We were just trying to figure a way to get a tree home," Ian said.

"No problem," the salesman told them. "We'll cover your car with plastic and tie the rope through the windows. Which one do you have in mind?"

"Something very pretty," Phyllis said.

"This birch is the best we've got. It's $15.00."

"That's good, but I don't know much about decorating a tree," Phyllis said.

"We've got you covered there, too. You see this garland? You criss-cross it all around the tree, and then these bulbs hang from the branches, and this tinsel—just hang it all over."

"If you're sure you can fix it so it won't scratch the car, we'll take it," Ian said.

"Just watch me," the salesman reached for the money Ian extended.

*   *   *

While Ian and Phyllis were struggling to get the tree

67

inside the house, Philip drove up. "What are you two doing?" he asked.

"Esmeralda is coming home tomorrow, and we wanted to surprise her," Phyllis said.

"Mera," Philip said.

"What mirror?" Phyllis asked.

"It's the middle of Esmeralda's name. Marty told me she likes to be called Mera. Her family and classmates calls her that."

Ian and his son Philip took the tree inside and Phyllis carried all the decorations. She laid the boxes on the sofa and asked: "Where do you think we should put the tree?"

"How about there beside the fireplace?" Philip suggested.

"That's vote number one. What do you say, Ian?"

"It seems to me that Philip has chosen the ideal place."

"I guess that is it then. The man at the lot said that the skirt would hide the bottom so let's try it both ways to see which looks best, with or without the skirt."

I suppose I should try rustling up some dinner while you two figure the tree thing out," Phyllis said as she left for the kitchen and began to search for leftovers. "Little girl, your new mama misses you already," she thought to herself, looking through several small dishes in the refrigerator. "What's this?" she asked herself out loud. "We had baked chicken two days ago, and there is plenty left. I'll make a chicken noodle soup."

Phyllis diced an onion, bell pepper, celery, and the chicken. She used the broth that was in the dish as the starter stock and allowed the vegetables to cook, before adding the chicken, canned tomatoes, and noodles. She added a little salt and pepper, and then thought about white vinegar. "I wonder why Mera uses white vinegar. Whatever her reasons are, she makes everything taste good. How much should I use? Maybe one tablespoon full."

After getting the soup on its way, she thought of making a tossed salad. "Any dummy can make a tossed salad. Hey, it's beginning to smell good in here. I'd better go check on the guys when I finish setting the table," she thought, thinking proudly of her efforts this day, from the tree idea, to the soup and salad fixings. "Let me see now," as she scooped up a spoon full of the concoction, blew on it to cool it down, and slurped it down. "Oh, good. I may get a passing grade yet, as mother and wife."

Meanwhile, the tree was coming to life with the skirt beneath it. Father and son seemed to be getting a great deal of pleasure in working on this project together. Ian noticed how diligently Philip was working, seemingly enjoying what he was doing, and Ian asked him: "How was your day, son?"

"My day was much less stressful. I've decided to let sleeping dogs lie. The issue may be there still, but the reason that caused it is dead."

"I'm glad to hear that. Your mother and I worry about you."

"I know you do, and I'm sorry. I'll see Marty as often as I can. He'll help me find my way back. I really miss the old gang sometimes and wish we could get together sometimes, but not like this."

"It's been a long time coming but we'll get there one day at a time. It won't be easy, you know that, don't you?"

"My little sister is to be thanked for whatever change you see happening to me. I can see her as a very brilliant and beautiful young woman instead of a threat."

"Praise God. I heard that," Phyllis said. "The tree is so beautiful. Do you think she'll think we're patronizing her?" Phyllis asked.

"We are in a way, but it's with good intentions. Besides, I've always wished I could celebrate Christmas like some of my classmates."

"You really felt that way?"

"Yes. I hated being a Jew. The kids called me a Christ

killer. I didn't want to punch their lights out; I wanted my own lights out forever."

"You had thoughts of suicide?" Phyllis gasped.

"I guess that is the reason why I got married. I thought it would change the way I felt. I even thought that the deep love and respect that I have for you and dad was abnormal. At least Annette told me it was."

"Oh, son, I'm so sorry. We didn't know," Phyllis said.

"I'm sorry, too. I've missed out on a lot by not having the courage to stand and deliver. The two of you are my best friends. You stood by me through it all."

"I'm sure that Mera will be pleased for sure when she sees this tree," Ian said.

With this said, they all formed a circle of embrace and held it as the tree glistened in the living room lights.

*   *   *

Esmeralda's visitor in her hospital room was somewhat strange to her. She remembered getting a glance of him at numerous religious functions, and wondered who he might be. He never spoke but smiled, and stared at her before disappearing. He was a white man of medium height and weight, light brown hair and dressed in typical clergyman's attire. His face was gentle and friendly, yet extremely concerned.

"Hello Esmeralda," the man spoke softly." I'm Rabbi Berak."

"Do you know me?" she asked.

"Yes. I know you in a way. That slogan you have on your van that reads "MY BOSS IS A JEWISH CARPENTER...well, my Boss is also the same Jewish Carpenter."

"But you're a Rabbi."

"I met your brother Clarence in Chicago several years ago when I was attending a conference there. He has been working through me to get your California businesses legally taken care of."

"If you've been doing this for years, why haven't you introduced yourself before? I've seen you on many occasions."

"I haven't introduced myself before, because it just now time, little girl. Didn't the Angel tell you?"

"In my dream, it said exactly what you've just said about it being time. I couldn't understand what it wanted me to do."

"You've done part of it when you turned the other cheek to Philip. You've also made wise investments to acquire the funds for expansion. The Ravin's are not aware that they were chosen to play an important part in this expansion in helping you lead the Jews to Jesus. Remember how all the wild animals mingled together in Isaiah 11:6, and God said that a little child shall lead them? That child is you, Esmeralda."

"How am I to do this?"

"Just follow the leadings of the Lord, and He will show you the way. I know you are aware that you are to enter a covenant with God, but the Ravin family is not aware that they, too, have been chosen to help you lead the Jews to Jesus."

"I know that I'm supposed to find a man called Terah. Can that be you?"

"I am Terah Berak."

Rabbi Terah told Esmeralda that he'd been helping her acquire her property holdings that she believed her brother Clarence was doing for her. Because of her age and race, no one would sell to her, nor would they sell to Clarence because he, too, was Negroid. Clarence had visited a conference of Messianic Jews in Chicago in answer to his prayers and had asked Rabbi Terah to look after his sister from afar.

Even though Esmeralda was aware that she owned

large parcels of land in Mandeville Canyon in Los Angeles, She was not aware that this included the synagogue where Rabbi Terah led a flock of both changed and unchanged Jews. She was told that the church would be the headquarters for her preparations; the steering committee was there, and they are the pivotal point.

"Your writing volumes are to be distributed to strategic areas throughout the world from the headquarters. You must also lead the teachings and lectures on Wednesday evenings and Sunday mornings. You are a novelty; your age, race, and intellect will be the key that shocks my people into listening.

"My people are not only very stubborn, but extremely superstitious. They may even think that you are not just a descendant of a prophetess, but the resurrection of the prophetess herself. On a negative side, they also believe in witchcraft. They may label you a young witch and try to burn you at the stake."

"I don't understand how The Emerald Corporation acquired your church. It is farther East than the property line," Esmeralda said.

"When the Emerald Corporation purchased the Mandeville Canyon property, even though the church is east of the property, it was tied up in an old deed that was never recorded as separate."

Rabbi Terah told Esmeralda that when he was told by Clarence to buy the property, he quick claimed it to the Emerald Corporation. "One reason the Angel told you it is time, the Emerald Corporation is $3 00.000.000 strong in liquid, businesses, and land assets. It is definitely time to use those assets to expand their teaching capabilities."

"Esmeralda, trust the Ravin family, they will protect you from serious harm."

"You said that you were aware that Philip hit me, didn't you?"

"Yes, I know it. That was God's plan to shock him out

of his depression. He will slump backwards from time to time with his dislike of you, but he will never hit you again."

"What should I do first, Rabbi Terah?"

"I have arranged for you to teach your first lesson the first Wednesday in January. You know what you are to teach?"

"Yes, I do."

Rabbi Terah blessed Esmeralda and hugged her before leaving, telling her that she was beset with trials and tribulations. "Just remember the teachings of Jesus the Christ."

He handed her a card with his telephone number on it and told her that she would need to call him often. "Volunteer at the Jewish home for the Aged; Uncle Zech can be helpful."

Esmeralda watched Rabbi Terah walk through the heavy door and watched it click shut behind him leaving her alone with millions of thoughts floating through her mind.

*   *   *

Saturday afternoon can be the loneliest day of the week, especially in a private room with no visitors coming in or going out. Dr. Lukas had told Esmeralda yesterday that she could go home today, but she was beginning to wonder where home was.

In her short fifteen years, she had lived everywhere. At home in Pittsburgh, her brother's friends wanted to take advantage of her, her mother was afraid of her, and the universities would not accept a child so young. She moved in with Clarence in Chicago, but his neighbors accused her of being his lover. And then she learned that UCLA would accept her at her age, so she moved in with her grandmother and two gay uncles.

She managed to get through several years with her

grandmother, but the inevitable showdown finally exploded. These uncles were afraid their friends would find Mera more desirable than they were, and they had asked her to leave.

She had lived for a short time with her only sister, who barely tolerated her because of sibling rivalry. Then her brother-in-law decided that he had the right to use her if she stayed in his home, so she had run away. She had not called the Ravins to tell them that she'd been discharged, for she was not sure they wanted her back.

No way could she call Dr. Heller, for she didn't want to jeopardize that friendship, and make his wife not like her. What a predicament to be caught up in. It was already past discharge time, and no resolution had entered her mind. She remembered an old song she used to hear her grandmother sing when she was making dinner rolls, and she began to hum it in her mind: "The lord will make a way somehow, It's when beneath the cross I bow. And I said to my soul, don't worry, for the Lord will make a way somehow."

He usually made a way in that run-down, raggedy old smoke filled stove in the country, for grandmother's rolls were always so tasty and smelled heavenly.

"Guess who gets to go home today?" It was Phyllis's voice as her face peeped around the door jam of Esmeralda's hospital room with Ian and Philip close behind. Esmeralda looked up towards the ceiling, as though she expected to find a messenger of the Lord fluttering there in the form of a bird.

"How did you know?" Esmeralda asked.

"A little birdie told me," Phyllis said. She and Ian took turns hugging and examining Esmeralda's face, but Philip thought it was best if he just stayed in the background. Esmeralda took several glances at him and wondered why he had wanted to come to the hospital also. Maybe he was feeling remorseful. Nah. Not this hard shell recluse, she thought.

Phyllis waved her hand at the two men and told them to leave the room so that she could help get Mera dressed.

"How do you know my nick name is Mera?"

"A little birdie told me that also... Now, hurry, let me help you with those."

"Why are we hurrying?"

"I'm just excited to have my little girl home again. Here, let me do that."

"I can do it, I'm better now. I think I'll need some papers from the office."

"I've got your paroled papers right here in my purse. All we need is a wheelchair. Look, here comes your carriage now."

Mera looked up to see a nurse pushing a wheelchair with Ian close behind. Philip had decided to stay outside the room.

The Ravin's Mercedes rolled to a stop in the driveway of their home, and Phyllis squeezed Esmeralda's hand. "Its s good to have you home again," Phyllis said.

Esmeralda wanted to say that it was good to be home, but she thought she'd better wait and see what developed.

"I made that nail soup you always talked about. It was delicious," Phyllis laughed.

"What on earth is nail soup?" Philip asked.

"That's a private joke between Mera and me. I've ordered dinner from the Calorie Counter. A messenger will deliver it about six." There was a long pause, and the family just stared at each other, seemingly waiting for just the right time or words to clear up their next question. "Mera, the Manager Booker told us that he's your uncle."

"Yes, ma'am."

"He also called you his boss."

"Yes, ma'am."

The Ravins seemed disappointed with Mera's answers for they were expecting much more explanation than she had offered, and they all looked at each other with a fixed puzzling stare.

"What does all this mean, Mera?" Ian asked.

"When I came, I told you that I could support myself, but I was just too young to live alone without parental supervision. I'm not ready to talk about it now, but if you're patient, it will be soon. Is that OK?"

"Whenever you're ready," Ian said.

"Soon, the time is very soon," she explained.

They all exited the car and started for the entrance, when Mera stopped, remembering that she'd left her attaché case in the car: "My books, I need my attaché case."

"Philip has it," Ian told her, calmly.

She turned to look at Philip, her eyes fixed on his in a hypnotic gaze, and it appeared that they were both in a trance, unable to let go of the gaze. Phyllis didn't want to know what this action meant, for she thought it would jeopardize her rights to have her little girl. Had her son really let sleeping dogs lie? Was Esmeralda ever going to forgive him? Would she eventually run away again?

Phyllis had no answers for her questions. She only wanted this tension to end: "Come on, child, we have a surprise for you." She pulled Mera's arm and led her toward the entrance, and the four of them entered the house. When they entered the living room, Mera's eyes lit up like two big green candles, and a slight gasp of air escaped her throat.

"You did this for me?" she asked.

"You've done so much for us that we thought..."

Mera interrupted Phyllis. "This is against your religious beliefs. You didn't have to do it."

"But we wanted to," Ian told her. "And now that it's done, we all like it."

Phyllis embraced Mera and kissed her cheek: "I think the spirit of Christmas is contagious."

"That is the most beautiful tree that I have ever seen."

Mera walked to the tree and kneeled down, bowing reverently.

"Ian and Philip did an excellent job of decorating the tree while I made that nail soup," Phyllis commented.

"Thank you, God," Mera prayed out loud.

CHAPTER VII

Enormous plans were under way for a big Christmas dinner. The twelve-seat dining room table had been extended into the foyer, with rentals attached. The aroma from the kitchen was simply heavenly. Everyone had been assigned a special task. Setting the tables, polishing the silver, washing the china, and stacking it in readiness were assigned to Philip and Ian.

Phyllis sat at the kitchen table, chopping fruits, vegetables and filling pans with the mixtures that Mera had concocted. The hutch in the dining room was filled with cakes, pies, halvah, and baklava, all sitting on a white linen table cover. The smell was just like that of an old fashioned Brooklyn bakery.

Periodically, Mera glanced into the living room to look at the beautiful tree with all of its wrapped gifts beneath its branches. Christmas music on the stereo was beautiful and soft but suddenly mixed with the ding donging of persistent ringing of the front door bell. When Philip answered the door, it was Marty, Evelyn and their two boys.

"I'm so excited, I couldn't wait for tomorrow," Evelyn exclaimed, bubbling over with joy, and her boys ran for the tree. Marty and Philip embraced, and Philip kissed Evelyn, inviting them to come in. As Philip started to close the door, another set of car lights flashed in his eyes.

"It's Joe. What's going on here? Tomorrow is Christmas. Come on in; I sure hope you brought your aprons, there's plenty work to be done, just check with Mera. She's a slave driver," he teased. Philip kissed Pamela and their little shy boy and shook hands with his best friend Joel.

Little J.J. ran to the tree to join the Heller kids, and there they stayed, transfixed for the remainder of the evening.

In the kitchen, Mera asked Evelyn to remove the first batch of baklava and chocolate chip cookies from the large oven and add them to the bakery on the hutch.

Is that the sampling batch?" Joe asked, as he burned his hand on a hot chocolate chip.

"If anyone gets to sample, it'll be me. I'm the one who always wanted Christmas, remember."

"You were too young to know the difference. I'm the one who taught you," Marty proclaimed. The sampling should be mine," he demanded.

Mera watched the men in amazement, putting the last of the stuffing into the large bird that took both she and Phyllis to slide it into the baking bag, and return it to the refrigerator...

"What's this?" Pam asked, pointing to the large number of pies sitting on the hutch.

"It's pumpkin pies," Joel explained.

"I hate to tell you this, boys," said Ian, "but I've got the cut samples over here, and it's not pumpkin, it's sweet potato. As Mera taught me some new jargon, it is so good; it'll make a Bull dog hug a Hound."

They all rushed for their taste sample, laughing at Ian's description.

"I had these when Marty was doing some research in Louisiana, but they didn't taste like this."

"So, who's coming tomorrow?" Joe asked Philip.

"All of those who've confirmed are Uncle Zech and aunt Winnie; Dr. Berman and wife; Ben and Tussah, Nathan, Marge and kids and Rabbi Terah Berak."

"Rabbi Berak is coming? Evelyn asked. We'd better be on our best behavior. Who invited the Rabbi?"

"Uncle Zech asked us to invite him. He will help us understand our first Christmas

"Oh ,God, please don't let anyone go into labor tonight, or tomorrow," Joel pleaded prayerfully.

"I tried to tell you about that specialty, but you wouldn't listen," Marty said.

"I really enjoy what I do. There is nothing more rewarding than seeing a new life for the first time, and that sweet little cry just tears at my heartstrings. I just want them to take it easy tonight and tomorrow. After all, I've never celebrated Christmas before."

Phyllis hugged Mera, saying: "Just look at the excitement you've caused."

"I'm so sorry. I didn't mean to cause family chaos," Mera said apologetically.

"Does anybody her appear to be in chaos?" Marty asked. "I've never seen a bunch of hook nosed Jews more happy than they are here tonight."

"You speak of your own nose," Evelyn said. "I happen to believe I have a very lovely nose."

"Me, too," Phyllis said.

Pam tugged at Joel's sleeve: "Joe, have you seen out kids starring at that tree? I don't know how we're going to get them to go home tonight."

"Why go home?" Ian said. "Mera has a big bed, and so does Philip, and there are sofa beds in the living room and den. A day bed is in Mara's and Philip's office."

"And there are plenty of blankets," Phyllis said.

"Are you sure?" Pam asked.

"I really don't care; I'm staying," Evelyn said.

"Mera, do we open gifts tonight or in the morning?" Phyllis asked.

"Usually, its early Christmas morning, but I don't think it really matters."

"Our gifts are in the car. We had planned to leave them tonight and return tomorrow," Joe said.

"Evelyn packed our gifts with plans to stay the night," Marty laughed.

"You know what, I have no problems with being a Jew, but sometimes there are limits to the lines we are not supposed to cross, so much we miss out, our kids miss out. This year, no matter what the Rabbi says, I'm going to live it up," Evelyn promised.

*   *   *

Mera was up early to put the turkey and prime rib roast in the double oven. Evelyn and Phyllis were right behind. Philip and Mera had slept in their offices, and gave their bedrooms to their guests.

"I thought I heard Pam up when I passed the door to their room," Mera said.

Evelyn scoffed and said: "Not that primadonna Jewish princess. It'll take her an hour alone just to put her makeup on. And she doesn't look any better."

"That's not nice, Evelyn," Phyllis reprimanded.

"But it's true." Evelyn did not bite her tongue.

"Mera, what's that black stuff you're putting on the roast," Evelyn asked with curiosity.

"It's cracked black pepper; garlic cloves go into the knife puncture holes, about a tablespoon full of salt for the whole thing, and then you cook it uncovered at 300 degrees for about five hours."

"How'd you learn to cook such delicious dishes at such a young age?" Evelyn asked.

"I learned by watching members of my family and by experimenting on my own," Mera told her.

"You're going to steal some man's heart away. You know what they say: the way to a man's heart is through his stomach." Evelyn teased.

"I hope I won't have to rely on my culinary skills to secure a relationship with the man I'll marry." Mera smiled politely, but she was entertaining deeper thoughts, recording in her mind questions she wanted to ask uncle Zech.

"I forgot to tell you, Mera. A package came the other

day from Georgia. It smells like meat, and is awfully heavy," Phyllis said.

"It must be a Tailmadge ham from Miss Edna. Besides the sausage, we'll have country ham, grits, scrambled eggs, hot biscuits, orange juice, and coffee. I hope everyone eats ham and sausage," Mera said.

"I know how to make good coffee," Phyllis said.

"I make some mean scrambled eggs," was Evelyn's reply.

"What can I do?" Pam's voice startled the others.

"You up?" Evelyn said.

"Of course, I'm up," Pam snapped.

"You can start the sausage to cook on the grill as soon as it gets hot. Cut the bag open and slice the patties about a half inch thick. When that's done, the ham will be your job also," Mera said.

Mera and Phyllis opened the heavy package from Georgia and cut open the gauze covering next to the meat.. Mera stood back and declared: "We need one of those surgeons for this operation."

"We're here," Joe and Philip said in unison.

Mera proceeded to tell them how she wanted the meat sliced and gave them two of the sharpest knives in the drawer. Joe cut the wedges, and Philip cut it into slices for cooking. After parboiling and drying the ham, they passed it to Pam to put on the grill.

Mera kneaded biscuits, rolled them out on waxed paper, and cut them with the edge of a drinking glass dipped in flour. She saturated them in melted butter, placed them on a large cookie sheet, and into the vacant oven. Phyllis stirred grits according to Mera's instructions, Ian poured orange juice, and Marty set the plates and forks with Joe and Philip's help.

"I like this assembly line," Evelyn said.

"Do you get the impression that we're in each others way?" Pam asked.

"Who cares?" Phyllis said. "It really feels good being together like this."

"What about the gifts?" Joe asked. "When do we do that thing?"

"As soon as the kids are up, we'll eat and open presents."

"Will somebody go get the kids up for goodness sakes," Philip said. "I'm too excited to wait."

"Why don't you calm down, buddy," Evelyn said, shaking her finger in his face. "It's my first Christmas, too."

There were a good many compliments throughout breakfast, but it was easily discernable that the new Christmas recruits were anxiously awaiting their turn to open a gift.

*   *   *

Breakfast was over, dishes washed, and everything cleaned up, for the crowd had gathered in the living room where the tree and gifts were displayed.

"Someone will have to play Santa, and pass out the gifts," Mera said.

Ian stood up, slapping himself on the chest. "That'll have to be me. I'm the most Santa looking guy here, besides I'm the oldest."

"You won't get an argument out of me," Mera said. "Now did Santa stack the kid's gifts together so they could be easily found?"

"When he sneaked in to cut a piece of cake, I think I saw him do just that," Marty said.

After the children had opened their gifts, they were busy playing with toys. The guests declared that they'd received just what they needed or wanted; it was now time for the Ravin family to open their big boxes from Mera.

Philip unwrapped several sharkskin suits in an array of

colors, matching shirts, socks, ties, and shoes made of Italian leather. Ian and Phyllis opened their packages which contained the same, except there were no shoes.

When Mera opened her gift that read from mom, dad and your big brother, she felt a hot tear boil over in her eyes, She really loved the new attaché case and 24 carat gold desk clock with pearls on the hour settings. The brief case she owned sustained numerous scars in the leather, and it was time she replaced it. She was truly happy with their choice.

Everyone had opened expensive trinkets and pretended that it was something they needed even if it was not.

"Go on, Philip, try one of your suits on. I especially like the small hound's tooth and black accessories," Evelyn prompted.

"Why don't you all try them on, so that I can see where we will need to alter them," Mera told her family.

When the Ravins returned, all three of them looked like the pages of vogue magazine. The fits were perfect, and everyone was amazed at how handsome and dapper Philip looked.

"My God, Phil, I've never seen you look so good," Evelyn said.

"Are you trying to tell me that you'd trade me in for a younger model?" Marty asked.

"If I wanted a boy toy, it would have to be someone less than two years your junior... Admit it. He looks good from head to toe" Evelyn remarked.

"He is looking damn good. What do you think, Mera?" Marty asked.

"The change is refreshing, she said cautiously.

*   *   *

The special guests were arriving, and everything was ready. The Ravin home had never sparkled so brightly, smelled so good, or heard so many happy compliments.

Uncle Zech offered the holiday prayer. He seemed to have had a revitalized physical condition since Thanksgiving. Everyone noticed it, and when he prayed, the new awareness seemed to take place in the minds of all who were present. They all raised their heads at the very precise moment and looked around the table at each other as the twelve Disciples must've done during the Last Supper, when they asked: "Lord, is it I?" The small children looked around with curiosity and impatience, their eyes fixed on Uncle Zech as he began the prayer blessings for the day.

"Almighty, Omnipotent God. God of Abraham, Isaac, and Jacob. We bow humbly before you to receive your special blessings. Thank you for sending your Messenger from Zion to open our eyes to the realization that Your Son, our Messiah, has come. As we celebrate His Birth here today, Lord God Jehovah, we offer these bountiful table settings as our praise and thanksgiving to you. May this house always be a beacon that will lead others to the truth and bring joy to all who enter. Amen."

Everyone sat quietly, obviously trying to understand Uncle Zech's prayers. Most of them stared at Esmeralda, wondering if the old Rabbi was talking about her as the messenger who had come.

Realizing their confusion, Rabbi Terah put his hands together prayerfully and said: "Lord, let us enjoy this mouth watering food that sits before us now, Amen." He rubbed his hands together as he spread his napkin on his lap, and a faint sound of soft laughter spread around the table.

Almost like battery-powered robots, the group was alive and started passing food around, as they spoke of the appetizing appeal it had and the excitement of the day.

Before touching her food, Aunt Winnie made an announcement: "Be it known to all that I'm divorcing Zechariah."

"You're kidding, of course," Ian said.

"Have you ever known me to make jokes?" Aunt Winnie asked.

"What has you so riled up, aunt Winnie?" Phyllis asked.

"Just look at him. Two months ago he had one foot in the grave and the other on black ice. He could hardly talk. Sounded like he had marbles in his mouth. Now he's spruced up and suddenly come back to life. Only a young woman can do that to a man. And when there's another woman, the wife can't do anything right anymore."

"Hush, woman! Eat this good food. You won't eat so good at the retirement home," Zech reminded her.

"I think he's in love with your pretty little foster daughter. Since Thanksgiving, he talks about her all the time. He's even writing a journal for her."

Unaware that Aunt Winifred was joking, Esmeralda stopped eating, and placed her fork down on her plate, breathing deeply to hold back tears.

One of the male guests smiled as he stared at Mera and teased a compliment: "If Zech plans to be unfaithful, he could not have chosen a more beautiful woman."

Esmeralda pushed her chair back, so that she could leave the table, but Rabbi Terah restrained her. "I think it is good that Rabbi Zech is writing a journal; it keeps his mind agile and his spirits uplifted. He's waited a long time for this day," Rabbi Terah said.

Forks were clinking against plates, but many did not understand what was going on in the minds the two Rabbis.

"Rabbi Terah, what is your opinion about Christmas?" Ian asked.

"It is a day when Christians celebrate the birth of Jesus the Christ. I'm not sure if he was born on December 25, because the Roman calendar that we follow has been changed many times, but just as the Jews celebrate Honniker and Thanksgiving, those days are also changed."

"You say the birth of Jesus the Christ like a person who believes He existed." Marty said.

"Oh, He existed alright. No one ever doubted that fact. Even the Jews do not dispute it."

"But I thought Jews don't believe in Him," Philip said.

"It's not that we don't believe in Him, the Jews don't accept the fact that He is the Messiah. So Jews are still waiting for their Savior."

"Do you accept that fact, Rabbi?" Philip asked.

"Come to Temple sometime, son. We are a group of Messianic Jews or Jews converted to Christianity. That is why Zechariah was suspended years ago. He had learned the truth and was teaching it in the Synagogue. I think the change Winnie is seeing in Zech is prophesy being fulfilled. He said in his prayers that a Messenger from Zion would come to lead our people. Zech and I believe that Messenger is here now."

Rabbi Terah patted Winnie's arm assumingly and whirled around to face Esmeralda, who was fidgeting nervously.

"Who are you child, and where are you from?" Rabbi Terah asked firmly.

"I am Esmeralda, from Georgia."

"These people are your friends. It is time that they know who you are. They can help you with your mission, but you must tell them now," Rabbi Terah demanded.

Reluctantly, Esmeralda whispered, just barely audible: "I am the great grand daughter of Huldah the prophetess, hundreds of times removed. She lived and taught in the Kings courtyard during the reign of King Josiah. Our people were exiled to Ethiopia by the Jews, due to their extreme astuteness. There, they became known as the Totem tribe and spread back into Israel and eventually the United States as American Indians.

"Why was Huldah so important to your mission to-

87

day?" Rabbi Terah asked.

"She was the only person who could decipher the meaning of the lost book of laws when the Priest Hilkiah found it in the Temple ruins. They wanted Jeremiah to try to understand the book, but the king sent for the Prophetess Huldah, who unveiled the future of a nation. She prophesied national ruin because of disobedience to the commands of God. Her prophetic messages and public readings of the law that others couldn't understand brought about a national revival.

"Many of my ancestors were teachers, engineers and doctors by the time they were twelve years old."

"My studies would never have come up with the answer to her advancement—why she has a Masters Degree at age fifteen," Marty said.

"If she'd had the support she needed from her family, instead of everyone wanting to sleep with her, she would have a doctorate at fifteen," Uncle Zech said.

"This gorgeous young thing will never get married?" Evelyn asked.

Rabbi Terah smiled disbelievingly: "She is human just like any other woman, just called to service as Uncle Zech and I are. What did the Angels tell you about your future as a wife and mother, as Huldah was?'

"She talks to angels?" Evelyn asked.

"The angel said that my husband and I will have four children: two sons and two daughters. The first born will be twins: a son, and daughter, and then a son and last a daughter."

"These are visionary conversations during her dreams. Just as Daniel, and Ezekiel had," Rabbi Terah said. "We all have these kinds of dreams, but we soon forget them. Esmeralda's dreams are prophetic because she has been chosen to help our people."

The dinner table had turned into a place for teaching and from time to time, Uncle Zech spelled Rabbi Terah from the arduous task of explaining everyone's questions. When they tried to stop the lesson, the curiosity became more intense. The question came up about humanity's and civilization's of black verses African.

They were told by Esmeralda that all black people are not African, and all Africans are not black. There were black people living on the continents of India and Asia, making reference to the Mesopotamian area. Cush, a grand son of Noah (Kish) is found in Genesis 2:13, and the ancient civilization of Sumer in the Land of Shinar in Genesis 10:10-11:1. The Sumerian civilization was made predominantly by Nimrod, a descendant of Cush.

"Are you saying that we could all be black?" Phyllis asked.

Phyllis was told that the two very distinct geographical territories were Africa and Mesopotamia in the Tigris Euphrates Valley. So it was from this territory that Cush's descendants migrated not from Africa, but into Africa. Archeological and historical facts say that the roots of all people are in Africa/Egypt. Abraham was a Shem descendant, a brother of Ham. Noah had three sons: Japheth, a pale white son; Shem, an olive complexion son; and Ham, a black son.

"It would be an untruth to say that all people would've been black, but somewhere between black and white probably. The pale white descendants of Japheth were said to be a curse, a reminder of leprosy for their disobedience, fornication, homosexuality and idolatry. As is the Negroid mark God placed on Cain for murdering his brother Able. Ham was cursed for laughing at his father Noah's nakedness.

*   *   *

While the Christmas celebration was going on at the Ravin's home, no one was aware that the evil group of or-

89

ganized protestors called the Yarmulke, for the purity of Jews, was holding a sinister meeting in another part of town.

This group was as secretive and more poisonous than the Ku Klux Klan. They were bent on stopping the further- ance of the kingdom of God and all who proclaimed Jesus the Christ as Messiah.

The intent of this group was to keep Judaism pure and free of the claim that the Messiah had come. They wanted no infiltration of foreign prophets and wanted to steal by force the information that Christian leaders might have.

The leader was a very dapper, false prophet named Daniel, who stood in front of his followers at a large Syna- gogue, proclaiming his power as ruler.

"Our aim here is to keep the Jews pure and to stop the conversion to Christians at all costs."

The crowd roared with excitement and applause.

"The time has come for us to pull together and stop the upcoming prophetess. She's fifteen years old and is about to lunch a full campaigned for recruitment to Christianity."

"Who is she?" a voice yelled out from the floor.

"According to history, she is a Cushite, extremely as- tute and her name is Esmeralda. This girl holds the key to knowledge that could change the history of the world."

"What is this knowledge that she holds?" a voice rang out.

"It is a secret that no earthly person understands except her, and one that our people should not be told about. It will defame the true Hebrew Torah. When you find her, bring her to me. Do not harm her. I must have her tell me the se- crets that she is holding—this prophesy of God."

*   *   *

The dinner was winding down at the Ravin home, and Rabbi Terah had just asked Dr. Heller a question that made

90

all heads turn: "We all have spiritual gifts according to God's scriptures. Dr. Heller, you should know something about Parapsychology, and those spiritual gifts."

"We are in the middle of that research but have not written the conclusive papers on it yet. Therefore, I hesitate to divulge my conclusions until those findings are registered," he said.

"Sometimes we are not aware of His callings and often anger Him with our stubbornness, and then we pay a high price during our lifetime with the choices we make. What we are today depends on the choices we made in the past," Rabbi Terah said.

Uncle Zech spoke up with determination: "Enough of this kind of talk. When it's time for you to make a change, God will notify you. Dr. Berman, how's your young protégée?" He gently jabbed Philip on his arm.

"I couldn't have prayed for a better assistant," Dr. Berman said.

Philip's face flushed red with the delight of such a compliment: "Thank you, sir. You just made my day."

This small talk continued for at least another half hour before the Christmas party started to clear out. With the assembly line in the kitchen and dining room, food was put away, dishes washed, and stored.

Finally alone in the kitchen, Mera started to remember the events that had taken place during the day, and she began to tremble. She thought for certain she would be labeled an evil witch. No assurance that Rabbi Terah or uncle Zech had made would convince her otherwise. What if this news would cause her new family to alienate her? she wondered, as she thought of Philip's hands around her throat, squeezing the life out of her.

Then suddenly her suspicions switched to the Rabbi. She thought of his charming smile that could so swiftly change to a murderous scowl. Maybe these people were holding her prisoner, she thought. If they are my jailers and

91

allowed me to die here, how could I fulfill God's prophesy? The Antichrist has deceiving powers. He could be orchestrating everything that is happening. Was God ready for me to confess my mission? The angel said "It is time." Was today the beginning of that time?

Esmeralda began to pray silently: "Please, help me, God. Still my trembling heart and remove my doubts and mistrusts. Speak to me now, and let me know what I am to do." She groped through the darkened service porch, trying to open the back door to take out the trash. For the hundredth time, she struggled with that door. She tried pushing it with her shoulder and all of her weight behind it, but there were no results except a near dislocated shoulder and bruised flesh.

Mera did not realize that the door was not locked. It was her own fears that had caused her dilemma. When Ian pushed gently on the door, it opened without any effort at all. She dropped the trash and let out a scream that would pierce an ice glacier.

No amount of assurance that Ian offered could calm her fears. It was only in Phyllis' arms that her whimpering turned to apologetic pity.

"It's alright, child. I'm here," Phyllis said.

"I don't know what came over me. I thought the door was locked."

"The guys will take the trash out. "Come with me and sit down... You've only been out of the hospital a few days, and this was a very tiring event."

Philip had difficulty taking the trash from Mera's hand but finally managed it: "I can truly say that I never had such a good time, thanks to you," he said.

"I'm grateful that you allowed me to be a part of your happiness," she said.

Phyllis assisted Mera to her room, helped her dress for bed, and then covered her with the blanket. Before leaving, she kissed her gently on the cheek, and then turned off the light as she watched her close her eyes.

*   *   *

On a beautiful Sunday morning in February, Mera was dressing to leave for church. When she passed Philip's bedroom door, she heard him singing Danny Boy. His voice was a low tenor and so melodious it seemed captivating. She stood still until he had almost finished the song, and then she went downstairs.

Phyllis and Ian were still in the breakfast area sipping coffee, reading bills and the Sunday paper as Mera looked in to say good bye.

"I'm sorry Philip missed breakfast. I'm going now."

"Don't you worry about him. We'll scrounge up something whenever he's up and about. He seldom gets a chance to sleep late. I think the rest will do him good."

"He's up now. I heard him singing. I'll be back about one o'clock to fix dinner."

"Is there something I can start preparing for you?" Phyllis asked.

"If you'd like, you can break the green beans and make a tossed salad. Baked chicken and macaroni and cheese don't take long. The chicken is dressed and ready to go into the oven. The beans and veggies are in the vegetable tray of the refrigerator. I made a pound cake last night. See ya."

"Drive carefully and say a prayer for us." Phyllis said.

Mera peeked back around the door smiling: "I always do." Then she exited.

"What's the problem, Ian?' You haven't said a word, and the furrows on your face are telling me something is wrong."

"It's another bad check. This one is for five thousand dollars. I don't know how much longer we can pay the office rent."

"Maybe you shouldn't talk about bad checks and hard

93

times in front of the kids. Philip blames himself for our dilemma, and Mera may feel that she's a problem to us."

"I really didn't mean to get carried away last night. Maybe we should try working with an established law firm."

"I've thought about that, too, but we're approaching fifty. I'm not sure a law firm would consider us at this stage of our lives. They're usually looking for vibrant young lawyers.

"Good morning, son," Phyllis said smiling.

Philip was casually dressed and entered the breakfast area. He poured himself a cup of coffee and then sat down.

"Would you like some breakfast?" Phyllis asked.

"Just toast would be nice and a glass of orange juice," he said.

Phyllis put two slices of bread in the toaster and poured a glass of orange juice. When the toast popped up, she applied butter to the sides of it, cut it in half, and set the plate before Philip.

"Where's Mera?" Philip asked, sipping his coffee.

"She went to church; she'll be back about one," Ian said.

"You don't dislike her now?" Phyllis asked.

"She's OK. Well... er... She's kinda sweet and er...helpful. Actually, she's smart and very pretty.

"When you visit Marty, have you discussed this special messenger thing the Rabbi's were talking about?" Ian asked.

"I thought I'd leave it alone and see what comes of it," Philip suggested. He spread his hands open and hunched up his shoulders. "Dr. Berman asked about it though. He strongly feels we should all become Christians. His son had embraced Christianity before he was killed in Korea. He said it is a good thing."

"What do you think, son?" Ian asked.

"I think we should just let sleeping dogs lie. By the

94

way, Dr. Berman has offered me a partnership in his practice when my State Board License is back. This will mean a sizable increase in salary. What do you think of my staying on here and paying rent?"

"Son, you know you can stay as long as you like. We're not asking for money," Ian said.

"I know that, dad, but it's only right that I do this. You've done so much for me."

"Whatever you feel is fair," Ian told him.

"There will come a day when your own home and family will need your support. So why don't you..."

"Mom," he interrupted. "I don't know if a family will ever be for me. Right now, I'd like to rule that notion out of my plans."

"You know what you want to do," Phyllis said. There was sadness in her voice that cried out for the grandchildren she felt she would never have.

CHAPTER VIII

At the Mandeville Canyon Temple, Mera was about to leave after the service, but a great many worshippers had her cornered near the exit. They were asking questions and praising her for the lesson she had just taught.

"When will your book be out?" a woman asked.

Esmeralda told them that her book would be out in March, and she thanked them for their kindness. She tilted her head when she heard her name being paged over the public address system. It was Rabbi Terah, asking her to meet him for a brief meeting in the library.

She was surprised to see another Rabbi enter with Rabbi Terah.

"Esmeralda, this is Rabbi John Schulman."

Esmeralda stood, extending her hand to the gentleman before her.

The new Rabbi was tall and slender and his early blond balding was covered by a small skull cap. His eyes were gentle, as he spoke: "I've been anxious to meet you," he told Mera.

She bowed respectfully, smiling up at him. "What is it that you want of me?" she asked.

"Rabbi Schulman is trying to establish a Christian Temple in San Francisco and has brought along sketches for you to look at," Rabbi Terah said.

Extending the folder, Rabbi Schulman told Mera that the property consisted of twenty acres in a very prime location. "Although the synagogue there is small, the property is rented, and the congregation is out growing the present building."

"Have you reviewed the sketches, Rabbi Terah?"

"I have and feel that the possibility is promising."

"When can I see this property?"

"What about next Saturday? You'll be out of school then," Rabbi Schulman said.

"I'd like to bring my foster parents, if you don't mind."

"I don't mind at all. My wife and I will meet you at the airport."

"I'll call you with our time of arrival, and hotel reservations."

"You won't need a hotel; you will be staying with us. Our kids are married and moved out, so there is plenty room.

Esmeralda took the folder with the sketches and financial statements and bade the men good day.

*　　*　　*

Sunday dinner at the Ravin home had become a tradition already. The table was set and dishes of delicious food steamed from their trivets waiting to be served, as the family took their usual places. They all bowed their heads as Mera prayed which had also become an acceptable tradition.

Phyllis was first to notice that Mera was picking at her food and asked: "What's the matter, child?"

"I need to go to San Francisco but will need an escort, and I was not sure if I should ask."

"When do you plan to go?" Ian asked

"Next Saturday. I have an eleven o'clock appointment."

Then you plan to fly up?" Ian asked.

"Yes, sir," Mera responded, flinching for she knew there was a problem about to be told as to why her parents could not go with her.

"I'm not sure we can afford it," Ian said.

"Just say you and mom will go, and the tickets will be

97

arranged. It's a business trip and will be paid by the corporation."

"What about hotel accommodations?"

"We're going to stay with Rabbi and Mrs. John Schulman. The business is at his request."

"What do you think, Phyllis?" Ian asked, turning to his wife.

Phyllis put her hands up in an agreement resolution: "Let's do it."

"What's so urgent in San Francisco?" Philip asked with skepticism.

Mera looked at Philip, trying to understand if he was just curious or was he trying to keep his parents from accepting the offer to escort her: "The trip is an acquisition."

"Acquiring what?" Philip asked suspiciously.

"It is corporate expansion," Mera said.

"Alright, honey. I think it's time you told us what's going on," Ian demanded.

"Yeah!" Philip chided. "A sewing factory, restaurant. Now what?"

Phyllis sat with her elbows on the table and her hands beneath her chin, awaiting the explanations she'd hoped Mera would talk about.

With a deep sigh, Mera appeared trapped or just too tired to fulfill her obligations without getting help: "The Christian temples are expanding rapidly and so is the rest of the Emerald Corporation. With my studies, teachings and company growth, it is getting to be too much for me alone."

"We'd like to help, but we need to know what it is you need," Ian said.

"After dinner, I'd like you to review the books and tell me if you and mom would consider being joint CEOs of a multi-million dollar corporation. We could start you with an annual salary of two million if that is satisfactory. Of course a contract would need to be drawn up with your salary demands and job descriptions."

Philip all but fell off his chair laughing: "You are truly a dreamer, aren't you? If what you just said was true, I'd be better off leaving medicine and joining your corporation."

"Please, Philip," Ian said, annoyed. "Mera, is that all you're going to tell us?"

"You won't fully understand until you've reviewed the books. I borrowed them from the CPA and must return them by Wednesday. For now, remember that my name is Esmeralda, which is Spanish for Emerald, or green. The business is called the Emerald Corporation. But first, please enjoy your dinner."

The Ravin family stared at Mera for a moment and then at each other before they took their dessert and coffee. Then Mera broke the silence: "I heard you singing this morning Philip, and was very impressed. I wish you'd record some music that I've written."

"I've heard you singing from time to time and think you should record your own music," Philip answered.

"I have a voice like Cinderella, and only Walt Disney would record me. Even then, no one would buy the records," she said.

"I'm not a singer; I'm a doctor," Philip snapped.

"That fact alone would sell the records. It would be exceptional for a white Jewish doctor to sing black spirituals. You'd rupture the charts."

"Where would we record it or sell it?" Philip asked.

"I'd take care of that. We'd record you, do a concert, and Ouch! You'd be bought everywhere. An overnight million record sale."

Philip shook his head disbelievingly: "Yeah, right."

Mera stood up, gently poked Philip's nose with her index finger, and then pointed both index fingers in his direction: "If I tell you there's cheese on the moon, you'd better take your crackers and wine," she teased.

Mera's joking statement made Phyllis and Ian laugh, and Philip looked at them as he decided to accept the challenge: "OK, where's the music?"

"Do you read sheet music?" she asked.

"Yes, I read sheet music," he said firmly

"The music is in my office. When I return from San Francisco, we'll do it. I'll call uncle Alvin, and he'll set it up with the musicians," she said.

"If I'm going to do it, I want my guys to accompany me."

"What guys are you talking about?" she asked.

"I'm talking about Joel, Marty, Ben and Nathan," he replied.

"Musicians? Mom, is this true?" she asked.

"They used to play pretty good in high school. Joe blew the saxophone, Ben lead guitar, Nathan played bass, and your friend Marty played mean drums."

"I can't believe Dr. Heller is a drummer. He doesn't look like a drummer. He's always so exact, so straight laced and professional. What about you Philip? Did you sing?" she asked.

"There were no singers in our band. I played the keyboard."

"So, that's your piano?"

"The piano is mom's."

"I've got to hear you guys play, and you need to learn to sing like a black person. You know, with the physical feeling in it."

"Let me see the music," Philip said.

"I'll get it; keep your shirt on."

*   *   *

Mera and Philip were playing around with the music in the living room; Phyllis and Ian were in their office upstairs going over the financial statements of the Emerald Corporation.

A cold wind had decided to push some darkened

clouds across the sky, covering what was left of a produc-
tive Sunday afternoon. The flash of lightening and gentle
roll of thunder brought shattering rain upon the window
panes and rooftop. Mera shook off the chill by rubbing her
shoulders, and Philip got up to adjust the heater thermostat.

"Let's build a fire," Mera requested.

Philip stopped to stare at the smiling face of his eager
little sister, and then thinking for a moment, he decided to
accommodate her wish. He stooped over to put logs on the
gas jetted fireplace and the open fire crackled quickly as he
adjusted the logs.

"I'll go make some coffee while you're doing that.
Maybe Mom and Dad would like some, also." She disappeared into the kitchen, and soon the aroma of coffee perk-
ing permeated the air.

Philip was still playing the untuned piano and mouth-
ing the words to the song, when Mera returned with a tray,
four cups, cream, sugar and a decanter of freshly brewed
coffee. With her back towards the outer door, she poured
Philip a cup, remembering how he took it...

"I'll have some with you as soon as I run some up
stairs to..."

"You can pour them all here," Ian said, startling Mera,
cutting her statement short.

Mera poured the two additional cups of coffee and
stared at her parents in disbelief: "You've finished reading
those files already?" she asked.

"Yes, Mera, and now its show and tell time." Ian said
with determination...

Mera looked around the room at her new family, and
tears began to flood her eyes, for dredging up memories as
painful as she was about to do was a most difficult thing for
her. She thought how happy Philip would be when he heard
of her trials and tribulations, and she knew if she was to get
her new parents to assist her in her business, they'd need to
know everything. So the sorted details began.

"Please sit here in front of the fire and try to relax, for this is a story I never like to talk about." When everyone was comfortably seated and the fire was adjusted, they all turned their eyes towards Esmeralda...

She told them that she was born on a three horse farm in Georgia... By the frown on their faces, she knew that they did not understand what the horses had to do with things, so she explained that the more promising the farmers were, the larger their farms and the more horses they needed to attend the farm. Every forty acres required another horse.

This was farmland and did not include the forest and pasture land which was probably another forty acres. Also, her father and many others owned tractors, but the land was still measured by horsepower, as today's cars are.

God had carefully laid his plans from the moment she was conceived. She had been born the seventh of eight children, and her mother had also been the seventh child in her family as well. In African and German folklore, this was an omen of special powers. Most people dismissed it as superstition. Not only was the child born with the mark of the Seventh child of a Seventh child, it shocked it's parents and midwife by being born with its bright green eyes wide open, finger nails long and folded over the tops of its fingers; it arrived still in the placenta sack. Again, many cultures call this being born with a veil over its face.

In 1932, babies had to have the doctors administer silver nitrate drops into the child's eyes to get them open, and then they were only opened several days after birth. There was a lot of controversy about the black baby who was born with green eyes. The child's mother instantly became afraid of her and thought she had given birth to a demon or witch.

The midwife explained to Esmeralda's parents that the child was prophetic and not of witchcraft: "Look at those bright green eyes, see how she is looking around. She's trying to grasp her surroundings, to figure out where she is. She'll know things before they come to pass. She'll be a blessing to you someday."

So often, Negro men accused their wives of carrying on with white men, and Esmeralda's mother wanted to set the facts straight for her husband by asking Aunt Becky, the Midwife, if she remembered it said that their great grandmother, Mariama, had green eyes, and the fact was confirmed by Aunt Becky.

As days went on and the child's need for its mother became more demanding, it was obvious that Carina was afraid of her and dreaded feeding time.

The child's father had a brother, Ed, who had served in Europe during WWI, and he had learned a little Spanish; so when he saw the pretty little girl baby with green eyes, he named her Esmeralda, meaning Emerald or Green in Spanish.

The child had daily visitors who came to be blessed by touching the miracle child. Her nine-year-old brother Clarence noticed the poor care and lack of love his mother extended to Mera, and he bought a baby bottle and began to take care of his little sister.

The town's largest landowner, Miss Edna Carpenter, came by to see the child, took her in her arms, and walked out to the well with Clarence close behind her. Clarence heard Miss Edna say to the child. "You are here, and I'm going to see that you get whatever it is that you need..." She turned to look at Clarence and told him that he was a good boy for taking such good care of his little sister and promised that she'd be back often.

Carina was lying in bed, her belly swollen with the nearing time for another child to be born. It was early January, and tiny Esmeralda, two and a half, toddled across the room, and laid her head on her mother's chest: "Mama, Mera loves mama," she said. The child was pushed away by her mother, and as she landed on her bottom with tears of rejection filling her eyes, she heard her mother say: "You've killed too many of my friends and relatives with your witchery!"

Confused and hurt, the tiny child looked at the photograph of Mary holding baby Jesus, and every way she turned, the eyes of Jesus seemed to be upon her. She spoke out in her tiny soft voice: "Yes, I'll help you Jesus."

Carina sat up in bed watching the child and asked her: "Who you talking to, Mera?"

"I'm talking to Grandma Mary and baby Jesus," she said.

Carina became fearful and said in a trembling voice: "Grandma Mary died when Papa was a baby, she was his grandmother. Lordy mercy, child, you are strange."

Esmeralda grew old enough to start to school. By the time she was four years old, Clarence and Miss Edna had already taught her to read and write. Her tiny hands could crochet and knit as fast as Miss Edna who'd taught her. Shortly thereafter, she was writing poetry and stories that were published.

With the wooden box that Clarence had made for her to keep her money in, they decided to take it to town to the First National Bank that Miss Edna owned major shares in. When she was asked by Miss Edna what she intended to do with all that money, she told Miss Edna that she had to help the Jews find Jesus.

"That is a wonderful thing you're doing," Miss Edna had said.

Mera thought Miss Edna was a strange, but very nice lady. She was always alone, except when she came to their farm to visit with Clarence and her. She appeared to be searching for something or someone, and her eyes seemed so far away sometimes. She had a leathery face, red from frequent exposure to the sun, and her dark brown hair was braided in the back and wrapped around her head.

Miss Edna also owned the cotton mills, shipping dock,

the only shoe store in town, and held deeds on most of the land around the county seat. Her home was an old colonial two-story building with spiral stairs that lead to the upper floor, and a well-kept storm cellar and lawn. The house was snow white with green shutters and a red chimney. Although she owned no horses, she always wore those riding pants and boots.

Miss Edna kept a photograph of her father, Samuel Carpenter, sitting on the coffee table in her home and on her desk at the bank. He was a tall appearing gentleman, with very distinct features and a prominent nose. One day when she saw Esmeralda staring at the photograph, she said: "He is a direct descendant of King Josiah. I, too, have a mission, and you'll understand as you grow older."

Nine years older, Clarence, who looked a lot like Esmeralda, was especially protective of her and helped her with her acquisitions. When she thought a property or business was a good deal, Clarence would consult Miss Edna, and she'd help him acquire whatever they needed. When the account in First National grew to alarming proportions, Miss Edna thought it would be best if the holdings were transferred out to her uncle's bank in New York. She knew that the stockholders at First National would try to take the assets if they were aware that it belonged to a couple of black kids.

Twice each week, Miss Edna came by the farm to admire little Esmeralda and bring her more teaching materials. Few had noticed how much Leticia, the Wilkins' older daughter hated Esmeralda and was jealous of the gifts that Miss Edna brought. She often called her evil names that she'd heard some adult say, and would push the child when she wanted something that was hers.

It was early Saturday afternoon when Miss Edna's car ticket tacked down the Frog Spring Road and wheeled into the Wilkins' farm drive path. Ralph was already dressed to go to town for supplies, and Ernest, their oldest son, was chomping at the bit to get going. Visitors were rare in those parts, and everyone ran outside to greet the arriving car.

Even Carina and the new baby, three-year-old Johnnie, came out. Molly and Dude, the youngest of the mules were hitched to the wagon and tied to the well post, waiting their departure. The ugha, ugha of the car's horn and out gassing hiss made the mules fearful and they whinnied and pulled against the post, almost dislodging it.

"Howdy Ralph, Carina," Miss Edna shouted, as she stuck her long green clad leg outside the car...

"Howdy, Miss Edna," Ralph and Carina said at the same time.

"Nice day, ain't it," Ralph continued.

Miss Edna exercised her lungs in the fresh air as she walked closer to the house: "I love it when the June Bugs and July flies are singing, the cool winds are blowing the tree tops, and there's not a cloud in the sky."

Little Esmeralda had been watching through the window pane in the kitchen, and when she saw Miss Edna take a package from her car, she became excited and started for the door but was tripped by Leticia's foot across her path and fell hard on the planked floor.

"You keep your witching tail inside. Nobody wants to see you. Miss Edna wants to see me. Those packages are for me, do you hear?" And she pushed Esmeralda down again when she tried to stand, but stand she did and ran to Miss Edna with Carina yelling at her:

"Come back here Esmeralda."

Miss Edna stooped and picked the child up in her arms, laughing: "She knows that I came to see her, don't you sweetie? We're gonna sit under that big old oak tree yonder, and listen to the birds singing, and I'll crochet while you read me a story; we'll have ourselves a good old time. Carina, you'll have one of the boys bring us a cool pitcher of lemonade, wont you? Here, I brought you some fresh lemons. You can also make a pie if you'd like."

106

Miss Edna saw that Leticia was watching with hatred on her face for her little sister and decided to ask her: "Leticia, would you like to join us?"

Pouting, Leticia responded quickly: "No ma'am"

"Very well, then. We'll just get on with our business. Ralph, why don't you go on and do whatever you have to do; we'll be alright reading, and crocheting."

Mera looked at the pretty colored yarn Miss Edna had in her tote bag and asked: "Crochet?"

"Yes, baby girl, I'm going to make myself a sweater."

"Mera make a sweater, too?"

Miss Edna laughed and hugged Mera: "Why child you've done well with the pot holders, but your little hands are too small to hold a needle for sweaters. Ralph, I said we'd be alright, now you go on, you hear. Y'all sure have yourselves a smart little girl here. She's gonna make you proud some day," she said.

Mera ran back inside to get her box of paper and pencils, and in doing so, she bumped into her mother who screamed at her. "Watch what you're doing," she pushed the child out of her way. When Clarence heard his mother screaming at Mera, he rushed to her aid and took her into his arms to console her. "Hush now, little Mera. Don't you cry. Bubba loves you, and everything is going to be alright soon."

Leticia had been watching and entered the bedroom, appearing happy that Mera had been scolded: "Why you gotta hold that little witch?" she asked.

"You're the witch," Clarence shouted. If you ever hurt Mera, I'll...I'll.. He stopped to look at his mother and then finished his sentence. "I'll wring your neck, just like they do the chickens. Do you hear me?" His teeth gritted.

"I'm gonna tell daddy," Leticia threatened.

With Mera safe in his arms, Clarence said: "You tell him, smell him, put him in a band box, and I'll help you sell him," reciting the childish ditty as he started for the door with Mera and her box of papers and pencils.

"Daddy and mama loves me; they don't want Mera, she's evil," Leticia shouted.

Clarence never looked back, but answered: "I love Mera, Miss Edna loves Mera, and God loves Mera. She don't need the rest of you hypocrites anyway."

When Mera and Miss Edna came to their favorite oak tree and were about to begin their reading and crocheting, Mera told Miss Edna that she'd found some pretty stones in the hills when Clarence took her fishing. They were digging for fishing worms and uncovered the bed of stones that were so pretty.

"Let me see the stones, Mera. I've heard that there was a lost diamond mine in Georgia," she said.

Mera removed the pine needles and red mud that covered the hiding place, and Miss Edna was surprised to see what looked like amethysts, rubies, and diamonds. "My word, if they are costume jewels, I'm sure someone can use them and will pay you a good price."

Miss Edna always talked about Kings, and a prophetess who lived around 800 BC, but this was foreign to the small child. Before Christ, meant nothing much to her at this stage. She knew that she was different from other children, but she didn't understand why.

At age eight, Esmeralda had outgrown the little country school where she lived, and Miss Edna tried to get her parents to send her to Massachusetts to a school she knew that taught exceptional children; she suggested that Clarence go with her to care for her.

Carina was all for the idea for she believed that Mera meant harm for her family,

Ralph, on the other hand, understood that he'd be loosing a good field hand in Clarence, and he wondered what the Lord would think of them getting rid of their own child due to fear.

As destiny would have it, Esmeralda was taking fresh

water and sandwiches to the field where Clarence and the others brothers were working, when old man Deveraux came lumbering out of the thickets. He was a tall, fat white man whose matted blond hair smelled like a wet dog, and his sweaty body was crusty with unbathed oils mixed with the red Georgia clay dust.

This drunken man whose intimidating grayish blue eyes had his sights set on molesting Esmeralda, an eight year old child whose physical makeup had budgeoned far beyond that of a normal child. As Georgia was considered a semi-tropical zone, and girls developed fast in these regions, nature had well endowed Esmeralda; and it is said that she was more shapely than a teenaged girl. Her father called her sinfully seductive.

Esmeralda fought and screamed as her brother had taught her to do, but after all she was only eight years old, and Deveraux was about two hundred fifty pounds. His snow white, potbelly protruded through the stretched-out shirt like yeast rolls rising to the heat.

His red sweaty face and stinky breath nauseated the child. He tried to put his nasty hand over her mouth to keep her from screaming, and unfasten his fly at the same time, but his actions required more effort than he had anticipated, and he had to get to his knees to orchestrate his maneuvers. As he slid his pants down, that now white, tipped one-eyed snake popped out fully erected and ready to be jabbed into the exhausted body of the struggling child. An odor came from his private parts that smelled like a whole sack of daddy long legs.

When Esmeralda's brothers heard her screams, they ran like the wind towards the sounds. As the boys approached, Devereaux pulled a pistol from his back pants waist and fired several times into the air. Three of the brothers ran, but Clarence kept coming like a downhill, out of control locomotive.

Devereaux saw that Clarence had a drawn pitch fork,

and he fired directly at the young man. Clarence staggered but kept coming, yelling: "Get off of her! Get off of her, now!" Devereaux snapped the trigger of his gun, but it was too late for the pitch fork entered his blubbery flesh making a swoosh sound, and the blood curdling scream that came from his throat echoed through the tall pine trees, bright red liquid covered his snow white skin.

Clarence managed to drag the heavy white man from on top his little sister before he, too, slipped into unconsciousness. Esmeralda propped Clarence's head on her lap and plugged the hole where the bullet had found its mark. Help came in the persons of her three brothers who ran, her father Ralph, Miss Edna, who just happened to be there to visit with little Mera, and several white farmers who'd heard the shots and came to investigate.

Before the men moved Mr. Devereaux, he managed to cry out to them not to harm Clarence: "Don't harm the boy. I thought this little girl was that uppity older sister of hers. My own little girl is eight years old, and I would kill to protect her. Leave the boy alone." Then he slipped into unconsciousness and never awakened again.

Clarence was taken to a hospital in Atlanta where the bullet was not removed due to the fact that it was too close to his heart. Leticia made sure she told Mera every day that she was the cause of the whole problem, and the child stopped talking. Miss Edna came by almost every day to console Mera.

One day when Miss Edna, and Mera were sitting beneath their favorite oak tree, Miss Edna read several passages from the Bible: "Mera, I want you to listen good, you hear. This is a passage in the Bible from Isaiah Chapter 11, 'And there shall come forth a rod out of the stem of Jesse, and a branch shall grow out of his roots.' Do you understand what this mean Mera?" she asked.

The wide eyed child looked at her with sadness, for she missed her brother Clarence and wondered what she had done wrong to cause such a tragedy.

"Are you listening to me, Esmeralda?"

"Yes, ma'am. It means that the servant Jesse's youngest son will be special like I am and will become the fore parent of Jesus the Christ who is the Messiah, and I must tell the Jews that he is."

"And what does Isaiah 11:6 tell us?"

"It said that the wolf also shall dwell with the lamb, and the leopard shall lie down with the kid, and the calf, the lion and the fatling together and a little child shall lead them."

Miss Edna took Esmeralda's chin in her hand and looked directly into her eyes: "And who is that little child, Mera?"

"I am she."

"Good girl. Now you stop worrying for Clarence will be alright, but you all must leave this place; you've outgrown it, and your family is no longer safe here.

Within a few months, Miss Edna and several other white people helped Ralph move his family to Pennsylvania, where some of their family lived, and Miss Edna had made contacts to get Mera in advanced schools.

*   *   *

As Esmeralda's mind drifted to recall her beginning, she could not stop the rivers of tears and choking sobs from her throat, for she always believed that her sins almost caused Clarence his life.

With the Ravin family so intently listening to the story that Esmeralda was telling, the fire had died down, and only red and gray embers remained. Phyllis shook her head in disbelief: "Oh, my God. How awful," she shuddered.

Ian and Philip were speechless for the moment, wondering what they should say to Mera. When Philip saw his mother and Mera with their arms around their shoulders trembling as though they were cold, he put another log on the fire and watched it blaze up again: "Has anyone tried to remove the bullet from your brother's chest?" he asked.

"Several doctors have examined him, but none dared to take the challenge. I don't think he wants to do it at this stage. He's lived with it this long."

"I'd like Dr. Berman to take a look at him to evaluate what is best to be done," Philip said.

Ian rubbed his forehead as Phyllis went to make more coffee. He seemed puzzled about all that he'd just heard and had so many questions for Mera to answer. "How did you amass such a fortune, child?" he asked.

"The Corporation's financial growth was due to investments, donations and diversifying. When God knew of an opportunity that was worthy, he'd plant the sketchy information in my dreams. I'd explain the dreams to Miss Edna when she was able, and she would acquire the holdings for me. Clarence met Rabbi Terah at a conference in Chicago because his dream directed him there, and the Rabbi has been fronting and quick claiming the holdings to the Emerald Corporation. The Calorie Counter Restaurants, and Emerald Hotels are in some of the hub cities around the world, and we are planning to expand to other major sites. The hotel designs are strictly my own and are very popular because they are suites, with food courts that are opened for breakfast, and lunch."

Phyllis soon returned with fresh coffee, but Esmeralda refused the second cup: "No, thank you. I only started drinking coffee when I came here, and I wouldn't want it to become a habit. I do like hot water with lemon or a decaf tea."

"I think that can be arranged," Phyllis said, and she returned to the kitchen and within minutes returned with a pot of hot water with a tea bag strings hanging out.

"What will this acquisition in San Francisco do for you?" Ian asked.

"The purpose of the whole exercise is to reach Jews for Jesus. In order to do this. there must be Synagogues where they can come together without being threatened. Most of the established Temples are hardened believers that the Messiah has not come and most definitely is not Jesus, one of their own. Just as Philip could be president of these United States, every Jew born could've been the Messiah if God so chose it to be."

"You say us, when referring to the corporation. Who are the owners?" Phyllis asked.

"Legally, just me, but spiritually, its God's plan. God can't have a lot of owners to fight over the holdings and possibly split the assets. I pay myself a very small salary to maintain living and support my education. Otherwise, it all goes for salaries to employees, expansion and training. It is like research and development." Mera told them.

"So what happens to Rabbi Terah if we decide to take over his part in this?" Ian asked.

"Rabbi Terah is as over extended as I am. He needs to be more responsible in the teachings and building of new temples around the world. Besides, he will be needed to take an active part in the television network teachings."

"Does the Corporation have its own TV network, too?" Phyllis asked.

"The initial deposits have been put into Escrow and papers are drawn, but I need someone to show up with power of attorney to sign the purchasing documents and those required by the government for airways permits. They won't let a child or a black person do this."

Philip laughed out loud: "This story gets better as it grows. Are you sure you are not dreaming all this up? Mom, dad, if you accept this fantastic opportunity, do you realize that everything you have could be lost forever," Philip said with doubt.

"My CPA said that we could pay each of you one million dollars a year to start. To set your mind at ease, we could pay you the first year's salary up front. If you need to do more checking, you may want to do a quick property profile on the restaurants, the clothing, the hotels, or what ever will help you with your decision," Mera said.

Philip was still playing the devil's advocate, and asked with skepticism: "That big hotel on West Amber Street, toward the beach, is called the Emerald hotel with a big green eye surrounded by crystal looking glass; don't tell me that is yours, too," he quipped.

"That was a hostile takeover. They wouldn't allow some black entertainers to stay there, but they were having financial problems; when my uncle told me about it, we moved in, offered the government the back taxes, paid the finance company off and remodeled the whole place; and yes, that is one of my sinful acquisitions, born out of anger."

"Let's see what needs to be done in San Francisco; then we'll talk more about your offer," Ian said.

Phyllis appeared excited and spoke up: "I've never seen a million dollars, least of all two million."

"Why didn't you stay at your own hotel?" Philip asked.

Esmeralda stared at Philip in disbelief. "You don't know much about life, do you? A young girl alone in a hotel would instantly wear the flag of prostitute. Women fear them and men hate them. They like the excitement, but it exposes their own weaknesses, so they abuse the prostitutes. Sometimes kill them. I've already been labeled that by my own sister and her husband, and dare I say you, too, Philip."

"I never called you a prostitute!" he said defensively.

"That thing you called me is in the same category. A very demoralizing accusation."

"Aren't you ever going to forget that?" Philip asked.

"Forget, no; forgive, maybe." She hunched up her shoulders.

Philip quickly changed the subject: "I take it your family is rich?" he asked.

Mera stared at him for a moment trying to decide if she should answer his smart aleck question; when she looked at her foster parents, she realized they, too, were wondering the same thing. So she decided to answer: "Clarence is the only one who's rich; the rest would be broke in a year. They all have moderate homes, paid off, of course, and good paying jobs.

"Even though my sister Leticia works for Emerald Fashions as a sewing machine operator, I did not buy a home for her. She is too ungrateful and mean. She's not aware that she works for me. She'd probably quit instantly if she knew. My uncles want me to sign the part that they manage over to them. This is not a family business, but a God planned business, and even though it is used to pay salaries, it's not to embellish my uncles homosexual life styles. They are paid fifty thousand a year; if they are unhappy with that, I'm sure someone else will be happy to earn that kind of money which includes a paid off home.

"Geese, you are hard nosed," Philip said.

"You can't run a business being a push over," Ian said. "I like that toughness I see in her; she seems to be a real business person. It takes the toughness in directing businesses and gentleness that she displays in her personal life, together with strong convictions. Little girl, I think you're going to be alright."

"You realize that this will not be smooth sailings. Jews, as you know, are adamant in their determination to prove they are right and will start a war to protect their beliefs. I'm going to be in serious danger from time to time, but I will try to draw that danger away from you. Oh, by the way, Philip, there is a security team already in force. You'll meet them sooner than you think."

*   *   *

The Wednesday night meeting at the Temple in Mandeville was packed with curiosity seeking Jews. They had come to witness a real live kid speaker, who was on her way to a doctorate degree in Engineering and had already received a minor in Religious Science. Word of mouth had spread throughout the entire Los Angeles area that a child had the gall to try to lead the Jews to accept Jesus as the Messiah. Most of Mera's teachings had been lead by the Holy Spirit, she claimed, and even though she spoke several languages, she spoke to this evening's audience mainly in English and some Yiddish.

She told them that she'd written a book on the history of the Jews and the Old Testament teachings, and it could be bought in the Temple entrance.

Attending this seminar was all of the Ravin family, their friends, Uncle Zech and Aunt Winnie. Being mainly professionals, the crowd remained courteous to hold their shouts of objections for the question period.

When the option was offered to ask questions, Rabbi Terah and Uncle Zech took the podium along side Esmeralda. In the second row, a hand was raised and recognized as several hands went up at the same time.

"Please stand so that everyone may hear your question," Esmeralda stated.

"How old are you, and what is your nationality, young lady?" the man asked.

"I am fifteen years old, and my race is Negroid," she answered.

"Why are you here meddling in our business instead of holly rolling to boogie woogie music in a Black Church?"

"I am here because God sent me here to help you regain your rightful place as his chosen people since your fall from grace."

"And He told you this?" the man asked laughing, and the laughter echoed throughout the entire Temple, as others joined in...

"You won't get another chance to condemn the Lord Jesus Christ to death. Because of your denial of Him and all of our sinful disbeliefs, he died on the cross, but you have a chance to redeem yourselves if you'll only accept that He is the Messiah. He is your own flesh and blood, but you are looking for a magical thing to claim as Savior. He has the magic power you are seeking if you'll only trust Him."

As the laughter grew louder, Uncle Zech stood and raised his hand for silence, but the congregation jeered even more...

"Sit down, old man!"

"Yeah. You were ejected once for your blasphemous teachings. I'd sure hate to see you tossed out on your decrepit butt," the voice rang out. The excited crowd stomped their feet and jeered vocal obscenities.

Esmeralda signaled for the sound technicians to increase the PA volume. And then she spoke clearly into the booming microphone. "God has sent his Son to be the Savior of the world. There will not be another opportunity for you to change your minds. You will find that God will remove His protective care from around as he did Saul, and the enemy will take away the lands that He gave to you as spoils of war."

Somehow, the static charge surged through the PA System and made a crashing sound that was equivalent to seven times the sound of a lightening strike. The building rattled, rolled, and shook; the over powering sound shut off the lights momentarily. When the lights were off, only Esmeralda's face could be seen clearly lighted through the darkness.

Everyone had seen this obvious miracle and became fearful. Their screams changed from mockery to fearful ones, and then they became quiet enough to hear a cockroach crawl on a cotton mattress.

When the lights came on again, Uncle Zech stood to

117

speak, but Rabbi Terah motioned for him to stay seated: "I think they will listen to her now," he whispered.

The sound was readjusted, and Esmeralda ended her presentation about God's plan for Salvation, and how the Jews had failed to listen despite His love for them above all other nations. Not one hand was raised with objections. The organist played and sang a song entitled, "There's room at the cross for you. There's room at the cross for you, Though millions have come, there's still room for one. There's room at the cross for you."

The Congregation was still for a few moments, and then Dr. and Mrs. Berman walked down to the altar, followed by Ian and Phyllis. There they stood with their heads bowed low, and Uncle Zech joined them there, whispering congratulatory words to them and embracing each as they came.

Before the evening was over, one hundred twenty had come to kneel before the altar. Included in this crowd were Joel, Marty, Evelyn and several others of Philip's friends. Philip and Pam were stubborn holdouts.

* * *

In San Francisco, Phyllis and Ian noticed that Mera was more quiet than usual as she stared out over the bay from the window of the conference room of the little synagogue. Phyllis walked to the window and placed her hand around Mera's shoulder; the young woman reached up, took Phyllis' fingertips, and gently brushed her cheek against the backs of her fingers.

"What's wrong, child?" Phyllis asked.

"Since Wednesday night, I've felt an enormous estrangement between Philip and me again. I wouldn't want to do anything to turn around the progress he has made."

Phyllis turned Mera's shoulders so that the two of them were facing each other: "Our son's pain is so deep, it's going to take a lot of love and patience to help him over it."

"Why must I always be the one to bring on the festering of his resentments?" Mera asked.

Ian walked back from the men's room in time to hear the last statement, and he walked to the window, took Mera's hand in his, and raised her chin so that their eyes met.

"Who knows why it works out that way, Mera. These feelings of resentment could be the brewing portions of healing that is within him. Sometimes we have to go temporarily blind before we appreciate out sight."

"I pray that he doesn't feel that I'm stealing his friends and parents," Mera said.

"In your presentation, you said that God offers us salvation through Jesus, but it is not ours until we actually accept it, feeling it deep within," Phyllis said.

"Oh, yes, that part about an effective prayer life. I'm eager to hear that lesson. Mom and I have been praying a long time. We need a change for the better in our business, but the answer never came. We couldn't see the forest for the trees until you came into our lives," Ian said.

"I'm not sure I caused the changes in your lives. God chose you to carry out His plan before you were born. He then put you two together because you were both obedient and curious. Perhaps you chose your own path and did not consult him before you did. It is important to wait for His answers," Mera said.

"I agree that you had nothing to do with the germination of our need to know the Messiah, but perhaps the fulfillment and understanding of our longing came through you," he continued.

"It pleases me to hear you say that, and it is an honor to know that I have in some way been instrumental in guiding you to His Cross."

They both took Mera into their arms and hugged her assumingly as the door swung open, with Rabbi John escorting several other executives into the room. "This is the young lady you've all been waiting to meet, Miss Esmeralda Wilkins. This is attorney, Myron Rosenberg and his secretary Linda Cox, Escrow Officer Jeffery Bateman, and Rabbi David Hess.

"I'm pleased to meet you," and she extended her hand to them all one at a time before she introduced her foster parents.

As the group exchanged hand greetings with Ian and Phyllis, attorney Rosenberg said:

"Excellent, I'm happy that you brought them along. Do your parents understand this acquisition?" he asked Mera.

"Yes, sir; I've explained it to them," Mera replied.

"Polite little creature, aren't you, and cute as a button, too," he complimented her. "Did Rabbi John give you the low down on what's happening with this property?" Myron asked.

"Yes, sir. He also gave me copies of the Platt maps and drawings of the main building. From what I can see, there is no earthquake protection, and the materials used previously are seriously outdated. My recommendation would be to take down the current building and erect a steel load bearing structure. Of course we'll need to have geological soil reports and perks. There seems to be so many underground pools of water in the Bay area."

"That's right, you are an architectural engineer. I should've known you'd see something we missed," Myron said.

"We'd also like a tour of the surrounding area to get an idea of the kinds of businesses and styles of buildings are in this area."

"Good idea. Linda, call for a limo," Myron ordered.

Linda walked to the telephone in the room; legal documents were spread out on the table. "Do you mind if I check these out," Mera asked.

"That's what they're here for," Myron said.

Mera visually reviewed the transfer documents and handed them to Ian and Phyllis for reviewing. As she continued searching all technical documents and church records, she handed each one to her foster parents to review, also.

Rabbi John noticed her inspecting the attendance and financial statements of the current Temple, and he appeared embarrassed: "Membership has been down since we started teaching Christianity," he said.

Mera looked at the Rabbi and smiled. "That's to be expected. What kind of deficit are we looking at?" she asked.

"Here are the court's foreclosure extensions," Davis said.

Esmeralda briefly reviewed the documents and quickly handed them to her parents. "Two hundred thousand dollars due in ninety days. You were cutting it close," she said.

"We never stopped praying and believing," Rabbi John said. "We continued to do everything we could think of to stall and pull ourselves solvent again, but God only knew the way."

The phone rang and Linda answered it: "Thank you," she said as she hung up the phone. "The limo is downstairs," she said.

They all took part in folding the documents and replacing them in the folders from which they were taken before they put on their top coats, gloves, and scarves, and then followed Linda down stairs and into the limo.

*   *   *

The Bay area hillsides were white with snow several days old, and there were cars criss-crossing in every direction. The ride was not long in distance, but timely due to the massive traffic jams.

There were numerous questions asked, especially about Esmeralda's background, but her foster parents were quick-thinking running guards at every turn. Mera liked not having to talk about herself and most assuredly enjoyed the protection her parents offered.

The proud look in her parent's eyes told Mera they were enjoying this parental and corporate legal aspect of their possible new positions.

Gosh, it felt good during the inspection, listening to their daughter itemizing all the building requirements. The terminology she used, sketches she'd made of the proposed Synagogue, shopping center, and retirement homes, just blew them away. They didn't say these things out loud, but each of them knew what the other was thinking, and Mera looked at them with gratefulness.

When the Ravins and Esmeralda had a few moments alone, Ian asked his daughter: "What do you think of this acquisition, honey, it's more than a quarter of a million dollars?"

"I think we should do it. It is not just twenty acres, but they are offering us the property next to it, an additional ten acres. From my observations of the area, it's a prime location to many conveniences and proposed business opportunities. Not but twelve miles from the major airport and a large medical clinic is within five miles. I believe it will pay for itself within two to three years," Mera said.

"You really sound like you know what you're talking about," Phyllis said.

"Did all of the legal documents appear to be in order?" Mera asked.

"They seemed to be, but I'd like to review them further and federal express them to Escrow later," Ian said.

"Then as my power of attorney, you'll sign the papers?" Mera asked.

"We will. Do you have the cashier's check with you?" Ian asked.

"Yes, I have it. Is there anything else we need to take care of?"

"Not until Escrow closes, and then we'll need the rest

of the charges paid in full before documents can be distributed," the Escrow officer said.

Esmeralda turned to Rabbis John and David and asked them to write down the following: "Before Escrow closes, we'll need surveyors, reports, geological reports with complete soil test, perk test to measure the ground water, and the Planning Commissioner's recommendations."

The two Rabbis were busy writing the instructions that Esmeralda requested: "We'll get that started as soon as Monday," Rabbi John said.

"When you know the cost, let us know, and we'll wire the money to you. You might want to write down my parent's office number just in case you can't reach me. They may be taking care of the business angles, anyway," Mera said.

*   *   *

Philip sat in his office after everyone had left for the day. He placed the EKG strips onto the glass lighted viewing panel and sat down to view them from afar. He studied the strips for a while, got up, and circled several negative PVC's.

Philip thumped the areas that he'd marked, sat down again with his hands locked behind his head. The phone rang and he stared at it, hoping it would stop. It did and he felt relieved. Tonight, he didn't want to talk to anyone; he wanted to be alone.

"Oh, my God, it's Saturday. Maybe it was an emergency call, and they tried to reach me at home," he said out loud. "Oh, well. No way to trace it now. I should've been home since right after noon," he said.

He continued studying the medical test strips with his lip crimped inside his teeth. "What's at home anyway? That little conniving witch has everybody twisted around her finger," he said out loud, sounding exasperated. "What if they take the job as CEO? They won't need me anymore. Why can't life be the way it was before she came? How can everyone fall for this crap of hers?

"If I say or do anything against her, they'll all think I've lost my mind. Marty said he'd see that I don't practice medicine. I'm trapped. Bitch!" He rolled up his lab coat and threw it across the room, just as the phone rang again.

"Hey Phil, what're you doing still there? I thought we were going to Jam tonight." The voice on the other end of the phone was Joel Markowitz.

"My folks are up north with Esmeralda, and it totally slipped my mind," Philip said.

"Are we going to do it?" Joel asked.

"Can I beg off, Joe? I'm bushed and besides we were supposed to do some music that Esmeralda wrote, but she's not here."

"OK, then, let me know when," Joel said.

Philip racked the phone, appearing relieved; then he sat down with a plump and folded his arms in defiance and anger. His lips curled to imitate Esmeralda: "If I tell you there's cheese on the moon, you'd better take your crackers and wine. Evil woman!"

"It's alright Philip. Get your act together. State Board Exams are in July; you don't need this," he said out loud.

*   *   *

The airport in San Francisco was awaiting a fog lift before the clearance could be given to board for departure. The Ravins and Esmeralda were already two hours late. They made use of the delay by browsing the airport shops. Phyllis reached out and took Esmeralda's hand when she noticed her examining medical equipment.

"A stethoscope," she said with understanding. "His stethoscope is kind of outdated," Phyllis added. "I've been planning to look for a new one."

Esmeralda nervously dropped the instrument back onto the shelf and wrenched her hand gently away from Phyllis's grip. She stepped back as though she was a shop-lifter caught in the act.

"It's alright, honey. I'm sure Philip would appreciate the gesture," Ian said.

Esmeralda shook her head from side to side, getting farther away from the instrument:

"No... He wouldn't understand."

"Oh, baby girl, haven't you seen the changes in him?" Phyllis asked. She turned to Ian for confirmation. "It's different, huh, honey?"

"He's definitely more relaxed," Ian answered.

Esmeralda shook her head and said firmly: "He's a clever actor who knows what his public expects, so he gives it to them. He's not ready to accept me or his old friends."

Phyllis took both of Mera's hands, smiling gratefully: "You've brought us all so much joy sweetheart..."

Cutting Phyllis short, she said: "Not Philip. He's in competition with everyone and refuses to play with the team. It's seems that it's all him or nothing. His acceptance of me is tolerant, not caring. My sister tolerated me, but when she felt threatened, she lashed out with all the venom of a cornered viper. Philip will do the same if we can't help him."

"What do you mean?" Ian asked.

"Everything pleasant that I do for him, he'll suspect it is a ploy to earn something from him. Sexual favors are the first thing on a man's mind," Mera said.

"You're just a child. Philip wouldn't do such a thing..."

Esmeralda stopped him: "You're a mature parent. You see me as a child, but Philip sees me as a physically mature woman. To many men, women are devious, cunning, and self centered profit seekers.

"I'm not blaming Philip, for he is what he is. Look into

the past that I've experienced. That old man in Georgia, my brother Clarence's neighbors, my uncle's friends, my sister's husband, even my classmates. Do you know they are taking bets who'll be the first to change my status from virgin."

"They're really just kids," Ian said.

"You really believe they're kids?" Let's see now. Most of them graduated high school at eighteen, then four years in Engineering, and two years in graduate school. That sounds like twenty-four to me. How old were you when you got married as a mature man?" Mera asked.

Phyllis looked at Ian with surprise on her face. "We were certainly not that old."

"Mom, Dad, I wouldn't be surprised to learn that Philip slept at the office last night, pouting that I've taken away his two special supporting friends. I don't want to do that to him; I want to be his friend."

Ian frowned and then pulled away to a phone booth to make a call.

"You're probably right, mom. I'm just being an over judgmental kid. You've known Philip all of his life; your experience counts more than my suspicions," Mera said.

Within a few moments, Ian returned from the phone booth with a surprised expression on his face.

"What's wrong, honey?" Phyllis asked.

Ian stared momentarily at Esmeralda before answering his wife: "It's Philip. He slept at the office last night. He said there was nothing to go home for."

They both looked for answers in Mera's face as she walked away, with them close behind. "You somehow knew. How can we help him, Mera?" Phyllis asked.

"Dr. Heller can help him, I'm not qualified. I'm his current insult, his most recent threat," she told them. "I can tell you what I suspect though."

"You think he's insane, don't you?" Phyllis asked.

"No ma'am, just hurting. Dr. Heller will have to take

126

him back to when the pain began and help him understand and cope with it. And when he's faced his demons head on, he'll know how to dismiss them as simple events and get on with his life. Don't you know I've had to get over the rejections and jealousy. As little communication as I have had with my father, he told me something that I shan't ever forget. He said that when a person hates you, you have something that they fear or wished they had."

"How did you deal with your problems, and how will be best for Philip to deal with his?" Phyllis asked.

"I have a Holy Psychiatrist, for my problems are never ending. I finally learned to accept the fact that I didn't cause my brother's near death experience. Prayer brought me through that and, of course, the constant counseling of gentle caring people like my brother and Miss Edna."

"Philip will have to realize he has a problem and want to be helped. Again, Dr. Heller will help him learn to walk again. We'll just have to love and support him without going overboard, or it'll appear to be patronizing to him."

A voice filtered loudly over the P.A system. "Flight #91 to Los Angeles is now boarding from gate seventeen."

"That's us," Ian said, getting up and gathering the three overnight bags, and then they all walked together down the boarding ramp.

CHAPTER IX

P hilip's weekly visits to Dr. Heller's office appeared beneficial outwardly, but deep inside, his soul cried out to be free of the cold chills that often swept over his entire body. Even before his outburst of rage against Esmeralda, he'd had these feelings.

As he sat in the psychiatrist's office, waiting for their next session to begin, he thought he'd reached the depths of despair. But he was wrong. Despair was a bottomless pit, and he could plunge further if he allowed it, he thought.

The wine cellar of his parents' home, as his father explained it to him so many years ago, was a solid edifice with thick walls of gray stone, and had been erected over a century ago when the vintners Costellos lived there. It was structured to be impregnable to weather changes, thieves, enemies bent on arson or harm, and most of all to protect the aging wines stored there.

Marty asked during their last session if he could try to remember when these fears had begun. That's it, he thought. It was the cellar. When the kids would tease and pick on him, he'd run down there for peace or comfort.

When the door closed, no sound could penetrate from the outer world. It was as dark as coal and as silent as a tomb. He remembered huddling there on the cold floor in a corner, struggling to keep a tight grip on himself and not allow the creeping hysteria to enshroud him.

When the session finally began with Dr. Heller, Philip was able to recount these experiences of how the chills and fear began. He told how he'd gone there when his ex-wife Annette made light of his sexual abilities and during the course of their divorce.

"I thought that if I'd do a three year stretch in the military, I could help myself. You know: "The Boys To Men" thing," he explained.

Dr. Heller asked as he looked over the top of his glasses: "And did that help?"

"The fear went, but the anger and chills stayed," Philip responded.

"When did you become impotent, Philip?" Dr Heller asked, readjusting his chair.

"I guess it was about six months after I got married." Philip squirmed nervously, for he did not like to talk about this subject. He focused his eyes on the old drum set sitting in the corner of the office and wished he could talk about them getting together again to practice their musical skills.

"Can you attribute anything to this cause?" Dr. Heller asked, following Philips gaze to the drums in the corner.

Philip wanted to see what Dr. Heller was writing. He wondered if any of this could be used to cause problems for him in the future. He craned his neck to see but was actually too far away to read anything.

"Philip, did you hear my question?"

Becoming aware again, Philip answered: "I believe it was when Annette made fun of my efforts to make love and often told me to hurry up and get it over."

"How old were you when you started hiding in the wine cellar?"

"I don't know. I was seven or eight, maybe even younger. I stopped hiding there when you and Joe moved into the neighborhood and taught me to fight the kids who picked on me, and when we started jamming."

"You were ten then."

"I think so."

Dr. Helter stopped writing, leaned forward, and twirled his pen towards Philip: "Do you know what I think, Philip."

Philip drew back as though he expected the pen to be a javelin being hurtled in his direction.

"I guess that's why I'm here."

"There are a number of things I see here. Your parents worked, and you were alone a lot while your sitter listened to soap operas on the radio. Your mother named you after her, and this Phyllis verses Philip is terribly confusing, and easy for children to use as fuel for teasing; you made a bad choice when you got married. Annette was much older and more experienced, and she was looking for a satin cushion to slide into life's easy chair."

"I can't say that I wasn't warned," Philip agreed, nervously crossing his extended legs at the ankles.

"She did a number on you for sure. That's a form of spousal abuse: sexual harassment. Your manhood was under attack!"

"I suppose you're right," Philip cringed.

"Philip, there's nothing more psychologically damaging to a man than to defame his sexuality."

"The things she said did hurt a lot. It made me feel small and insignificant," Philip admitted, staring down at the floor while cracking his knuckles.

Dr. Heller took in a deep breath and then rocked back in his chair: "You said you'd thought about having sex with Esmeralda."

"I think I just wanted to hurt her, put her in her place, but I'll never hit her again. I'm really sorry about that."

"Have you decided what her place is, Philip? Is it because she's Negroid, you'd like her to behave more like a servant? Preparing the family meals and for your guest also, washing your dishes, doing the laundry, cleaning the house, shopping for the family, and getting everyone's cleaning done. Sounds like a servant to me."

"Do you want her to suffer with your hatred because you hate Annette so much that you want to punish all women for what that one did to you, or maybe you're jealous of the rapport she's developed with your parents."

"I think it's the pain thing and maybe some jealously." Philip answered.

"You accused her of practicing African voodoo on your family. Do you still see her as a witch?"

"That was jealousy and resentment for... I really don't know what for," Philip shrugged his shoulders.

"Perhaps you don't want her to penetrate that protective barrier you've built around yourself that keeps you from getting involved with women in general!"

"I'm not sure."

Dr. Heller lifted his eyebrow and leaned forward with his elbows on his desk:

"She's drop-dead gorgeous, Philip. She is humble, not forward, doesn't mind doing hard work, and smart, too. Those kinds of credentials would turn the key of desire in the hearts of most men."

"Are you saying I'm falling in love with her?" Philip asked loudly, his voice trembling.

"I didn't say that. Only you can answer that question." Dr. Heller paused for a moment, as he noticed Philip's confusion. He thought he'd better explain his last statement for he sure didn't want to put notions in Philip's mind.

"Philip, love has several sides. There is the side that is made up of respect and admiration. The love that one have for parents, other family members, and friends. Then there's the side that has physical and emotional gratification. Acting on the law of nature, one would want to protect this love and support it emotionally and financially, even have a family with this lover."

"Now there is the one you talked about. 'Put her in her place.; That's evil, sinful, spiteful and destructive. Rapists have this kind of obsession. Has Esmeralda hurt you so much that you want to destroy her?" Dr. Heller continued.

Philip's face twisted with the thought of destroying anything or anyone. *Have I become this monster that I'm hearing about? he thought.*

"Oh, my God. Did I say that?" Philip asked.

"You did," Dr. Heller answered.

131

"I truly don't want to hurt her. I mean seriously hurt. No, I don't want to hurt her at all."

"Philip, my concern is that she has the God-given right to grow up, become educated, and not have to fight for her chance to become a decent woman, maybe a wife to some deserving man."

There was a lengthy pause, a long uncomfortable silence, as Dr. Heller waited for Philip to lead the conversation again. But Philip focused his eyes on several objects in the office rather than look at his friend. They both knew that Esmeralda was not the problem and were waiting for the real reasons for his anger and chills to surface. Finally, Philip broke the silence.

"You haven't told me why I'm cold all the time. I've had all kinds of physicals, and no pathology was indicated."

"Are you cold all the time, Philip, or just when you feel threatened?"

"I guess it's not all the time."

"During those times, does your memory of that icy cellar come back where you'd hide when you felt scared or lonely?"

"I think so."

"As far as I can tell, your fears started with the neighborhood bullies. Let me tell you something. Kids are cruel. My boys are three and five, and they fight like the "Hatfield's and McCoy's" sometimes. Little Victor is as mean as a rattled hornet. I have to take him by the seat of his pants and swat his behind.

"Philip, life is a bitch, and it's time you realized it. It's a time gain, time to decide on further actions. You stop at the water's edge and don't take a chance on it being too hot or too cold. You want your little corner of the world to always be safe. That's not reality. You are a man of science, making life and death decisions every day. Why not practice this in your own life? Take the bitter with the sweet.

Roll with the punches. When you've learned all these things, you won't need me as your therapist but instead your friend.

*   *   *

Philip drove down the boulevard towards his home, stared through the windshield of his car and into the darkened sky. He felt certain that someone had locked him inside an inescapable dungeon. Could the escape key be in his mind? he asked himself. "I don't know." He admitted confusion and shook his head as though emerging from too long in deep water.

"I just don't know," he repeated. "Perhaps Marty is right. I am expecting too much without giving anything."

Now he was thinking deeply, the way Dr. Heller had suggested he do. He gazed up towards the sky.

"Hello, God!" Are you there? Everyone wants me to believe you are!"

"Well, here I am, full of sin. You heard Marty, God. I'm evil and selfish. I need a new life. I want to be the new creature that Esmeralda talked about. How did she say it? Oh yes. 'If any man be in Christ, he is a new creature. Old things are past away, behold all things are become new.'"

"Make me a new man, God. Take away my need for self-satisfaction. Take my life in Your hands. Forgive me for the pain I've caused."

Philip did not understand where the words were coming from. All he knew was that the most powerful feeling swept over him, a delightful feeling that he wanted to savor forever.

While rapt in prayer, his awareness had temporarily escaped him, and he found himself on the wrong side of the road while blinding car lights faced him, and deafening horns blaring shocked him back to reality. He managed to steer his car to safety on the side of the road with only minor weed scratches. Before he drove off again, he stared up toward the night sky, chuckling softly.

"You took me seriously when I said take my life, didn't you, Lord?" he yelled.

For the first time since he bought the car, he decided to play the radio. The music was not spiritual but was certainly spiritually uplifting. He tapped his fingers on the steering wheel and bobbed his head joyfully as he drove along. His immediate thought was that his family would probably be waiting dinner for him.

On a chilled night like tonight, maybe Mera had made that delicious Yankee pot roast, and that Georgia corn bread. "God, that girl can sure cook some good food." Maybe they would even be worrying about him and why he was late.

The approaching month of May was full of promises for the Ravins and Esmeralda. The spring afternoon was more joyous than one could imagine for a Saturday in late April. Esmeralda and her classmates had completed the remodeling on the outside of the home and had converted that old dungeon of a wine cellar into an exercise gym, and spa...

*   *   *

Ian seemed happy as he returned from a tour of the new changes, with a group of excited and pleased guests. They all seemed surprised to learn that a young girl had orchestrated such a beautiful job.

The first public performance of Philip and his boyhood musician friends was about to begin. They had taken their places on the makeshift bandstand at the north end of the flagstone patio and just above the lovely sparkling swimming pool.

The lingering aroma from the built-in barbeque pit and warmer instantly made everyone take notice and certainly stimulated their appetites. The elevated sun deck gave rise to the beautiful foliage hand planted nearby of philodendron, African and Australian fern, and a host of multicolored roses and lilies.

Mera and Phyllis had several oven pans of prepared shish-ka bobs, steamed wild rice, Western beans, several kinds of salads, and numerous types of cookies and cakes. There were plenty of all kinds of beverages chilling in the galvanized new horse trough filled with crushed ice.

There were pretty serving dishes with various and unique hors d'oeuvres placed conveniently around the sitting area. As the patio began to fill up with guests, Esmeralda was inconspicuously watching each person who arrived and paying a lot of attention to the tuning exercises the band was making.

Several of the Raven's friends and neighbors arrived, and there was a fuss over the whole changed homestead.

Gazelda Hoffman was an eloquent woman whose appearance bespoke of wealth and glamour. She was a petite blond with tell-tale dark roots and a very jolly personality. She reminded Esmeralda of Dr. Heller's wife Evelyn. Gazelda's husband Stephen was a classmate of the Ravins from law school, but it was apparent just by looking at him that his law practice of Hoffman and Goldstein was thriving well.

Phyllis introduced the Hoffman's to Esmeralda: "This is our foster daughter, Esmeralda. Mera, I'd like you to meet out dear friends Gazelda and Stephen Hoffman.

With all the how do you do's and glad to meet you out of the way, Stephen said: "We've heard a lot about you, young lady."

"Pray tell me why they call you Meer-ah?" Gazelda asked.

Esmeralda smiled, for she knew that a lot of people were wondering the same thing about her name: "It is part of the spelling of my name Es-Mera-lda. The Mera in

Spanish, means look, and the letter e is pronounced as a; when you pronounce an r in Spanish, you twirl the letter with your tongue against the roof of your mouth. So they are calling me Ma-rah."

"I thought they said you were Negroid not Spanish," Gazelda stated.

"And you're right, but my uncle was stationed in Spain during WWI and learned a little Spanish. When he saw that I had green eyes, he named me Esmeralda which means emerald or green in Spanish.

Gazelda took Mera's face in her hands, turned her from side to side and then said: "By golly, they sure as heck are green." She held Esmeralda's arms to be sure she didn't move until the inspection was over...

"Now I get it; the Emerald eye jewel that appears on the fashion labels, the bank, hotel, and other businesses around belong to the Emerald cooperation," Gazelda continued.

Not wanting to have the entire group know that she owned these businesses, Mera looked away from Gazelda and toward the strange man who'd just entered the patio, at which time, Philip came to let them know that they were ready to perform. He stared at the strange way that Gazelda held onto Mera and was instantly triggered to understand that she needed to be free.

"Mera, we are ready for you," Philip said as he tugged his sister free of the curious woman who held her captive. Esmeralda politely excused herself and gladly followed Philip to the patio area. She thought to herself: *Will I always be a curiosity piece to everyone who looks upon me, or hears of the Emerald Corporation, and how I'm to use these financial opportunities to bring the Jews to Jesus?*

The Angel spoke in a dream, and said 'Narrow is the pathway, and full of thorns, your feet may be bare that walketh upon it.' 'I already know that I will suffer hardships for His sake and I know that my cross is not nearly as

136

heavy as the cross He bore for me.

Philip noticed the dazed state that Mera was in, but before he could ask if she was all right, she'd already tripped on the door jam and was falling headlong and embarrassingly onto the floor of the patio.

Several guests, including Philip, rushed to assist her as she displayed a minor abrasion on the elbow. The injury was quickly cleaned and bandaged by Philip. Marty rushed to investigate the incident with suspicions: 'What happened in there?" he asked with mixed expressions of anger and curiosity.

"I'm just fine, really. I had my mind in the clouds and not looking where I was going," she stated.

When Esmeralda looked back, she saw Phyllis, Ian and the Hoffmans exit the door and come onto the patio. They seemed surprised to see Philip dressing the minor wound that she had sustained in the accidental fall...

Convinced that the problem was of a minor nature, Ian whispered to the sound technician to turn up the sound a bit for an announcement.

"Please, may I have your attention," he began. "We are celebrating here today for several occasions; our new daughter has written all of the music that you will hear the guys perform here today." There was applause and yells before he continued: "All of the construction renovations that you've seen here today were done by our daughter and her classmates. The interior and exterior all look brand new.

"It is hard to believe that Esmeralda has never had a birthday party. She has been so busy learning adult things and growing up before her time, that no one stopped to celebrate her childhood. Although it's a little early, we'd like to celebrate her sixteenth birthday, which will be on May 28, and Evelyn and Pam have a cake for the occasion."

The ladies arrived, carrying the large cake that bore

sixteen blazing candles and placed it on the table prepared for it. While the group sang Happy Birthday, Esmeralda made her silent wish, proceeded to blow out the candles, and then the band played the song Sixteen Candles; again, there was a round of applause and shouts of congratulations.

Ian shouted for the crowd's attention again: "Last but not least, most of you here know that the life of this little girl has been prearranged for her. She is building a shopping center, a retirement home, and restoring an old synagogue in the San Francisco area, as well as working on her PhD program. And if that is not enough, she is our musician's song writer and manager..."

Following the long applause and shouting period, Ian continued with surprised announcements: "The good news is that she has steered the musician towards a late August Concert, to be performed as a Television Special.

"Since Esmeralda will be busier than a one arm paper hanger, Phyllis and I have sold our client interest in our law firm to Stephen Hoffman and Associates and will be joining the Emerald Corporation as joint CEO'S at the end of June."

Everyone stood to shout approvals with mixed loud applause, and Esmeralda could not stop the happy flow of tears that streamed down her cheeks. Several people, including the members of the band, came to hug and congratulate her.

"And now... And now..." Ian held up his hand for the audience to quiet down so they could hear what he was about to say to them. "Thank you. I'd like to turn the entertainment over to the reborn childhood group entitled Philip Ravin and the MD's.

Marty came to whisper something in Ian's ear, and he gestured for the attention of the crowd again. "I just got word that the MD's first recorded dub has just reached the number one spot on the record sales charts. It looks like we pack our crackers and wine and head for that cheese on the moon. A private joke between Esmeralda and Philip."

Despite the loud applause and shouts of congratulations, Philip gave the cue to the musicians, and they began playing the beautiful music that Esmeralda had arranged for them.

Several times during the performance, the group looked at Esmeralda to be sure they were using the body language that she'd taught them during rehearsals. Each time one of them looked at her and saw her pleased smile, they were encouraged and seemed to develop their own Afro/American entertainer's style. Most of all they were feeling the rhythms and enjoyed it, as did the guests...

The party continued for an endless time, and no one seemed to get tired. These people needed a tension release and were certainly getting it. But as all good things must come to an end, this wonderful occasion was surely destined to do so. Esmeralda felt a sharp sense of uneasiness and backed against the side wall as she stared at the stranger whom everyone else appeared to have overlooked.

She had no way of being sure, but she wanted to be ready just in case. Quickly she entered the house, slipped off her sandals, and laced on her construction boots, preparing herself for battle.

The reason she had done these things was something she could not begin to understand or explain. How could she convince anyone else that trouble was brewing, when unconvinced she was herself.

With her tight sweats on and laced working boots, she found the chain she used in Tai Kwan Do and now felt ready for battle. She reached the front hall and moved through the kitchen looking out to assure herself that the stranger was still there. She found that he was, but also noticed that he'd moved toward Uncle Zech, with his hands on Zech's chair. She exited the house, displaying awareness.

Mera saw Rabbi Terah and Marty looking at the way she was dressed, and only they knew why. They followed her gaze as she quickly scanned the crowd and became fixed on the stranger hovering above Uncle Zach. Then their eyes followed Esmeralda's gaze around the patio. They saw them also as she had seen.

My God, there are three of them. How am I going to get them together? I've never seen a terrorist, but I believe they'd look like those three strangers, milling around hoping to be unnoticed by anyone. It's me they want. I've got to protect the family and their guests. God, send your mightiest angel to help me.

With that prayer, it seemed that God had prompted her into action, and she dashed away from her standing post, brushing into several guests, deliberately pushing them out of harms way, and then she leaped several feet into the air. When she hit the ground, she rolled, tumbling summer salt into the man standing over Uncle Zach, knocking him off his feet.

Her Tarzan-like screams caught everyone's attention, especially the two other strangers. When they came closer with their weapons drawn, everyone screamed and moved back. Esmeralda held tight the choke hold, arm twist of the now standing terrorist near her who was groaning painfully as she tightened her hold on him.

The two other strangers waved their weapons around towards the crowd threatening to shoot if Esmeralda did not release their friend.

"Let him go, or we'll kill them all," one of the men shouted.

There were screams of terror from the guests as Marty tried to calm them down, assuring them that Esmeralda could handle the situation.

Esmeralda sized up the distance between herself, the man she held, and the two other criminals; she inched her way forward pushing her captive before her. Satisfied that she'd closed enough space between them, she made a jerking twist of the man's neck and arm, pushed him into the other two men, and they all fell to the ground.

She quickly kicked the fallen pistol out of the way, and Ian picked it up, aiming it at the terrorists. Before the second terrorist could ready his gun for firing, she landed her right foot into his midriff. When he doubled over with pain, she put her hands together, pulled him towards her as she bent his body painfully into her flexed knee, then upwards, and the man fell down bleeding from his mouth and nose.

With an acrobatic side kick, the second man fell down unconscious. When the first man retrieved another gun, she managed to grab his gun hand, twisting it so painfully that he flipped in mid air, and the bones in his arm actually compound fractured with a loud cracking sound.

Rabbi Terah had slipped off to call the police and paramedics, and the sirens could be heard in the distance..

Esmeralda backed away from the shocked crowd apologizing for her behavior, leaving the three terrorists lying helplessly wounded on the ground.

Several guest, including Phyllis, Ian, Marty, and Evelyn hugged the terrified young woman. "It's alright, sweetheart. Thanks to you we're all safe," Phyllis said.

Joel was heard whispering to his wife Pam: "That should convince you to stop feeding information to that piece of dung Philip used to be married to."

Another voice in the crowd asked: "Who are those men?"

"I don't know; they were certainly not invited guests," Ian said, as he walked around the patio to be sure everyone was safe. He was joined in picking up several overturned chairs and tables, and other items that had been shuffled about during the melee.

"How on earth did she know they were undesirables?" Pam asked Philip, but before he could answer, Uncle Zech heard her and spoke up in his feeble voice: "Like all devil-driven demons, they smelled bad, and Esmeralda is a special person who has the gift of discernment. She can tell what you're thinking just by looking at you."

Gazelda was still standing with her mouth wide open in amazement": I wondered why she'd changed into her sweats and work boots. She obviously recognized them right away."

Someone heard Joel whispering to his wife Pam: "Keep your mouth closed and eyes open."

Several uniformed police officers and paramedics entered the patio and made assessments of the needs. The police tried to take statements while the medical team busied themselves with the injured men groaning on the patio floor.

When the injured man with the broken arm saw Sgt. Darling, he called out his name, but the sergeant stepped on his injured arm to keep him quiet, and the man cried out in pain. Even though the sergeant tried to make it appear like an accident, there were three people who were not fooled by his actions; they all three kept an eye on him. Mera, Uncle Zech, and Rabbi Terah all watched his every move.

Trying to throw suspicions off himself, Sgt Darling said: "Their descriptions fit the gang who crashed several functions of wealthy people and terrorized some Synagogues around the county. How'd they sustain such serious injuries?"

Ian stepped forward: "They were threatening our guests with loaded weapons, but someone here knew martial arts and surprised them."

"I'm afraid I need to talk to that person," Darling said as he kept his eye on the crowd that had gathered around him. He felt uneasy, and thought it necessary to place his hand on his weapon.

Esmeralda saw that a commotion was about to begin all over, so she walked up to the sergeant and confessed: "I'm the Tai artist, sir."

Darling looked at the young girl and laughed out loud. "No way can a little girl do this much damage to big grown men. You had help, of course?"

"No sir, I did not."

"Are you Black Belted?"

"Yes, sir, I am and Master Tai."

"You do realize that is considered a deadly weapon?" Sgt. Darling slightly pushed Esmeralda, and the whole musical group descended upon him as he drew his weapon and stood back to point it at the group. "Now we're going to have some order here." He beckoned to his partner: "Don't hesitate to fire at them. Now Miss...er...What's your name?"

"My name is Esmeralda Wilkins, sir.

"Well, Miss Wilkins, we're going to have to place you under arrest for assault with a deadly weapon."

Ian stepped between the sergeant and Esmeralda, telling the policeman to remove his hands from his daughter. He explained that because of her bravery, a lot of lives were saved. The policeman only laughed and explained that he didn't make the laws, but he surely intended to enforce them. Her life would have to be in direct jeopardy, he told them.

"I believe it was her life they were after all the time," Uncle Zech said.

Sgt. Darling wig wagged his finger between Ian and Phyllis, and in gesture of humor, he asked them if they expected him to believe that big time terrorists were out to take vengeance on a poor little black girl with no real parents. Their story needed to be better rehearsed, if they expected someone to believe them.

A crowd had gathered around that made the policeman nervous before Rabbi Terah spoke up: "Perhaps I can shed some light on the situation."

"And who are you?" the policeman asked with skepticism.

With a voice of authority, Rabbi Terah vocalized: "I am the child's mentor."

"Don't tell me she's got another set of parents?" Sgt. Darling scoffed.

"She's a prophetess," Rabbi Terah declared.

Sgt. Darling slapped his forehead in disbelief, while pointing his finger around: "You're her mentor, you two are her parents, and now you want me to believe that she's a black Jesus. As I recall, the most anger Jesus displayed was turning over a bunch of tables in a Temple, not breaking necks and arms. What kind of dope do you think I am?"

Philip returned from within the house with newspapers that featured Esmeralda converting large numbers of Jews at her lecturing crusades. The sergeant and several others read briefly before looking around at the large crowd. "So you think these men were here to stop her."

Uncle Zech elbowed his way through the crowd, and spoke up: "Unequivocally. The Apostle Paul had Steven killed for the very same reason. Jews don't want anyone telling them that they're wrong, and this girl has the proof locked in her mind from century's back that will prove they are leaving out a good part of God's commandments."

Surprised and filled with disbelief, Sgt. Darling appeared to be having a mild heart attack: "Are all of you people Jews?"

"Most of us are," Philip answered.

"And you're here to be converted to Messianic Jews? What do you do, young man?" He walked around the patio twirling his night stick.

"I am a resident physician in cardio vascular surgery," Philip replied.

"Are there any more doctors here?" Sgt Darling asked as he moved around the patio, facing several people eye to eye.

"Yes," several voices responded at the same time... Sgt. Darling whirled around and laid his stick in Dr.

Markowitz's chest. "What kind of doctor are you, son?"

"OB/GYN," Joel answered.

"What's that?" the policeman asked with his head cocked in manner of bewilderment.

"I take care of female problems and deliver babies," Joel said.

With a reddened flush on his face, Sgt. Darling voiced pretentiously: "I knew that. I just wanted to know if you'd tell me the truth. All of you professional people here, and you believe in this saintly hocus pocus. There's no wonder why cults are taking over the world."

"She's not a saint, she's a prophetess." Uncle Zech faced the policeman with defiance.

"You want me to believe there's a difference?" the sergeant asked scornfully.

Esmeralda walked up to the policeman with her hands up and wrists together: "Please arrest me if you must, but don't humiliate these good people."

"We're not just her parents, but my wife and I are attorneys, and no one will arrest anyone here except those terrorists." Ian stood between Esmeralda and the policeman.

"Is that a threat? Or are you just trying to keep me from doing my job?" Sgt. Darling drew his weapon again and aimed it towards Ian.

Ian said calmly: "Sir, I'm just trying to get you to do your job properly and get those evil men off my property."

Steven Hoffman entered the arena declaring: "I'm Steven Hoffman of Hoffman and Goldberg Law Firm, and I agree with Ian."

Sgt. Darling's anger seemed fueled by the lawyer's request, and he decided to offer a challenge: "Why don't you consult your prophetess here to see if I'm going to make several arrests: hers, as well as yours for obstructing arrest? Missy, you tell them what is about to happen," Sgt. Darling said laughing.

Esmeralda closed her eyes, raised her head towards the sky, and breathed deeply as she had done before attacking the terrorist, and then she said: "Why not show you the message that God has sent to me." She stretched out her hand towards the sergeant and his gun holster, belt and night stick fell to the ground; and his assistants had the same problem.

Ian yelled to the stout gentleman behind the crowd: "Harold, can you get this idiot out of here?"

Most of the guests were in stunned shock from what they had just witnessed, and as Harold stepped forward, he too seemed amazed. His mixed gray hair, a mass of waves on top of his head, was slightly disheveled, and his heavy black eyebrows were arched from surprise. He was immediately recognized by Sgt. Darling who spoke up:

"Oh, Judge Craven, I didn't see you there. Did you witness this fiasco?" He cowardly picked up his fallen equipment.

"I saw it, and it was as told to you. I'll take this up with the DA."

Sgt. Darling hastily started for the exit: "OK, men, our work here is finished." He stopped and turned around with one last word of advice, wig wagging his finger: "You'd better do something about that girl; she's a witch if I've ever seen one."

When the policemen left, the crowd was too stunned to speak but watched Esmeralda with curiosity. Uncle Zech got their attention by using the PA system: "Listen everyone; we have a serious problem here. If they sent those goons here, they'll send others. Esmeralda will need full time security."

Esmeralda broke down crying: "Oh, no. Please not that. It's too costly."

From curiosity, Pam spoke up loudly: "Who are they that you speak of?"

Rabbi Terah took the microphone: "They are a group

of dissidents who call themselves Yarmulke. They are organized to keep the Jews true to Judaism." Rabbi Terah put his arm around Esmeralda to comfort her: "We've lost too many teachers who were forerunners of your coming. The Emerald Corporation can afford security. We must act quickly."

Esmeralda looked up at him imploringly: "What about Mom and dad, Philip, you and uncle Zech?"

"They don't want us sweetheart," Terah told her, "it's you they want to stop. As they did in the Seventh Century, they buried the Book of Laws to avoid obeying Gods Commandments, and now you are here to interpret those laws to the modem world of non believers, they'd die first before they would allow a child to lead them.

"Just as we betrayed Jesus the Christ so many years ago, they'll stop at nothing to stop you also. We must keep you safe until the time is right. I'll notify your brother."

"Do you have to upset Clarence?" she pleaded.

"Yes, child. He'll need to step up security on the east coast holdings and Temples.

"It Has Begun!"

CHAPTER X

When Sgt. Darling knocked on the door to Doctor Wallace's office at the Los Angeles County prison hospital ward, he appeared extremely anxious. He swallowed hard and closed his eyes when he heard the lock click, and a baritone voice within inviting him to come in. He pre-rehearsed his opening statement, just in case the terrorist with the broken arm had talked too much.

Dr. Wallace, an extremely over weight gent in his early sixties, seemed anxious to meet Sgt. Darling, and he attempted to raise his cumbersome body off the chair with extreme difficulty: "Sgt. Darling?"

Realizing that the doctor was having difficulty lifting himself, Sgt. Darling waved for him to keep his seat: "Please sit. I'll need to take a statement from the prisoner. I believe he can tell me who was behind the raid they did on the West Los Angeles home," Sgt. Darling said.

Doctor Wallace kept his eye trained on Sgt. Darling, and his every move made him aware of his involvement with the criminal: "Those were the very words he spoke to me. That's one reason I called you. He kept saying your name."

Extremely anxious, Sgt Darling sat forward in his chair to ask: "He wanted to confess to me?"

Dr. Wallace tilted his head and twisted his lips suspiciously: "He sounded more like he was accusing you of something."

"Probably because I personally made the arrest." He removed a pack of cigarettes and asked permission to smoke, hoping the nicotine would quell his nervousness.

Realizing how upset the sergeant was, Dr. Wallace

thought he'd better say something to keep Darling from knowing that he suspected him of being a part of the problem: "Sometimes, the heavy sedation makes him confused, and little that he said made sense. The only lucid thing he said was get me out of here, Darling, or I'll blow the whistle."

Sgt. Darling stood and walked around the office, shaking his cigarette ashes wherever he had a mind to: "Did he say anything about who he had planned to blow the whistle on?"

"He was muttering a lot of nonsensical words about a group called Yarmulke. I'm not even sure if he understood what he was saying."

Sgt. Darling extinguished his cigarette on the bottom of his shoe and threw the butt in the trash can: "Yarmulke is the terrorist organization that we're investigating."

"I've heard they're fighting against the conversion of Judaism to messianic," Dr. Wallace stated, as he poured himself a cup of black coffee, extending a badly stained cup toward Sgt. Darling.

One look at the cup turned off any desire for coffee that the sergeant might've had, and he blocked it with his hand: "No, thank you, but I would like the opportunity to talk to the prisoner. What about the other two?"

"Both men had emergency surgery for internal bleeding and injuries. Bantz had a ruptured spleen and required a spleenectomy. Lapidus is in traction. Fractured cervical vertebra. His jaw is also broken and wired shut. He'll be out of commission for quite a long time."

Darling shuddered when he thought about the damage that Esmeralda did: "Surely there's something we can do about that girl and the murderous martial arts she used to cripple these men." His voice displayed hatred and defiance.

"Why would we want to do anything? Looks to me like she did your department and the city a favor by getting rid of that evil trio," the doctor said, sipping his coffee.

Suddenly angered by the doctor's statement, Sgt Darling stood abruptly: "It sounds to me that you approve of violence, doctor!"

Dr. Wallace shook his head in disbelief, for he knew instinctively that the policeman belonged to the old school of Judaists: "You said you wanted to question the prisoner, sergeant?"

Sgt. Darling quickly agreed to visit the prisoner, for this conversation was going no where and was causing him more anger: "I came for that reason," he snapped.

Extremely suspicious of Darling, Dr. Wallace stated: "I'd like to be present when you question the prisoner, and I think a police stenographer should be there to record what he says."

Feeling trapped, Sgt. Darling looked down at his watch and then suddenly declared: "Gee whiz. I've got to be at another appointment in forty minutes. But I'll be getting back with you at a later time." He rushed for the door, and Dr. Wallace pushed the security lock to permit him to leave, then bade him farewell: "Good day, sergeant."

When Sgt. Darling left the jail ward, Dr. Wallace dialed his phone, then waited for a response: "Security, this is Doctor Wallace on Prison 15. I've just experienced an attempted breech, and would like twenty -four hour security on the patient in room 1523. I think the prisoner's life may be in jeopardy."

"Right away, doctor," the voice said.

*   *   *

In the modest middleclass home of Sgt. Rupert Darling, the off-duty lawman was sitting in a lounge chair listening to a Dodger Baseball game on the radio, while sipping a bottle of beer.

Mrs. Celeste Darling entered the room, dressed in a

cotton two piece suit and two inch heels. The attractive red head leaned over and kissed Rupert's forehead, patting him on the shoulder.

"I'm off to Temple, honey. Rabbi Jacob's subject tonight is going to be about that girl who was in the news last weekend."

"You be careful now, Celeste, and wake me when you get back home to let me know what happened." Rupert never really paid much attention to his wife for fear he'd miss a call of the game.

"Ok," Celeste yelled back when she walked out the door, as Sgt. Darling settled back in his easy chair to enjoy the winning Dodgers and his bottle of beer.

The phone rang several jingles, stopped, and then rang again. This was obviously a signal just in case someone else answered the phone and to let Sgt. Darling know that it was the "Big Boy" calling.

"Yeah, Rupert Darling, here."

"I assume the problem has been taken care of." The accented voice filtered through the phone receiver.

"They're all three very critical, and I was not able to get to them to really evaluate the situation."

"How many days has it been since the incident?" the voice asked.

"Almost a week now. I have several boys on watch for other activity within that Messianic group. They have been keeping me informed. When I get something conclusive, I'll report it as soon as possible," Darling said, stalling.

There was a long pause before "Big Boy" spoke again, and this made Sgt. Darling very nervous. He'd known members who'd gone to work and never showed up again when the orders of their leader had not been carried out to his satisfaction.

Darling quickly lit another cigarette and inhaled deeply, exercising his lungs with the smoke to make himself more calm: "Are you still there, sir?" Darling asked anxiously as he breathed deeply into the phone. I promise you those guys are unable to talk to anyone in their condition, and I've got someone on the inside reporting to me everything that happens there."

"You make sure they never talk again. I don't want the girl dead, just stopped. Do you understand? Those three dumb Coffs who let a little girl subdue them are of no use to me. You can use your own discretion; I just don't want to hear of them again. Am I understood?"

Darling nervously lit another cigarette, drew in the smoke deeply, and then blew it out before answering: "I understand and it will be done." The phone clicked and buzzed, indicating that the person on the other end had hung up. Darling held the phone for a moment, and then racked it abruptly, before kicking the big orange cat that wrapped itself around his leg.

"Get the hell out of here! Can't you see I've got problems?"

*   *   *

Phyllis came to the door of the Engineering office of the Ravin home where Esmeralda was working late on the San Francisco project: "Mera, someone named Domani wants to speak with you. He has a strange accent."

"Thanks, mom," Esmeralda answered and reached for the phone. Noticing that Phyllis was concerned, she explained that Domain was her martial arts instructor.

"I just wanted you to be all right. His accent sounded Yiddish."

"He's from Jordan," she smiled as the concerned woman left her alone.

"Hello, Domani,"

"Mera, I've been worried. I couldn't get an answer on your phone," his concerned voice filtered through.

"I'm not taking calls on my phone; there have been a

number of crank calls."

"From the newspaper account, it sounds like more than just cranks. Do you need me to hang out with you for a while?"

"Thanks, Domani, but my foster parents and the two Rabbis' have ordered twenty-four hour security."

"What's your itinerary for the near future?"

"I have two more weeks of school, a July Concert with the MDs at the Hollywood Bowl, And San Francisco for two weeks; but my foster parents are going with me up there."

"Do they fight or carry weapons?"

"No."

"Then they're just what lawyers are called, mouth pieces."

"I guess so."

"When are you speaking again?"

"June 23, 8 p.m.

Domani asked for her schedule for San Francisco, and when he understood the place, he recommended changing it at the last possible moment. Also, he recommended that she would need some new martial arts strategies and told her to schedule it as soon as possible: "Otherwise, you're OK?"

"I have an abrasion on my left elbow."

"How did that happen?"

"I tripped on the door jam and fell out doors before the party began," she laughed.

"You klutz."

"I'll talk to you soon. Good bye."

*   *   *

Esmeralda's face was a dull gray as she stood in the Ravin kitchen, preparing the large rib roast for baking.

She stopped, suddenly aware that she was being watched. Without moving her head, her eyes roved to the

153

shadowy figure standing just outside the kitchen door.

Body guards everywhere, she thought

Her hands clinched into fists. There was a certain feeling that if the bodyguard had not been present, she would've struck the piece of meat.

The large police dog beside her seemed to sense his new mistress's rage. He quivered, bristling, prepared for any command she might give.

Esmeralda stood motionless. Her hands stilled as she looked at the face of the bristled German shepherd in shocked surprise at how he could be trained so quickly to protect her. The meat lay across the sink, its limp bulkiness awaiting the preparation needed.

She felt a wave of sickness and revulsion as she looked at the meat and equated it as being a whole being which had probably met a violent quick death within the strong hands of some death crafts person such as herself.

Was I pleased watching those men wretch in pain? Did I smile? What sort of game was I playing? Oh Lord I think I wanted them dead.

She closed her eyes and felt the room whirl about her. The lights dimmed. She held onto the sink to steady herself. The dog barked, and the guard rushed to her side.

"Are you all right, Miss?" the guard asked anxiously.

"Yes," she managed, "but tired.., not much sleep... I think I'll lie down. Please help me get the meat and potatoes in the oven."

The guard lifted the heavy dish into the oven and placed the wrapped potatoes inside. He watched the dog lick Esmeralda's hand.

Outside the kitchen, she leaned on the wall for a moment to gather enough strength to climb the stairs. The dog barked and followed her up the stairs. The guard watched them until they were out of sight.

*   *   *

The Ravins finally came home, and Philip sat in the kitchen listening to his parent's plans for keeping Esmeralda safe.

"Why should this stranger come into our home and almost get his family killed? Philip thought.

His mind was churning with the recent promise he'd made with God to help him change and the uncertain feelings he was having now.

Haven't they suffered enough when he trusted another female intruder?

Ok, Philip. She is setting up some good moneymaking music gigs for you and your friends, and if this Officer thing works, two million in salary for mom and dad could end all of their financial stress.

Why can't I like or trust the girl? Is all the money in the world worth the suffering we could be in for?

Philip heard his parents talking, but he didn't understand anything they said. He was too involved in his own negative thoughts.

"Son, are you all right?" he heard Ian ask.

"Yeah, dad, I was just caught up in thought," he responded.

"You still don't care for her, do you, son?" Phyllis asked.

"It's not that I dislike her; I have reservations about her involvement in the kind of operations that would invite criminals into our home, threatening the lives of our family, and friends," Philip said defiantly.

"Son, she could go back into her world, become the mother of some illegitimate babies, be mistreated by her black men, hated by their women. I'm sure God could find someone else to carry out his mission. Would that make you happy?" Ian asked.

"What makes you so sure that God has anything to do with what she's doing, dad?"

"I believe that she has a special calling, and I'm proud to be a part of it. You need to learn to trust, son."

Philip got up and poured each of them another cup of coffee, taking care to set the pot down without incident.

"I just can't see it yet, and I won't be suckered in by a few eye popping experiences and another pretty face."

"Philip, I thought I was beginning to see a change for the good in you, son," his mother said with disappointment in her statement.

"What you saw, mom, was compromise. I'll always keep my eyes open. That is if she doesn't get us killed first."

*   *   *

Esmeralda slept for almost two hours, and it was hunger that finally drove her downstairs again at nearly seven PM.

It was clear that her family had been discussing her for their voices ceased as she walked into the kitchen, and they watched her in silence. She noticed that the potatoes had been removed from the oven.

"I'm going to finish the dinner," she informed them.

She then proceeded to work, watched by three pairs of eyes that were uneasily aware of the unflinching hostility of the dog. She put the peas in the boiling milk and in her nervousness, allowed it to boil over. The Ravins watched in silent amazement as she mopped up the stove.

"Ok, Mera. Sit down, and let's discuss what's bothering you," Ian demanded, as Phyllis took over the cooking.

"Not too complimentary for that domestic science ability of yours to allow a simple pot to boil over," Philip heckled.

With the peas on a low fire, Phyllis sat down: "What they're saying, sweetheart, is that we're here for you. Talk to us, please," Phyllis begged.

"There is nothing to say that you don't already know."

"There is something more than what we know that's eating away at your insides," Phyllis said.

"It's not going to get any better until you talk about it," Ian continued.

The doorbell rang, and Esmeralda jumped to a standing position. The huge German shepherd stood growling.

"I'm not going to be able to handle this," Esmeralda cried.

"Can't handle what?" Ian asked with sympathy.

"The dog and guards are always around. What's going on out there anyway?" she asked as she leaned to listen to the voices talking in the entrance.

"It is just a regular security clearance," Philip told her, yet his face displayed pleasure that this troublemaker was suffering as he was.

"Ian spoke up to put her mind at ease: "It is probably Rabbi Terah. I asked him to come over."

"Why would you do a thing like that?" she asked suspiciously.

"We both thought that he could give you some answers we are not capable of giving," Phyllis told her.

Rabbi Terah and the security guard approached cautiously under the protective growl of the mighty dog Maximus.

"Heel, Maximus," Esmeralda said firmly, and the huge dog lay at her feet with his teeth bared.

Phyllis and Ian stood to greet the Rabbi, speaking jovially: "Rabbi Terah, it is good to see you."

"Good evening, everyone." He quickly turned his attention to the withering young girl there: "Esmeralda, can you tell me what has you so tensed?"

Tears began to flow in large streams down Esmeralda's cheeks, and her chest heaved up and down under the tension. "I can't sleep without nightmares. I almost killed those men. I'm a Christian, and I had no problem with ending it for them," she confessed.

"Child, do you think David had problems sleeping when he killed Goliath?" Terah asked.

"That was different," she told him.

"How can it be different? Like the Philistines, war was declared, and God stepped in. Those terrorists had declared war, and many good people would've been hurt, or even killed," Rabbi Terah told her.

"But why me?" she asked.

"You're the one God sent. The only one who had the training to take those goons out. No different than David's slingshot. We were all at their mercy. Dozens of us could've been seriously hurt or killed."

"I'm only causing the Ravin family problems," she cried.

"That's the only sensible thing she's come up with," Philip said with sarcasm.

"I always looked at Jews as passive, loving people; I never realized they could be so cruel and insensitive," she said, squinting at Philip.

"Remember Esmeralda, the Jews were not alone in their judging of the Christ, but they had a strong hand in sending Our Lord to that cruel cross to die such a heinous death," Terah also rolled his eyes at Philip.

"I was told that Domani wants to schedule fight change strategies, I think that is a good thing," Terah told her.

"Martial arts require a lot of concentration and I can't keep my mind on it right now. Domani wants me to train Tung Su Do and Nun Chuks"

"What are those like?" Philip asked.

"Tung Su Do is trigger points that put out lights with touching vital blood and oxygen flow points. Nun Chuks is using hidden weapons, such as stars, blocks with chains, and blinding explosions."

"How long have you been studying martial arts?" Terah asked.

"I began six years ago, but never realized that I would have to use it. The old lady who helped us on the farm told my brother how to find the masters, and each time I moved, I was given a letter of recommendation and how to find masters in the cities where I went."

Esmeralda told them that it was a secret order and were warned not to talk about it to any one. "Sometimes the enemy will be trained also, so the element of surprise can mean the difference between life and death."

"The terrorist who came upon us last week were Jews. I guess I hadn't realized how ruthless and uncaring they could be," she said.

"You just keep in mind the part they played in sending the Lord Jesus the Christ to that cruel cross to die."

*   *   *

In the Las Feliz Jewish Home For the Aged, uncle Zechariah busied himself at the desk in their room writing proof and reference Scripture.

Aunt Winnie checked her watch and wrapped a crocheted shawl around her shoulders: "Honey, we'd better go down to dinner; they stop serving in one hour."

"I just need to finish this one page. I won't be long."

Winnie looked at the papers and reference books stacked in front of her husband and shook her head in sheer disbelief. "I've never seen you so intense. When you were teaching at Temple, you didn't spend so much time studying the Torah."

Uncle Zech raised his frail hand as though he wanted to apologize to his wife. "There's so little time, Winnie, and so much to be done. That child can't do it all."

"You've forgotten how the Yarmulkes tortured you when you were more able to be active. I don't want you to get hurt again."

"I'm an old man now, Winnie. If I should die in my

last days serving my God, then my living will not have been in vain."

*　*　*

Outside the retirement home, a limo pulled into the parking lot, and four passengers exited. These men were dressed in long black coats, English derbies, and wore beards down to their chests. The uniformed march and precarious way they looked around the retirement home, dispensed an aura of suspicion and suspense.

The visitors checked each room as they passed, glancing frequently behind the doors, then continued on. The man in front checked a slip of paper with writing on it, in a foreign handwriting, and then gestured to the right.

*　*　*

Winnie felt a sense of foreboding, and the tiny hairs on her arms stood on end. She had the urge to embrace Zech from behind, while he sat at the desk still working. She thought that basically Zech was a kind-hearted man, but he could be short tempered and moody at times. He often worked too hard and used to study the Torah 'til the early hours of the morning.

When he was trying to convince the Jews that Jesus was their Messiah, and their hearts were closed, he sometimes would go days without exchanging a word with anyone and often ate only a dry bagel and a cup of tea. Too many times he'd tried to explain the coming of the child. He prayed for God to send him a sign so he'd know who she was.

From all references, he learned that according to Psalm, Ham is synonymous with Egypt. He had learned that the child's ancestors came from African decent and were out of Egypt. He knew that she held the key to

160

Daniel's translations and the buried Book of Laws. She would have the proof that the Jewish Messiah was Jesus.

He also knew that she alone could interpret the Old Book's Laws and lead the Jews to Jesus. The task would be a difficult one, and her life would be in danger.

Zechariah reached up and patted Winnie's hand. "Do you love me, honey?" he asked out of the blue.

"Of course I love you, you old spoiled Gefilte fish. Why else would I bury myself in that God forsaken Temple for so many years?"

"Would you love me if you thought I was black?"

"I read some of your reports years ago, about the people of earth's beginning was on the African Continent. I've known all that time of your theory that Noah had three sons, one black, one olive, and one white. How could that be unless Noah's wife was a woman of color. I loathed that dark, damp and dreary living quarters, but I loved you and put up with it, even though it stole you away from me."

Zechariah smiled up at his loyal wife of many years. He appreciated her truthfulness and faith in him. "You know, honey, I'm not of a nervous disposition, and I haven't your colorful imagination, but even I felt uneasy in that Temple. It was not a happy place, and I always had the feeling it never had been."

Winnie pulled up a chair and sat in front of Zech, took both of his hands in hers, kissed them each and put his palms on her face.

"There was about..." Here she paused, groping for the right words to express the intangible. "There was a scent of evil," she concluded.

Zechariah stared at his wife. She was not given to extravagances, and it seemed a strange, a very strange expression for her to use. "A scent of evil?" he repeated slowly.

"That sounds silly. I don't quite know how to explain. Anyway," she concluded briskly, "I was very unhappy there. When I was pregnant with Isaiah, I resented bringing

161

him up in that place."

"You never said anything. You never shared your feelings with me and I always thought you were OK with my work."

"Your work was hard, and I understood that. It gave you vitality... Like now.

Look at you, gesturing to the piles of books and papers. You're alive again. The Temple organization never gave you any support; you were always fighting alone."

"You're right, sweetheart. Yarmulke has always been driven by an evil force, and they had the Temple superiors terrified."

She squeezed his hands and said defiantly: "Our only son moved to Israel because he felt the sense of danger here."

"You never talk about Isaiah, Winnie. Why?"

"I knew what he meant to you, and I didn't want to upset you, but sometimes my heart cries out to hold my baby, my son."

"How long has it been since we've heard from him?"

"When he graduated law school with Ian and passed the Bar. About 25 years, I think. Oh, Zech, a day has not gone by where I've not prayed that God would let us see him before we die," she cried with real tears.

Zech stood, embraced his wife, wiped away her tears with his finger, and kissed her forehead tenderly.

"Remember, sweetheart, God will allow us to meet him in Paradise."

"You think that he's dead, don't you, Zech?"

"Why else would he not contact us? Maybe he hated the life I led, but he knew how much we loved him."

At that moment of tenderness, the door to their room burst open, and the four men in black stepped inside, closed, and locked the door behind them. "Why don't you keep this door locked, old man?" the stranger in front asked sternly.

"Who are you? What do you want with us?" Zech asked, stepping in front of his wife to protect her.

"We've come to meet Esmeralda," the outspoken stranger declared.

"How should I know who that is?" Zech answered.

"For years you taught of this child's coming; now you forget."

Waving from behind her husband, Winnie shouted: "You leave my husband alone. He's an old man. His memory is not good."

The stranger took Zech's shoulders, shaking him gently. "We don't have much time. It's important that we speak to the girl."

"You spare my wife, but I'll tell you nothing. You Yarmulke devil."

The outspoken stranger stood in front of Zech, removed his hat and beard. "Dad, I am not Yarmulke. I'm Isaiah."

"My son. Oh, my God. My baby," Winnie shouted.

"Be careful of false prophets, sweetheart," Zech warned, holding his wife back.

With hands outstretched, Isaiah pleaded: "I am your son. Dad, Mom. I'm here from Israel with a mission to merge our efforts with Esmeralda's. We know that you are helping her when we read about her encounter with Yarmulke" at Ian's home."

"Who is Fu fu, and Tad?" Zech asked suspiciously.

"Fu fu was my lamb, and Tad was my green frog with red measles spots," Isaiah answered.

"Isaiah, my son," Zech cried, as he embraced his son. "Come, sit here, and tell me what you are doing," Zech pointed to the love seat on the opposite side of the room.

Winnie hugged her son and praised God for answering her prayers: "Thank you, God. You've answered our prayers."

Isaiah took his mother in his arms, and they hugged for

an endless time before he replaced his disguise.

"We were just going down to dinner. Would you like..."

With his finger to his mouth, Isaiah signaled his mother to be quiet: "Shee.. We can never be seen together in public..."

Uncle Zech inflated his chest and grit his teeth, as though ready for battle: "What does the girl have that you want?"

"It is like I told you; we need to merge our efforts. Her teaching tracks are spreading all over Europe and the world, but there is something more that she knows that Yarmulke does not want known. We've got to protect that secret. Like in the Seventh Century, it could change the future of the Jewish Nations, even the world."

Stacking his books, in getting ready to go to dinner, Zech checked the tiny clock and looked up to speak to Isaiah: "I will arrange the meeting. How will I let you know when and where it will be?"

"We'll contact Terah for your appointment."

"He knows that you're here?"

"He does not know yet, for we didn't want a leak or to put him in direct danger until you'd identified us."

"Son, please don't upset the girl. She's worried enough already. She believes we hate her because of her racial ties to Ham and the Cushites.

"The Ethiopians are our first cousins, dad. Noah and his wife were grandparents to us all."

"It shouldn't matter today that these people were forced into slavery and made to believe they were less than human. Even if some escaped the flood, they were still out of the dark nation of Nod, East of Eden where Cain fled, married and multiplied a nation of people who were the descendants of Adam and Eve. Still making us related."

"Isaiah, there's an old adage that says: 'You can get the man out of the country, but you can't get the country out of the man'. This applies to slavery in some cases. I think she will always be a slave. We'll never get her to change the way she feels."

"Dad, I think as a servant, it gives her a humbleness of heart, putting her cares to be Christ-like."

"Perhaps you're right. We should all be more like her, especially my young nephew, Philip."

CHAPTER XI

Phyllis took down the freshly baked pound cake and began to slice it into small slices, arranging them on a plastic platter. Esmeralda had followed her into the kitchen, removed the Deli chunked turkey, roast beef, and Swiss cheese. She looked her usual calm self, but her hand was trembling as she wheeled the knife to slice the meat, and she almost dropped it.

Phyllis reached for and secured the knife, but when Esmeralda took the knife, Phyllis made no protest, but moved swiftly about the room assembling knives, forks, chips and pickles on trays.

"You heard us arguing last night, didn't you, Mera?"

"Yes, ma'am. I knew it had something to do with me, but I didn't want to know why."

The big dog repositioned himself close to Esmeralda's feet and sized up the situation between the two women before relaxing.

"I'm glad the guys are playing golf; it gives us a chance to talk. Sometimes women need to share what's on their hearts, don't you think, Mera?"

Esmeralda neither agreed nor did she disagree. She was always on guard these days and didn't want to cause trouble.

"Ian is such a good husband. I only hope that you'll be fortunate enough to find a man like him someday. He was so handsome, and also a man of great charm and plausibility. He could do no wrong in my eyes."

"But you still fight sometimes."

"Philip has always caused us heartaches. Ian thinks he should be out on his own... Don't get me wrong, I believe this, too, but not while he is so full of... full of..."

"Do you mean hatred? Is that the word you are searching for, Mom?"

"Well... He's so unhappy, and he wants to blame everyone except himself. He can't seem to move away from his past."

"I don't think it's hatred; I think it's fear. That's why he wants me gone."

"You've brought a change in his life for the better. The clothes, and the way he's learned to coordinate them, and his hair is so attractive long and wavy like that. I never knew I had a son so handsome. The music you write and the managing of their group has brought him enough money to replace what he lost during the divorce."

"Sometimes the changes you're expecting never come. It takes away their manhood... Most men don't like aggressive females. It represents another kind of threat to them. A dictatorship. It is like a harsh tug, rather than a gentle push.. He probably feels that I represent a threat with his friends and parents."

"You are such a wise, little girl. Dad and I were flabbergasted when we examined the complete assets of the Emerald Cooperation. It is hard to understand how you did it all."

"It was by the grace of God in furthering His kingdom."

They demolished a small tray of cookies and a half pot of coffee as they talked about schools, and the idiosyncrasies of the Emerald staff of employees. They talked about Phyllis's ancient first car. They talked about Uncle Zech, and Aunt Winnie's son Isaiah who disappeared right after law school, and now reappearing.

They talked about Esmeralda's four other brothers beside Clarence, and her grandparents. They talked about Esmeralda's first day in school when they moved from Georgia, and how she'd searched for the Colored restroom until it was almost too late.

They laughed about the white doll Esmeralda got for Christmas when she was four years old, and the doll had no hair, just paint. Their sharing that started out as a sad thing became a hilarious laughing session.

Before they knew it, they had filled several deli trays for the guys' ravenous appetites upon their return from golf knowing that rehearsals would bring the band there and all of their wives and kids.

Even Maximus seemed relaxed for his tail began to wag as Phyllis allowed him to sample the roast beef.

*   *   *

While Phyllis busied herself with something in her upstairs office, Esmeralda sat very still at the piano, staring at the notes she'd written on musician's arrangement paper. Alternately watching the small Tiffany lamp flicker occasionally, she felt a glow of excitement webbing up inside her.

It had been a very happy day, a day when she'd been given a gift beyond price. It had been the gift of a mother, a sister, and a dear friend all wrapped up in Phyllis.

Discovering more about herself was not an easy task, but the time alone that followed, the gradual pieced together reluctant scraps of information about herself, and the picture of what she'd been became more clear.

Esmeralda knew that God had put this family in her life, because they were all in need of something very delicate that must come from each of them, to fill the voids that were eroding in the others. Phyllis had always longed to have a daughter. She and Ian both needed their son to be whole again. Philip needed someone to love him in spite of his doubts and fears, uncle Zech, and Aunt Winnie needed to feel useful again, and Esmeralda needed the love and care of real parents.

How wise the Father in Heaven is. He knows just what

each of us need, and as he tells us so patiently in Deuteronomy, "It is good to both hope and wait on the Lord."

As Esmeralda's mind was deep in thought, and her fingers glided over the piano keys, she hadn't noticed that the men folk had arrived and made a mad dash to the dining room table where the trays of food were set up. Maximus objected only when the group, with food in their hands, made their way to the living room where Esmeralda was playing music.

As she transferred the last note onto the music sheet, she heard Marty's voice in the background: "Mera, that sounds terrific. Will you be done with it in time for the concert?"

Appearing startled, she responded: "Yes, but there is a slight problem."

"What kind of problem?" Philip asked.

"I wrote in a keyboard."

"So, what is the problem with that? I play keyboard..." Philip asked.

"You're singing. We'll need another person on keys," she said

"What about you, Mera?" Ian asked.

"We don't want this to become tacky. It's a guy thing, dad, remember? Dr. Philip Ravin, and the MDs."

"Nat King Cole plays and sings."

"That's his MO, besides he's not a sex symbol. Because these guys are bi-vocational, and with their inability to travel a lot, they're going to have to hit their audience hard and heavy. Make them freak out to get the little time you can give them."

She reached for the fashion design portfolio. "You all need to go see Juan at Emerald Fashion, or maybe he can come here for a design fitting."

"Why can't we just rent tuxedos?" Marty asked.

"Like I said, the image has to be just right. Something they'll remember."

At that moment, the wives and kids showed up, and Mera had to leash Maximus before they could continue.

Mera zipped open the portfolio and showed them the royal costume she'd designed.

"How are we supposed to breathe in that?" Philip asked.

"It's stretchable sharkskin fabric. I'll have Juan add a centimeter or so to make you feel better. Oh, there is one more important matter that needs to be discussed."

"Here come the conditions," Philip added with skepticism.

"No conditions, it's a requirement. Have you all noticed how Dean Martin goes flopping around the stage in Boxer shorts? Well, you guys are wearing Jockeys when you perform."

"What does a young virgin know about such things?" Philip asked.

"Even a two-year-old knows the physical difference between boy and girl. Not only that, I know that men watch women's chest and butts, and women visualize mating with guys and look at certain parts of their bodies to see if they have padded socks in their shorts."

"You need to wear Jockeys. As a fashion designer, I must know the inner feelings of all age groups. Older men are going to look at you and remember when, younger men will wish they could make the women scream like you can. And the women will try acting out their sexual fantasies when they remember what you look like. End of subject. I'm going to call Juan and you find a keyboard person."

As Mera went to use the phone, the guys were still laughing and making fun of her demands, but they seemed delighted that she'd told them off.

Ian laughed with the guys: "All I can say is that she has a lot of chutzpah."

"Here, here," Evelyn shouted, "I've always hated those Irish skirt looking under plunder you men wear." The other women applauded.

"What do you think of Nate playing. He used to jam with us, and he played well at the birthday party," Marty suggested.

Joel spoke up with concern for he'd learned to love the music gigs; it took some of the tension away from his failing marriage: "Do you think he'll go for it?"

"We'll never know until we ask. Go call him, Philip," Marty urged.

Mera returned with two kinds of good news: first, Juan was on his way over, and the news about their Gospel record was explosive. "Your Gospel recording has surpassed Gold and heading for Platinum. I have been working on your publicity, and it's looking good."

The room was filled with applause, and everyone hugged each other, complimenting Mera, who quickly bowed towards the musical group with her palms up and open, giving them full credit.

*   *   *

The Hollywood Palladium was packed. There wasn't a vacant seat in the house. Outside, limos were lined up at the curb; it was plain to see that publicity was successful, and thousands had already heard the new group's singles, and were curious to see what a group of Jewish doctors looked like singing black spirituals, blues, and jazz.

By the number of expensive cars lining the valet section outside, these new performers had come to the attention of some very wealthy talent scouts.

Mera, her foster parents, and her tightened security occupied a special boxed section to the right of the stage.

When the announcer came to the podium, he picked up the microphone. The crowd went crazy with excited expectation, and the time was endless before they could be quieted. The soft deep baritone voice began his announcement:

171

"Ladies and gentlemen, tonight we are going to experience a phenomenon. This is something that has never been accomplished in the history of entertainment."

"A group of successful physicians, ranging from heart surgery, OB/Gyn., Pediatrics, Orthopedics, and Clinical Psychology, are singing and playing black spirituals, blues, and jazz. So you wonder what's so different about this group. Well, get ready folks. I give you our Jewish brothers; Dr. Philip Ravin, and the MDs."

The curtain raised on the instrumental group, and Philip ran to the microphone and bowed graciously, as the audience stood up with a roaring applause and shouts that lasted several moments. The eyes of the audience could not stop starring at the good looking, well fitting tuxedos the musical group wore, and the women appeared aroused as they screamed.

Philip gestured to the band, and they began to play a long and loud introduction to his first jazz tune; "The Same One." Between each song, Philip talked to the audience about some experience they, or the audience must've had that related to the words of the song he was introducing. This practice brought screams to many men, and tears to the eyes of the women.

About midway through the performance, Philip introduced his back-up team and their medical specialty. He introduced his little foster sister, as their manager/song writer, and this brought a lengthy applause.

As he sang; "I need your love," several women ran down to the front of the stage yelling: "Here I am, daddy, take me."

When security came down to remove the women, Philip took his handkerchief from his tuxedo pocket and handed it to the woman nearest the stage. She almost fainted as she was being ushered away.

Philip's wrap-up song was a spiritual entitled "Walk Around Heaven." He did this with so much feeling, all the voice, and physical gestures that a black soloist would use, and many of the people were wiping tears from their eyes; a voice from within the audience yelled out with sincere appraise: "Get down, white boy, you know you've got what it takes!"

Philip blew the woman a kiss, and turned to his band to join them, and many voices in the audience in laughter. He took the time to blow a kiss to his sister and parents, for he knew that Mera's dedication had made a professional out of him, and he would be eternally grateful.

Philip's gestures caused frenzies in the audience, and a screaming young woman fainted. Reporters' cameras flashed on every scene at the end. Philip had to be escorted off stage by security to avoid being stripped nude of his clothes as souvenirs.

*   *   *

Later, Esmeralda went back stage to congratulate the group, and she found Philip swamped by several good-looking white women. Her heart fell, and she whirled to leave.

"Mera, Mera," Philip called to her, but she was out of the dressing room area before he could break through the crowd surrounding him. "Why'd she run away?" Philip asked.

Marty exchanged an understanding look with Joel and then said sadly: "I think that someday it'll be told, but not now, not anytime soon. It has to do with her feeling of worthiness, I think."

*   *   *

Two days after the performance, it was dinnertime at the Ravin home, and Mera was very quiet. Even Maximus could sense that there was an unsettling churning within his mistress. She had deliberately made appointments that kept her out of the Ravins' way. The unsettling was felt by the entire family, and they only exchanged looks throughout the meal.

"Is anything the matter, Mera?" Ian asked.

"No, sir," she answered, breathing deeply.

Phyllis took Mera's hand, searching her face for an answer: "You've been awfully quiet, dear. Was the performance as you expected?"

Mera looked at Philip and then back to her plate of almost untouched food. "The whole performance was magnificent. Congratulations, Philip; you have arrived at performance perfection."

"From the way you hightailed it out of there; I thought I'd done something wrong."

You didn't do anything wrong; I did, for hoping that I mattered to you more than just a little sister servant. I wanted to be held in your arms and told how much you appreciated me.

"Philip, when I tell you there's cheese on the moon... Remember. You were outstanding in every way. The gestures, the handkerchief, the little vignettes. You showed a caring spirit that no other entertainer has. You'll go far and fast. I must remind you however, you men are starting late and your active performance time out there is probably fifteen years max, and then it's little old ladies' tea parties."

Ian unfolded the entertainment page of a Sunday *Times* newspaper: "You should see what was said about those costumes. They loved them, and a French designer is after them. Also, they were so impressed with the performance, that movie studios are looking to put you guys under contract. Looks like we've got ourselves a hit team."

"You bet they are, and the Thunderbird Hotel in Vegas called to set up a Thanksgiving performance for four days. That's a long time to have them away from their practices. Do you want to talk to them, dad?"

"You're their manager, you do it."

"Well, I thought a man would be better at this kind of thing."

Philip looked disappointed; "I must've done something wrong, so now you want to dump us." Philip's pleading was not only for himself, but for his group, for he knew how much they enjoyed playing professionally.

"When a little girl has enough gall to demand that the men change their underwear, she should handle the rest with a snap."

"Ian didn't tell you that he went out and bought a dozen pairs of Jockey shorts, in various colors," Phyllis confessed.

"This is embarrassing. I only meant for them to wear the jockeys while on stage."

"It appears that you've set a fashion trend, my dear," Phyllis said.

Seeing the disappointment in Philips eyes, she knew she'd started something that she'd better follow up on: "I'll call everyone, and arrange a meeting for tomorrow night. Maybe a dinner meeting at the Calorie Counter that would be less work."

Mera excused herself to arrange the meeting and then suddenly turned to face her family before leaving: "I need to ask if I may entertain my brother Clarence here next Saturday and Sunday?"

"He will be staying here?" Phyllis asked.

"No, ma'am. He will be staying with Rabbi Terah."

"Why Terah?" she asked.

"Clarence will be bringing papers that Rabbi Terah needs to review before he gives them to you for legal perusal."

"You're sure you don't want your brother to stay here?" Phyllis asked.

"Yes, ma'am. We're trying to avoid heavy East Coast security by keeping Clarence and me apart as much as possible. Oh, yes, who is Isaiah?"

"Are you testing our Biblical knowledge?" Ian asked.

"No, sir. Isaiah is here, searching for me."

With a puzzled frown on his face, Ian asked: "He, where Mera?"

"He's in the Los Angeles area, my sources told me."

The Ravins stared at each other without speaking for a few seconds. "Uncle Zech and Aunt Winnie have a son named Isaiah, but he's been missing more than twenty years. We think he's dead. He was my first cousin. We finished law school together, passed the Bar, and poof, he was gone."

Mera smiled at Ian, saying: "He's not dead; he's an ally to the cause."

"Who told you ... Never mind, child. I should've known better than ask how you know these things," Ian said.

Esmeralda smiled at her foster family, squeezed their hands individually, and then she ran off upstairs with Maximus trotting along.

*   *   *

So the evening passed by, and no more was said about Isaiah. It was only when the phone rang with a typical signal that everyone stiffened with suspicion. There was one ring, and then two, and now one more. Everyone sat very still staring into the faces of each other, while security checked the origin of the signaled call.

Realizing the tension the call had caused, Esmeralda made a feeble attempt to calm the family by announcing that the entire MDs had confirmed to meet at seven PM tomorrow at the Calorie Counter for dinner, and discuss the Vegas gig.

Even Esmeralda was only half-interested in what she was saying, for all eyes were looking for the news from security.

The sound of Jack's footsteps seemed to echo a foreboding mystery as it dickey docked down the corridor toward the kitchen area which was a favorite gathering place for the family.

Not one hand moved to pick up a coffee cup, but the deep tense breathing was shared by all four humans and Maximus.

With their eyes pealed on the doorway, they waited with baited breath as Jack entered and spoke.

"Beg pardon, folks, but I need to move the Mercedes out of the garage, for special and secretive guests arriving. They want to go straight into the garage where they'll enter the house unnoticed."

"Who is it?" Ian asked.

"All I know is they have clearance, and Rabbi Terah will be escorting them."

Jack opened the pantry, removed the set of keys, and then disappeared through the pantry back wall.

"I guess we should move to the dining room and set out some crumpets and tea. It's five of them," Esmeralda said.

Philip stared at Mera perplexed: "I didn't hear the guard say anything about how many were coming."

Ian looked at Mera with a question on his face: "You know who it is, don't you, Mera?"

"I think it is Isaiah." She continued to work without giving thought to what she'd just said; she finally stopped to look at the family staring at her is shocked disbelief, without speaking or moving their eyes away from Mera.

Not another word was exchanged while the family prepared a teakettle, coffee, and cookies. Chicken salad sandwiches were prepared, cut into tiny pieces, and placed on a tray. Ian and Philip set up the circular lazy Susan in the center of the large dining room table, and all of the hors d'oeurves were places on the carousel. Cups, saucers, and dessert plates were placed around the table also; with cloth napkins at every setting.

Finally, just as the family prepared to seat themselves by placing a cut glass with lemon wedges, sugar, and cream , the pantry door sprang open, and Jack came through followed by Rabbi Terah, and four gentlemen dressed in typical Rabbi attire. Esmeralda had to restrain Maximus, for he had never seen such a sight before.

The speaker for the group immediately recognized Ian and Phyllis, and spoke a Yiddish greeting to them.

"Shalom, cousin Ian, Phyllis." He embraced both of them.

"Shalom, Isaiah. Is it really you?" Ian asked.

"It is I, but how did you know? I told Mom and Dad not to say anything."

"It was out foster daughter who told us that you were alive and searching for her; your parents never said anything."

Isaiah greeted Philip. "Is this the little boy who always ran into the cellar when he was afraid?" Isaiah inquired.

Philip's face flushed with the exposure of a deep-bedded secret he'd rather not be reminded of, but here they surfaced nevertheless. Isaiah pointed with curiosity towards Esmeralda, and Rabbi Terah introduced them: "This lovely creature is our child prodigy, Esmeralda."

Blushing, she spoke up; "I was told that you'd be coming. I'm pleased to meet you, sir." Mera stretched forth her hand, but was surprised to find herself enveloped in the fuzzy man's arms, receiving unwanted juicy kisses to Maximus' objections.

"At last we meet, but how did you know I'd be coming? We told no one," Isaiah said completely perplexed.

Phyllis moved to embrace Esmeralda, saying: "She is amazing."

"And she's beautiful, too," Isaiah added.

Ian asked if everyone would be seated in the dining

178

room, as Isaiah introduced his companions who turned out to be security from Israel. The story of how he'd been called to service for the motherland unfolded. It had been one of heartaches and loneliness. For he'd longed for his family. He told how he'd watched his father being scorned for teaching Christianity, and he'd prayed to God to allow him to help bring the truth of the Messiah's birth to a nation of unbelievers.

When God spoke to him about the mission he'd planned for him, his heart was broken for it meant that for years he'd have to desert those he loved best. He appeared sad and dabbed at his eyes with his handkerchief before continuing.

"Dad and Mom look well, or better than I expected giving all they've had to endure," Isaiah commented.

"Mera is responsible for a lot of their new vitality," Ian said.

"Mera?" Isaiah asked.

Phyllis spoke up quickly: "It's a nickname for our little girl." She explained to Isaiah that Mera meant to look, and certainly was well befitting the make up of the child's abilities for she was always on guard. She explained how much hope and joy she'd brought back into the lives of uncle Zech and Aunt Winnie.

"He fought so hard to tell people that this child was coming some day; I can see why he'd be excited," Isaiah told them.

Rabbi Terah told Mera that Isaiah was here to discuss a merger between Emerald Corporation and Eureka, their European crusade.

"What is the Eureka Crusade?" Esmeralda asked.

"It is what we call our European Crusade. Eureka means "I Have Found It.""

"I know what it means, but why Spanish?" Mera asked.

Isaiah told her that the name was just a diversion. The

struggles in Europe were more difficult than here, and the Zionists were more adamant about keeping Judaism pure and alive.

Esmeralda told him that she could understand their desire to merge the two corporations, because the larger they are, the more clout they'd have, but her spiritual source had not talked to her about financial mergers. She thought it would be better if they each had their separate financial independence; as for as sisters allays, it should be known that we are one.

"The Eastern US manager is scheduled to be here this weekend, and we'll discuss this possibility with him before we make a decision. We'll pray about it; I'm sure God will tell us what to do."

"I'll leave my contact information with Rabbi Terah; he'll notify me of your decisions."

"Very good, sir; it was a pleasure meeting you."

They all stood as Esmeralda excused herself: "I have a full day tomorrow, and rest is my only hope of staying alert. Good night, all."

*   *   *

A unanimous decision amongst the musicians had changed the dinner meeting from the Calorie Counter back to the Ravin home, and spaghetti had been requested. Mera's specialty spaghetti dinner was one of the music group's favorite. It was thick rich sauce made from fresh tomatoes, onions, celery, green bell peppers, mushrooms, basil, Italian seasoning, chili powder, and cooked sliced Italian sausage, with salt and pepper to taste. French bread toasted with garlic butter was hot and ready.

The salad was thin sliced vegetables of firm tomatoes, bell peppers, white onions, and large fresh mushrooms, seasoned with rice vinegar, salt and pepper and a dash of cayenne. Their dessert of choice was Gingerbread, topped with whipped cream cheese.

The musicians' mouths' drooled as they entered the front door, and no one stopped until they'd taken a seat around the famous Ravin round table in the dining room, dirty hands and all.

Pam yelled loudly: :Whoa, did you guys wash your hands?"

They all rotated their hands as though inspecting for a visible foreign organism.

"They look clean to me," Joel said.

"OK, guys, line up for the wash basins," Pan ordered, drying her own hands on a kitchen towel.

Marty looked at his wife Evelyn filling plates for the kids in the kitchen, and he appeared exasperated. "Damn, man, by the time we all get washed, all that good food will be gobbled up," he complained.

"Sounds like one of my lab professors to me," Chris gripped.

But they all rushed to a sink somewhere nearby and began to run water over their hands, shaking the water off for the lack of a towel to dry them.

After sitting down and swinging the massive lazy Susan around to fill their portions, Marty asked: "Why is it that we always have to wash our hands at home, but no one washes in a restaurant?"

Now that the children were eating in the kitchen, Evelyn had joined the group at the big table, and said: "I'm going into Midwife practice to stay healthy because you doctors will bring home the infectious upper zetas."

"Please don't say that," Joel said. "Pam already thinks she's going to catch pregnancy when I touch her."

"I thought you had to do more than touch to catch pregnancy," Phyllis laughed.

Everyone laughed except Pam and Mera. "Prayer time," Mera yelled to cut the tension. Forks and bread dropped onto plates, and heads bowed with eyes on Mera.

She looked around waiting for a volunteer, then realized she'd better do it if it was to get done

"Most Gracious Heavenly Father. We thank you for the insurmountable blessings that you gave to us, especially when we do not deserve."

Philip felt a toe being stepped on and he cut a quick glance at Mera and then around the table where he noticed all other eyes were closed

"Thank you, Lord, for the overwhelming response that the music group received, and help them to be grateful to you. We thank you for helping us receive so many new offers to perform and at so many places. Help us to make the right choices and develop the appropriate music.

"We thank you and praise you for brightening the hearts of Dear old Zech and Winnie in bringing their son home again. Let my brother have a safe trip here and return. And Lord, thank you for my new family and friends, and let Philip not dislike me so much. Amen."

Philip was the only one not reaching, grabbing, and passing food items around. He breathed deeply and reached for the big bowl of white spaghetti when he noticed that even Mera gave no further thought to the statement she'd made concerning him. He thought it was better to say nothing but eat.

During this dinner, several entertainment engagements were decided upon, and the Vegas trip was the most exciting one for them all.

*   *   *

Late Saturday afternoon, and the black limo with tinted windows had received permission to park in the garage of the Ravin home. The pantry door was already opening when Esmeralda noticed that Maximus stood ready to attack the arriving guests.

"Heel, Maximus," Esmeralda shouted with urgency,

182

and the rest of her family stood ready to receive the guests.

The kitchen smelled delightful with all the favorite foods that Esmeralda remembered her brother liked. There was golden fried chicken that she had soaked in seasoned buttermilk for 24 hours, before sprinkling with seasoned flour. She had prepared creamed white potatoes using sour cream, and cabbage seasoned with white vinegar, hot peppers, and ham hocks laced with pods of whole okra, fresh black-eyed peas, braised short ribs, and peach cobbler.

The guests consisted of Clarence, east coast Attorney Darin Solomon, Rabbi Terah, uncle Zech and aunt Winnie. The dining room table had place settings for nine, so the Ravin family, and Esmeralda would complete the count.

The guard led the arriving party through the secret panel and into the kitchen. Esmeralda could not stop laughing and crying as she embraced Clarence. He was a six-foot, muscular gent, whose dark tan skin and jet-black curly hair was exactly like Esmeralda's. He had high cheekbones and light brown eyes that painted a perfect picture of his early Nod descendants.

"Baby girl, I'd like you to meet Attorney Solomon; he's directing the east operation," Clarence said.

"I'm pleased to meet you, sir," Esmeralda said and she stepped back to introduce her new family to Clarence and Solomon. Solomon reached for Ian's and Philip's hands and then kissed both of the ladies' hands: "I'm pleased to hear that you two have taken over the running of the west coast operations."

"We're pleased to be on board," Ian said.

Old Maximus seemed jealous of his mistress and the attention she was receiving from Clarence, and he growled often to remind everyone that he was territorial master here.

Although Clarence greeted Philip with respect and cordiality, he did not release his hand until a thorough inspection had been completed. Philip felt a twinge of uneasiness.

On a small table against the wall in the dining room entrance, sat a wooded two-sided bowl that contained warm wet washcloths that Mera dispensed with a forceps to each guest as they entered and sat down around the table. They dropped the used washcloth in the open side of the bowl, taking their seats.

The center lazy Susan was filled with the prepared dinner items before Phyllis and Mera took their places.

Ian opened the conversation by asking with curiosity: "So Darin, you already knew Rabbi Terah before coming here?"

Darin explained that he'd known Rabbi Terah for many years. Zech had contacted him when they were first disrupting the efforts that he'd started; he tapped Zech's shoulder and smiled across at the frail gent beside him. "Of course, there were too little funds available to undertake such an operation," he went on to say. "Those efforts fell by the wayside."

Phyllis asked how he knew to come on board this new operation, when so many things could've gone wrong. Darin smiled again at uncle Zech and then across at Phyllis before he answered.

Darin's decision had been made due to the teachings that he heard from uncle Zech many years ago about a young girl that was to come to lead the Jews to Salvation. Her powers in business would be unchallenged, her astuteness in learning was to be unmatched, and her beauty, love, and compassion were indescribable.

"Her brother Clarence did a great job of covering her steps and getting her places where she could complete her education. Edna Carpenter did the purchasing and banking for them through her own corporation."

Clarence finally found an opening to bring Mera some bad news: "That's one thing I came to talk about, Mera baby." He dropped his head, his eyes saddened as he paused. "Miss Edna is dead," he finally said with a great deal of effort and regret.

"I usually know of such things. Why did this escape me?"

"You knew when it happened. Remember last week you called to tell me that you were worried about Miss Edna and that she came to tell you something important, and then you wanted to hang up because you smelled embalming fluid. I received the news as soon as you hung up the phone."

"The funeral, I'd like to be there," Esmeralda cried.

Esmeralda learned that the funeral was over, and that Miss Edna made a special request that she not be there for safety reasons. When the town's people learned that most of the property and businesses, including the bank, had been willed to the Emerald Corporation, there would surely be consternation.

Beside the holdings in Georgia, Miss Edna had made sizable investments in towns throughout the United States, and they, too, had been transferred to the Emerald Corporation.

"We don't anticipate problems in transferring the investments in the northern holdings; but Georgia will be a problem, for those residents are already filing claims against the estate."

Phyllis and Ian were asked to go along for the trial that was set for thirty days from this date. It was estimated that they would have more than just Zionists fighting against the acquisition, but American WASP as well, who would be trying to eliminate the girl.

Uncle Zech recommended stepping up security for there was another group from Israel called the Eureka's who wanted to merge with Emerald. Even though the leader had been his own son, Zech was not sure they should be trusted.

Esmeralda suggested that they merge the two groups together, as long as it did not require sharing funds. "We don't need them; they need us, but surely as we grow larger, we will become more powerful in size. I say buy them out."

"Before we undertake another segment of business, it would be wise to finish what we have most pressing. The buy out of Eureka is a good idea; however, we should do some investigating of their practices first," Ian recommended.

Everyone agreed that Eureka should wait, and Darin spread papers on the table for inspection, but stopped momentarily. He knew that he presented a lot of new business for Esmeralda to think about, but he had still another question that needed to be settled.

"Esmeralda, do you know someone named Neal Landis?" Darin asked.

All eyes were pealed on Esmeralda, waiting her reply. Phyllis went to refresh the coffee cups, and Philip eyed the girl with freshly summoned suspicions.

"I've heard that name before, but can't really remember where," she said.

"According to the letter from his attorney, you met this gentleman at a train station in Dalhart, Texas, and you assisted him somehow," Darin said.

"Now I remember the incident. The train stopped for two hours, and all the passengers got off. I went into the gift shop, and when I was just about to leave, some young men attacked a man out front. They beat him up pretty bad. I sort of disabled the perpetrators, called for an ambulance and the police, stopped the bleeding from the large knife wound, and prayed with the injured man and calmed him down."

"You gave him Clarence's address and then disappeared," Darin stated.

"It was time for the train to go, I had to hurry on board."

"According to this letter, he later converted to Christi-

anity, but is dying from some rare cancer, and has been trying to find you before he dies," Darin said.

"Where is he?" she asked.

Darin Solomon told them that the sick man was at the
White Memorial Hospital in Boyle Heights and asked if she
knew where that was. Esmeralda had never heard of the
hospital, but Ian knew where it was.

"May I go to see him, Mom, Dad?" Mera asked.

When Ian hesitated for security reasons, Darin told him
that it would behoove them all to go as soon as possible,
since Neal's lawyer had described his assets as sizable. The
legal team and Esmeralda would be designated to go. The
rest would wait at home. Darin called Neal's lawyer and
arranged a meeting right away.

*   *   *

The limousine that carried Esmeralda and the legal
team, plus several security persons raced through the area
called Boyle Heights, down Brooklyn Avenue to 1720,
heading east away from downtown Los Angeles.

The street was a bumpy mess of cement over cobble-
stone and streetcar rails. The hospital sat on the south side
of Brooklyn against the towering site of the La County
General hospital.

Bakery shops, delicatessens, laundry/cleaners, shoe repair, and numerous fast food eateries laced the cluttered
sidewalks, together with cast aside trash and a few va-
grants.

The depressiveness was almost overwhelming for Esmeralda, and she was happy when the limousine finally
parked in front of the hospital.

Two security guards accompanied the group up the
elevator to the fourth floor and then down the east corridor
to room 422.

After the security searched the patient's room, they

187

stood outside the door which displayed a sign: N. Landis, as the interested group entered.

Beside the bed sat a well dressed, suspicious appearing middle aged man, his legs crossed, and he stopped examining the documents he'd spread out on the tray table and began to examine the arriving party who entered. He stood and extended his hand: I'm Mark Swartz, and you are?"

"Darin Solomon," and reached out to receive the extended hand as he introduced the rest of his party.

"So this is the little girl who made such an impression on my client?" Mark asked.

After showing Mark her birth certificate and Master's Degree, Mark was extremely impressed and amazed. They all turned with Mark to the sick man who was making gurgling sounds, trying to respond to the commotion he'd heard.

Mark leaned in close to the patient and called his name loudly: "Neal... Neal, she's here."

"You don't have to shout; it's not my hearing that's going, it's my heart." The dying old man gurgled with determination. He struggled to raise his head so that he'd be able to see Esmeralda. Mark cranked the head of his bed so that Neal could see well.

Neal reached a trembling hand towards Esmeralda, whispering: "Come here, child." Esmeralda reached for the extended hand of the trembling old man, and he squeezed her hand tightly. "Praise God you came before it is too late."

"I'm so sorry I can't take away your pain," Esmeralda said sadly.

"You're still as pretty as a bug's ear. It's all right, child. You saved my life in more ways than you know..."

Esmeralda could think of nothing more to say but that she hoped they put the criminals who'd attacked Neal away for a very long time.

In a raspy and weak voice, Neal told Esmeralda that

she should not fret about that incident. It was as he deserved. He explained that she had saved his life spiritually for he'd been so selfish and full of greed. The more he accumulated, the more he wanted. He actually hated poor people and envied those richer than he was. He then choked with the stress of talking.

"Please don't try to talk; you need your strength," Esmeralda pleaded.

Neal asked with determination what was he saving his strength for? Was it to create more evil in the world? With sadness, he said that he had everything a person would ever want, except a family. He'd thought a wife and kids would get in his way of becoming richer, keeping him away from his first love: money.

Now that he was dying, all the wealth in the world couldn't save him: "I want you to have my wealth. I want to help you lead others to the Savior, before it's too late.

"That is a beautiful testimony, Mr. Landis," Esmeralda told him as she held his head in her arms.

"Just call me Uncle Neal, child. You see, I have no other relatives, so you're it... I want to Quit Claim everything to you."

"What kind of assets are you talking about?" Darin asked.

"I have a half interest in a Shipping Magnate, interest in a gold mine in Alaska, plus a diamond mine in Africa...also insurmountable property and stock holdings here in the States."

The severe coughing began again and through the breaks from coughing, Neal asked:

"Where do I sign, Mark? You're my lawyer and notary. Let's get it done now so the government won't swoop down and take away it all."

The necessary papers were spread before Neal who signed with trembling determination. Phyllis, Ian and Darin witnessed them, and then Mark notarized the areas necessary. Esmeralda signed the area marked beneficiary.

Neal seemed pleased that it was finally done and laid back on his bed, a peaceful smile parted his lips, as he closed his eyes in a final curtain of satisfaction.

*   *   *

Clarence and Philip sat across from each other, stealing an occasional glance and trying not to let it be obvious that they had unresolved animosity and questions for each other.

The food had been put away by Philip, and Clarence had cleared and washed the dishes. Uncle Zech and Rabbi Terah continued talking while sipping tea and really not noticing the tensed feelings the two young men had for each other.

Philip decided to speak up first to break the silence: "Esmeralda told us that you still have a bullet lodged in your chest."

Clarence paused and stared at Philip, then to Terah, and uncle Zech before responding: "I'm not educated like my sister. What I know was country grammar school and some night classes recently. And, of course, Mera helped me a great deal..."

"I didn't mean to offend you by asking about the bullet..."

"Yes," Clarence interrupted. "Nine years it has been in my chest. The bullet that is."

"I wish you'd allow me and my associate take a look while you're here."

"No need, for several good doctors have already made studies of the situation and given their recommendations, which sounded logical to me. More probing doesn't interest me," Clarence told Philip.

Philip seemed to be pleading his case: "I am a qualified heart specialist, although I must confess that I've been

190

in practice with a seasoned specialist for a short time, but my prep studies are extensive. I'm not a Christian Jew like my parents are, but it is possible for Jews to practice medicine with a fair degree of skills."

Realizing that Philip has been somehow insulted, Clarence tries to apologize to ease his tensions: "Look, I have no doubts about your capabilities. My mission is to keep my sister safe until she can look after herself. Until that time, God will help me stay healthy. No insults intended."

"None taken," Philip replied. "I think that medicine has advanced so much that..."

Clarence interrupted: "You're probably right. I'll look into it some day soon and when I'm ready, I'll let you know." Clarence seemed concerned that Philip was insulted, and his sharp brown eyes stared at him with suspicions and indignation.

Philip began to clear soiled dessert dishes from the dining room, and even from the back view, his anger was clear to see; the three men seated at the table rolled a rueful face at each other as Philip savagely kicked a fallen spoon, and it shuddered across the room.

CHAPTER XII

In the Spring of 1949, a meeting had been scheduled in the conference room next to the plush offices of Phyllis and Ian Ravin. It was the Corporate headquarters of the West Los Angeles division of the Emerald Corporation.

The Ravins and Esmeralda stood aside while the security team examined every possible hiding place for listening devices and explosives. Assured that the executive suite was clean of harmful devices, the entourage of bodyguards escorted Esmeralda and her foster parents into the room.

Esmeralda was carrying an attaché case, and dressed in impressive business attire. Accompanying her were Rabbi Terah, Uncle Zech, Cleavon, her CPA, and Security. Ian smiled approvingly when he saw Zech's polyester stripped suit, matching tie, and slicked back hair. It had been a long time since he'd seen his uncle look so vibrant.

Bianca, the Ravin's efficient and attractive secretary entered the room, carrying a steno pad, and pencils which she immediately handed over to the security for examination, before taking her seat at the large conference table.

The rest of the group sat around the table, where Esmeralda had spread her dossier on the top and was passing clipped copies to each member present.

Ian called the meeting of the West Coast Emerald Corporation together, explaining that they were here to discuss expansion possibilities. He made them aware that sizable donations and means of supporting this expansion effort were now available, and that they each were holding copies of the proposed plans, cost and requirements.

They were asked to follow along as they stepped through each item and to feel free to ask questions at any point.

The major objective of the Emerald Corporation was to expand the Jews for Jesus, or Messianic worship centers, as well as the acquisition of the Eureka Corporation, headquartered in Israel and spreading throughout Europe. The Director of Operations there was Isaiah Ravin, Uncle Zech's son.

Rabbi Terah was assigned to oversee this operation but cautioned to work closely with the Engineering Department.

A question arose from the side of the table representing the accounting department: "We have an Engineering Department?"

"Yes, we've always had an Engineering Department; that is where everything sprang from, although it has been a tremendous overload for our President, trying to handle everything alone. She has asked us to hire qualified, dedicated engineers as soon as possible." Ian explained.

The second item mentioned on the agenda was the need for training and teaching supplies. Uncle Zech was assigned to supervise this endeavor, together with Esmeralda, Rabbi Terah, and the new recruited Rabbi's brought on board.

It was recommended that secure housing be found for Zech and Winnie, and secretarial and domestic help be made available to them. Zech stated that with the materials that Esmeralda had already developed and those he and Rabbi Terah added to the supplies, there should be enough to get started, after copies are made.

The third proposal had to do with Esmeralda. It was noted that she would be seventeen within a few days and would need to devote more time towards her Doctorate Degree which would require two more years. She would need engineering and architectural assistance.

Since Esmeralda had designed Emerald Suite Hotels and proposed that they were built in strategic sites in all Hub cities immediately, the Corporation would need engineering scouts, who will find the best sites throughout the world.

"There are other business endeavors that we have had in mind, but too much too soon can be a hindrance rather than an asset. Phyllis and I, of course, will be looking into insurance, real estate, and medical centers, as well as finding out how we can set up our own financial institution with the FDIC and FSLIC."

The members were so busy jotting down notes, twirling pencils, and underlining their particular assignments, there had been too little time for questions. Ian told them that he would expect a preliminary report from each of them within four weeks and that the Vice President of Human Resources should be on board within a few days, he and Phyllis had already interview several candidates.

Ian examined the faces of each person there, trying to understand if they had understood what was expected of them. His curiosity was not satisfied, so he asked: "If there are no questions, or other business you'd like to discuss at this time..."

He was cut off by Uncle Zech: "I'd like to ask a question, please; what do you consider a hub city. And what is so important about these hotels that Esmeralda has designed?"

"Hub cities are those with major airports. Usually a large amount of business is conducted there, and a large amount of business people meet there. Mera, our bobby sox baby, as I've heard some of you call her, has designed comfortable lodging, with adequate working rooms. Each is a suite with kitchen stocked with refreshments and dry food to be rotated weekly. There is a small conference table in the living room. On the first floor is a full buffet breakfast and lunch bar, and for dinner is an available dining room.

Phyllis raised her hand to speak: "As for the bobby sox baby, I'm very happy to call her my daughter. I can't say that I know any grown-up who has accomplished so much in such a short time."

Again Ian spoke up, this time with a more serious look on his face: "Phyllis and I will be accompanying Esmeralda to Georgia, where she has received a summons to appear in court. Please direct all problems to the Accounting Department, and we'll get with you as soon as we return. Thank you for coming."

*   *   *

As the security limousines arrived in Sugar Creek, Georgia, the little old-fashioned town which used to be the shopping center where Esmeralda was born, she could feel that evil things had happened here, and evil people live there.

Clarence mentioned earlier that when Miss Edna was very near death, she was hallucinating like someone had fed her drugs to force her to hand over the titles to key properties. Those evil plans had failed therefore, a court trial was necessary.

Overlaying the chill, the damp, high, haunting smell of death and decay was an overwhelming sense of awareness that evil forces were at work and had been throughout the years.

Even black people who borrowed money, food and other items from Esmeralda's parents when they lived there and who had worshipped and prayed together with her family years ago, stared at them with evil disrespect.

Clarence and Esmeralda's being there could mean reprisals by whites, and disturbances of the black way of life. They wished the Wilkins kids had not returned: *Who do those straight haired Niggers think they are anyway?* they thought.

Those eyes, red and black scowled faces starring at the two limousines were like the piercing daggers of a knife-throwing artist, staving dangerously close to the chauffeured cars. At one point, Esmeralda dodged as though an eye with a piercing blade had penetrated the armored car.

Phyllis noticed her apprehension and gently took her hand squeezing it, smiling reassuringly: "It is a quaint little town, but the people don't appear to be friendly at all."

Ian had been staring out the tinted window and quickly turned to look at the passengers in the car, grunting an agreement with Phyllis's statement.

This introspective opinion was Esmeralda's first reaction to Sugar Creek, Georgia where they'd come to settle the affairs of a very special woman. A woman she'd loved so much. This woman had been her rock on solid ground. She'd taught her so much far beyond the abilities of any other child.

At first she believed as Clarence did that it was only Miss Edna who'd been threatened and kept in a drugged state so that she could not will the holdings she'd owned in this town. Later, when the hearing began, she learned that she and Clarence were the targets, the intended victims in a terrifying and deadly plot.

*   *   *

Judge Godfrey, a red faced, wiry haired blond told the court assemblages that he never heard of such a ridiculous claim. He twinned, speaking in a windless jerky Southern accent that sounded like he had a clamp on his nose.

Those faces again, red faces and pale white faces, lined the musty old courtroom. Esmeralda heard the shotgun-toting spectators urge the black faces to move on for they wanted no Nigger sympathizers hanging around.

When Judge Godfrey announced the docket for the day, Esmeralda only faintly heard what he was saying, for she was staring at the frayed drapes and peeling faded wall paint. There were overall-clad deputy sheriffs holding shotguns by their barrels. Behind Esmeralda, standing near the deputies, were several security persons who'd removed their jackets to expose the powerful multiple repeating German Lugar's.

Most of the spectators wore scowls on their faces as they starred at Esmeralda and Clarence. There were several well-dressed white men who sat at the back of the room with their eyes on the armed deputies. Esmeralda wondered who these men were but felt at ease when she noticed one of the strangers making eye contact with Clarence. She later learned that these men were FBI agents.

The stifling and musty air was overpowering for Esmeralda, and she wondered if she could edge quietly out of the room before the atmosphere made her sick and faint.

Just as she reached the outside hallway, she turned to see if her security guards had followed her; she felt a large strong hand deliberately cover hers, and she shot around in a startled surprise to look into the twinkling brown eyes of a very tall and remarkably handsome young man.

The man had black curly hair, and Esmeralda recognized him as one of the instructors at Domani's School of Martial Arts in Los Angeles.

The man kept his hand firmly over Esmeralda's hand as he signaled to the guards and grinned down at her. He had perfect white teeth in a smooth tanned face, and as she tried to remove her hand, his grip tightened.

"Domani didn't introduce us, so I must do it myself. My name is Cesar Malachi, and I must tell you, it was like holding a ray of sunshine seeing you standing there in the doorway."

"How do you do, Mr. Malachi," Mera mouthed the words stiffly, embarrassed by the hand that held hers in a vise.

"How do you do, Miss Esmeralda," he echoed, and she blushed at his mimicking of her prissy voice.

There was mischief in his eyes. "It is refreshing to meet a girl who is knowing how to blush. Now my dear

Miss.. might I be having the pleasure of calling you Mera? I know you'd care to be away from this circus, but you are the one on trial, and Domani wants you kept close. So you'd better return to the room."

Esmeralda hesitated, feeling a little shocked at the impudence of the young man who still held her hand captive. "There are many things I'd like to show you later," he coaxed gently.

"In that case, I'd better get back inside." Together, they walked back to the courtroom door where she halted suddenly, pulling him up short: "I'd like to go inside, but would you please let go of my hand?"

Cesar turned her hand over in his, studying it and apparently considering her request.

"Why?' he finally asked.

"Because I don't walk around holding the hand of strange young men," she told him firmly.

"There's nothing strange about me," he insisted. "Honest to God, I'm not a bit strange. You can ask my mommy if you don't believe me," he teased.

"You're a stranger to me, and you're hurting my hand," she assured him.

With this request, her hand was released abruptly, and the smile wiped from Cesar's face. Feeling an emotion she feared, Esmeralda almost ran back inside the courtroom

*   *   *

Attorney Shepherd Baldwin stood before the jurors to make his opening presentation. His speech was whinny and jerky as a Georgia accent. His outdated cotton suit and greasy looking neck tie were far too small for his bulging weight gain, and his big feet made him appear like 'Lil Abner' of the comic book world.

"Ladies and gentlemen of the jury, it is not customary in the Georgia legislature that a Negro child can be the heir of property willed by a white woman. As you can see, this here child is not old enough to sign legal papers, so how can she be the heir of such a mass fortune?

"If Sugar Creek was to honor such a request, most of the citizens would lose their jobs, homes, farms and businesses." He turned to laugh at Esmeralda mockingly.

"Why, as the City Attorney, I'd be working for a Baby Nigra. Can you imagine how many other of those black devils would be getting uppity."

Ian stood to object: "I object to Counsel's statements. They are degrading and disrespectful."

"Objection overruled," the Judge yelled. "Mr. Ravin, I allowed you to sign on as the attorney for the defendant simply because no lawyer in his right mind would attempt to represent her request, but need I remind you and your wife that you are not licensed to practice law in the state of Georgia."

One of the well-dressed men from the back stood and spoke out loudly: "Beg your pardon, sir, but I am also representing Miss Edna Carpenter's Estate, and I am licensed to practice law in Georgia and any other state in the union. I agree with Mr. Ravin. We are not here to demoralize the beneficiary but to dispose of the estate of Miss Carpenter. If she saw fit to will her holdings to a cat, it's the duty of this court to honor her wishes."

"What is your name, sir?" The judge asked squinting suspiciously.

All heads turned towards the speaker from the back of the room. There was a mixture of surprise, hatred and fear on many of the faces of the spectators.

"My name is Christopher Greenberg. I'm legal director for Estate Affairs with the Federal Bureau of Investigation... er... May I approach, sir?"

The judge appeared shocked and waited several moments for a good reply to reach his brain before speaking. Christopher had begun to walk forward when the deputies raised their shotguns about waist high, and all of the strangers quickly put their hands on their German Lugers.

"Just a minute, young fellow," the judge shouted. "Listen everybody. I ain't gonna have no foolishness in my courtroom. Now, all of you put those guns down! I said rat now!"

Christopher spoke up quickly: "Your Honor, my men are licensed by the federal government law enforcement to bare arms. Might I ask if these men with shotguns are licensed?'

"They are deputized by me to keep order during this here trial, and they will keep their guns and do their job, ya hear!" the judge shouted.

Chris shook his head at such child-like proceedings: "I hear you, sir. Your City Attorney was just telling the jurors that their homes, jobs and farms could be in jeopardy. What about the lives of your families as well? We realize that your local law does not respect state and federal law, so we've surrounded your town with troopers. Your whole community could be wiped out in a heart beat with the sound of one shotgun."

The judge stood wig wagging his chubby finger toward all the visitors: "You whole bunch of bungling Christ killing ass Jews have no jurisdiction in my court. I am the law here!"

"You're absolutely right, sir, as long as you practice law and not that white-opinionated Southern bigotry," Chris shouted back.

The judge turned towards Clarence and pointed his finger accusing him and Esmeralda of murder: "That boy Clarence is wanted for murder. He killed one of our community's leading citizens years ago, leaving his little children and wife without a breadwinner. Arrest him and that girl there; she was his accomplice."

Ian, who was still standing ready to assist when needed, spoke up in Clarence's defense: "Your Honor, if the leading citizens here are child molesters, it doesn't say much for your town. That dead man was trying to rape this girl when she was eight years old—no older than his own daughters—and he shot Clarence first for trying to help his sister.

The judge's voice had begun to get hoarse from the stain of yelling, but he yelled to his shotgun-toting deputies: "Get all of these arrogant Jews out of my courtroom."

To avoid serious injuries from gunfire, Cesar, Domani, and the martial arts team burst through the door and began to physically eradicate the Southern deputies and their armed sympathizers.

Amidst the chaos, screams and people running, all semblance of a trial had ended, but with all the confusion, no one saw the armed man behind the witness stand, who had aimed a .38 at Clarence and was about to find his mark, but Esmeralda happened to see him in time, crying out to the heavens: "Empower me, Lord, and forgive me, please."

She did a double flip, landing in front of Clarence as Phyllis screamed out; "Oh, God, no!" Just as the discharged bullet neared Clarence's chest, Esmeralda stretched forth her hand, and the bullet landed in her palm leaving no scars.

When she looked at the gunman about to fire again, her green eyes became two green spikes of fire heading straight for the guilty man. The fire balls hit their target, and the gun exploded, sending pieces of the man's body flying about the courtroom.

A shotgun fired and a guard fell, but before Esmeralda could do anything to the gunman, her guards were all over the man. She went to help the fallen man and seeing that the spray of pellets had not hit vital organs, she picked up the shotgun and twisted it into melted lava.

The security had rounded up all of the deputies who'd attempted to fight into a huddle; a few stood cowardly, holding the barrels of their shotguns. Mera looked at the

201

deputies, and their guns melted, burning their hands as they yelled painfully.

Esmeralda whispered to Ian and he approached the bench. "Esmeralda wants to Quit Claim your town back to you." The judge was so humiliated; he wanted vengeance, not compromise. Therefore, he yelled for any backup deputies who could take the visitors out of his courtroom.

There was no one who had enough courage to fight any more, as the judge persisted in his quest to harm the visitors. Esmeralda stretched forth her hand towards the judge, and his entire clothes fell off, leaving him standing there butt naked. He reached for any object to cover himself.

With his hands covering his private parts, he yelled to Attorney Shepard Baldwin: "Let me sign those documents and get that witch out of my courtroom, out of my town and out of my sight forever."

He saw a bunch of uniformed officers enter the courtroom and heard heavy equipment moving about outside. The medics quickly attended to the injured guard and got him on his way, but the judge was still yelling to the top of his voice: "Who are those people, and what do they want in my court room?"

The troopers hauled away deputies as the judge yelled: "What's going on now?"

"I think it is the State Troupers that Mr. Greenberg told you about," Shepard explained.

After all papers were signed, the team of supporters and Esmeralda were leaving, the courtroom photographers had their cameras flashing. The injured guard had been bandaged properly, and they were on their way, another victory won. Esmeralda paused, waved her hand, and the film in the cameras rewound, exposing all shots that had been taken.

The buses and limousines started their trek back towards the Airport in Atlanta, when Phyllis asked: "Esmeralda, what happened back there?"

Mera put her finger to her lips and whispered: "God sent his angels to protect us. I hope it won't be needed again soon."

Clarence smiled proudly at his little sister: "Miss Edna told me that these powers would be developed in her someday. I'm glad it was now."

"Why can't we use these powers on Yarmulke?" Ian asked.

Clarence took Ian's hand in his, smiling at him: "Yarmulke can rationalize; these Southerners don't know the meaning of the word. We need divine intervention when dealing with Yarmulke."

"I guess that means we have to fight Yarmulke on our own," Ian stated.

Domani spoke up in response to Ian's inquires: "As you know, God is paving the way for the battle to be won. The victory in Georgia was another means of strengthening Emerald Corporation. The means are hard at times, but we are growing, praise God."

"Our baby here has so many powers, and she knows not to misuse them," Clarence told them. "The people in this town won't remember that she summoned angelic assistance. They'll only remember the fights, fires, and signing the papers."

This was the first time that Ian took Esmeralda in his arms, although he wanted to many times before, and he whispered to her: "My sweet, sweet, little girl." This loving gesture brought smiles to the lips of all passengers in their limousine.

*   *   *

Only a week had passed after returning from Georgia, and Esmeralda maintained her position huddled up in a corner of her bed; the Bible lay open, and the highlighted scripture was Daniel 9:27. It had some meaning to her as she stared down at the pages.

Each moment that passed seemed longer than the last. Her watch was a large dialed sweep second hand one, and she moved her eyes from the Bible page or stared at the hands of her watch which had surely never moved so slowly. Each second that passed before her eyes was like a small eternity.

It was now six o'clock pm. Her foster parents were sick with alarm and anxiety. Dr. Heller was on the way, as well as Rabbi Terah, and Uncle Zech, she'd been told.

The realization of why these men were coming made Mera feel for the first time a measure of comfort. Her nightly fears and screams had made her feel so uncomfortable. Philip would be wondering, perhaps worrying what had happened in Georgia.

She felt amazed that she worried what Philip thought. Why should she care what he'd think? This sensation was new to her. Was God trying to tell her something?

Her trembling ceased for a moment as Maximus whined and licked her hand. She remained motionless, then leaned over, hugging the large canine to her and felt a warm relief within her own spirit as well as the dog's.

She recalled the first time she'd screamed so piercingly that her foster family and security had rushed to her bedroom. Philip had arrived first, since his room was just across the bathroom from hers.

She recalled how attentive Philip had been. She hardly knew him at all as this new caring personality. That was the truth of the matter. Mera had always looked at the evidence that pointed to him being a strange eccentric uncaring and selfish man.

In that brief moment when he sat there with the two

upper buttons of his pajama shirt open and the thick hairs covering his muscular chest, she felt hypnotized listening to his soothing voice quelling away her fears.

Noticing her obsession with his hairy chest, Philip opened still another button, and Esmeralda nuzzled her cheek passionately into the fuzziness. He'd appeared genuinely concerned and fond of her. Perhaps it was part of her sixth sense, but for that moment she knew many things about this tall, fair-haired Jew.

As the face of Cesar flashed before her with his smooth pushiness, she felt from that very evening that she could trust Philip with her life. Beneath that exterior hard shell, he was basically kind, gentle and good. He was good not in the priggish way, but in the broad more real sense of the word. He is good in a world where it is a precious and rare commodity and often underestimated for its worth.

It was now eight o'clock pm, and Esmeralda heard a slight scuffling sound that heightened her terror to absolute panic. The murmuring down stairs that had Maximus restlessly growling was only just possible to hear.

She plunged blindly towards the door that closed from the inside, and she began hammering on it with her fists and praying out loud. Suddenly it was opened from the hallway; as she fell backwards, she felt strong firm arms around her and heard a familiar reassuring voice.

"You're all right, little sister. You mustn't cry. It's all right."

"The door was locked. I tried to open it, but it was locked," she gasped.

"You were excited and pushed the door the wrong way. Come along, everyone is waiting for you in the dining room," Philip told her, smiling down at her with tenderness in his grayish blue eyes.

*   *   *

205

At last Esmeralda took a seat around the table. She was sufficiently recovered to hear what her mentors had to say to her, and Terah was first to speak.

"Esmeralda, I cannot get your parents to tell me what happened in Georgia, so I need you to tell me."

Esmeralda seemed surprised that her foster parents had kept her secret, and she stared around the room into the faces that were glued to her, as Zech urged her to talk.

"Child, we already know that because of your faith and obedience to God's call to service, you will have unimaginable powers. If you have called upon God to allow you to use these powers, it's alright."

Dr. Heller took Mera's hands speaking gently: "It's alright to talk about it, angel. I know that you fear human reprisal, but understand that we are your friends."

Hesitantly, Mera whispered: "I killed someone. Not with my hands, but my eyes."

Philip watched Marty holding Mera's hands, and a flood of resentment flushed his face; it was almost obvious that he wanted to scream out loud for him to release her immediately.

"Was this person trying to do someone bodily harm?" Uncle Zech asked.

"He fired a gun at my brother; I caught the bullet with my hand and caused his gun to explode which took him out with the explosion."

Zech continued consoling Mera in his raspy aging voice: "Remember what our Lord said in Matthew 17:20: 'If you have the faith of a mustard seed, you can move mountains.'"

Rabbi Terah added Mark 9:23 where Jesus told the people that all things are possible to him that believeth. "This is just the beginning of the display of the powers given to you. It may be a hard task, but we will overcome."

Somewhat brighter in spirit, Esmeralda smiled and thanked the men who'd come to cheer her up: "I am so grateful for your faith in me, and I am as sure as you are that we will overcome." She tilted her head and smiled at Philip. "I'm going to write an instruction booklet on how to open a door. Thank you for helping me."

"Mom, Dad, I have been thinking about those holdings in Georgia. I'd like to send a construction crew in to re-model the Administration building and bank, but if I'm right, those people will never advance above upper pover-ties level. Any new development will just sit there and rot due to their lackadaisical attitudes. Their feeling that they should leave well enough alone. I would, however, like to upgrade the bank and find a competent person to run it.

"Maybe we should think about doing something for the educational system and a twenty four hour Emergency Medical center. Farm accidents could be brought there, and women in labor could get emergency help. We'll train and build an apartment complex for our employees. The rest of the farms, and little businesses, we'll quit claim back to the persons who rented them from Miss Edna."

"Good idea," Ian said. We'll get with Shepherd to find the names and addresses of everyone who has a title and quit claim them immediately."

CHAPTER XIII
(Twelve months after Georgia)

A lthough dressed neatly in casual slacks and shirt, Sgt. Rupert Darling, a secret member of Yarmulke, and his wife Celeste were among the spectators at the Mandeville Temple rally. Their leader, also there, was disguised so that he could not be easily identified. The men exchanged glances but made sure they had nothing to do with each other.

My mission here is to look for security breaches, for both sides, Darling reminded himself and he searched every foot of the Temple as he ushered his wife to a seat down front. He thought as he made his evaluations that there were two entrances in the choir loft one on each side of the podium, and three at the rear.

Darling also noticed that there were two armed security guards at each doorway who were not part of his team. This made him a bit nervous with the auditorium soon filling to capacity. There were a number of groups whispering about the melee in Georgia, and Darling strained to hear part of what was being said.

Following the prologue, Rabbi Terah, Uncle Zech, Esmeralda, and the great dog Maximus were escorted out onto the podium by six armed guards, and the entire auditorium stood and began holding up their hands in praises to God, praying in Hebrew or chanting in English, while some simply booed and rapped on the back of the seats with metal items to drown out the prayers.

The armed guards took places on each side of the speakers so they could see what was going on from their vantage points. Rabbi Terah stood and waved for the audience to be quiet, and take their seats. They reluctantly

208

obeyed. When Esmeralda was introduced as main speaker, the commotion began anew with applause, cheers and disgruntled boos.

Esmeralda raised her hand for the audience to simmer down. "Thank you... thank you," she said repeatedly. It was nearly two minutes before she could get the group to settle down.

"My message to you today was to show you thirteen steps to Christ; due to your obvious doubts, I feel many of you are not ready to accept this message. Therefore, I'm going to open this meeting with a question and answer period. First, I'd like to ask a question of you who feel that you already know the Messiah."

"Are you sure you know who He really is, or do you only know about Him? Are you curiosity seekers, or simply bent on doing harm if you get the chance?" She paused momentarily searching her mind to find a way of reaching this group of dissidents and malcontents, and she decided to use a pun.

"I heard a story about a woman who was teaching non Christians about Jesus. When she asked them if they knew the Man Jesus or only knew about him, a man in the back raised his hand, stood and speaking in a Brooklyn accent, said: 'Yeah, I knew Him, I heard He died or sum' pin.'

"Surprised at the man's statement, the teacher who appeared genuinely concerned and mixed sadness replied: 'Lord! If I'd known He was sick, I'd at least sent Him flowers.' This woman didn't really know Him either."

Esmeralda noticed that only a scattered few laughed. There was a serious void in their sense of humor, and she knew she'd have to really answer their questions.

*   *   *

In the foyer, Domani and his martial arts group recognized Sgt. Darling pretending to be a sympathizer on patrol,

209

and they secretively gained upon him. "Pardon me, do you have authorized passes?" Darling asked.

Domani removed a pass from his inside pocket and extended it toward Darling. When the sergeant diverted his eyes to examine the pass, Domani quickly took him by the head and applied knuckle pressure to his carotid. Darling trembled, rolled his eyes, and slumped into unconsciousness. Then Domani dragged his limp form into a sound closet, remover his weapon, stuffed him inside, and locked the door.

*　*　*

Inside the Temple meeting area, several other suspicious men gestured toward each other and looked at their Yarmulke leader, who nodded towards the empty seat beside Celeste Darling.

The man on the right whispered to his companion,. "He wants us to wait for Darling's signal. By the way, where is Darling?"

"Now that you mentioned it, I don't see Neal and Patrick either," the man on the left commented as he looked around suspiciously.

Several worshippers put their fingers to their lips, frowning, and shook their heads for the whisperers to be quiet during the lecture.

*　*　*

Outside the main meeting room and slightly down the corridor, Domani and Cesar Malachi dragged two more police officers into the storage closet, removing their weapons. While the door was opened, more than eight uniformed police officers could be seen stuffed inside.

*　*　*

"Tell us what happened in Georgia, witch," a voice rang out from the seated audience in the Temple.

"Instead of completing the speech I'd prepared, I told you we'd make this a question and answer session. I suggest you ask one question at a time, and no group shouting if you expect an answer."

Rabbi Terah and Uncle Zech nodded toward Esmeralda with shocked and surprised expressions on their faces. Rabbi Terah indicated that she should not have the questions, but she smiled back at him with confidence.

The man who'd asked the question, yelled out again: "Are you going to tell us about Georgia?"

"Of course. I'd be glad to explain. We were there for a property hearing, and it appeared that the community and court didn't want to honor the last will and testament that named me as heir. Someone tried to murder my brother, but God stepped in and shocked the court and townspeople. Everything turned out as my benefactor had stipulated in her will."

"Why are you preaching in a synagogue? Women are not to make spectacles of themselves in public," another man pointed out.

"Sir, would you please stand so that I may know who to address when answering your questions."

A shy appearing man stood but looked around to see if he'd gained sympathizers with his question.

"Thank you, sir; it pleases me that you asked that question. I know that you at least have read some of the New Testament. Now about your question, I believe it was the Apostle Paul in the New Testament Scriptures who defined woman's place.

"In the Torah, Genesis 2:18, God said He would make for man a 'help mate.' We are not in man's shadow or to be his subordinate, but his other self. The Hebrew term is K'negdo which means at man's side, his associate, or corresponding to him.

"Also in the Torah, the Hebrew word for woman is Ishah; man is Ish. God explained that he endowed woman with a greater intuition than He did man. The male was given greater physical strength, but they are to depend on each other to make the whole person that God intended."

Several people stood and began talking at the same time. Esmeralda pointed to a man on the right, and the others sat down, appearing disappointed.

"Why did you decide to undertake a task so far out of your league? You're obviously not a Jew."

"Are you Jewish, sir?"

"Yes, I am."

"I would suggest that you understand your own ethnicity, for anyone can be Jewish which is a belief or a religious following. Your biological background is Israelite. I would suggest that you also read your Torah, for you see, sir, all peoples before the Flood were descendants of Adam. After the Flood, we were all descendants of Noah. That makes you my brother, or most assuredly, my cousin.

"I believe you also asked why I chose to teach in a synagogue. I did not make that choice, God chose me. I was born to assist you in regaining your rightful place as God's favorite people before it is too late."

Another angry man stood: "How can you say that you can help us regain our rightful place? Do you mean that Judaism is wrong?"

"Not at all, sir; it is not wrong but incomplete. Jews were the only people of the earth who worshipped the one true God and were promised a Messiah, but due to their unbelief and other sins, you've fallen from grace, a relationship that needs to be rekindled."

"How is it that a child speaks about helping us regain our rightful place? Why didn't God send a more convincing adult?" a doubtful observer asked.

"Josiah, a son of David was crowned king at age eight, and God also called Samuel to service at about the same age. I'm sure you'd be unhappy with anyone, regardless of age.

Esmeralda heard Maximus whine and saw him topple over as though dead, a dart filled with succinal coline, had lodged in the back of his neck. When she stooped to help her dog, another dart lodged in her shoulder, and she slumped to the floor. She looked to the ceiling, closed her eyes and prayed.

Several people screamed and pandemonium broke out in the synagogue. The security rushed to assist Esmeralda; she waved them away, placed her hand over her shoulder and a pale blue light was seen flaring from beneath her hand. Instantly, the dart was gone, and the wound healed. She treated her dog the same way and he stood ready to attack.

Several cripple people who had come because they believed in the young child were filled with sorrow and went to assist her, but as they touched the girl who was still surrounded by the mysterious greenish blue light, their infirmities were suddenly made whole. The stooped old man's back straightened; the woman whose fingers were so deformed from arthritis became perfect again; and an obvious blind person could see.

Many people who'd witnessed the exercises looked on in shocked horror, many bolted for the nearest exit.

"My God, she is an angel," some said.

"Or a witch," said those who refused to believe.

As many of those who had physical problems came to be blessed by the miracle child and were healed. Uncle Zech took the microphone: "She is a messenger from God," his raspy voice boomed over the PA system. "Repent before it is too late. Remember how your unbelief caused the death of Jesus the Messiah so many years ago. Has it dawned on you that someone wants to control your minds, even the way you worship?"

"Don't you want this freedom?" Rabbi Terah pleaded.

"No one here will force you to change. Salvation is a personal gift from God, but it is not yours until you accept it. Esmeralda teachings are to bring you the truth, not to force you to do anything that you don't want to do."

Esmeralda spoke directly to those who were waiting to get out of the crowded doorways. "Running away is exactly what Satan wants or expects you to do. Why don't you break his chains that bind you to a world of unhappiness and sin. Remember, he that believes that God sent his son to be the savior of the world, God lives in him, and he in God."

A great many of the audience turned and headed for the altar, but the stubborn ones malcontents pushed and cursed them.

Although small for the number of people attending, a victory was won among the hundred or more converts who'd come. Esmeralda saw Dr. Heller sitting in a pew a few rows back with his head down all during the meeting; he finally decided to come up front again, for he'd joined the church before. He has been so rapt in sorrow, he had not witnessed the healing miracles performed through Esmeralda.

The tears that Marty shed were not tears of joy, but they were deep tears of sorrow. She could feel his pain, but for some reason she could not penetrate his thoughts. She was disappointed that God had given her this mission but had not given her the ability to discern the inner pain her dearest friend was feeling.

For a long time, Esmeralda had the feeling that Evelyn, Marty's wife, silently resented her because she felt their close friendship was hinged on a more intimate relationship. She looked around the Temple but did not see Evelyn. She prayed silently for God to erase any doubts or domestic problems with her friends.

*   *   *

Esmeralda moped around the house for days without eating more than toast, tea and occasionally a glass of juice. Although she had no appetite, she always prepared good meals for her family.

It was the spring of her eighteenth birthday, and this fall would be the beginning of her last year before receiving a Doctorate Degree. She took no pleasure in that thought, only felt useless and unfulfilled.

It didn't make sense for her to feel so depressed, for the men's singing group was doing well, especially since Emerald Corporation bad launched its own television and radio networks, and the MDs were the featured celebrities. Besides, several movie studios had used their talents. They were now all millionaires.

The Emerald Corporation was heading for big things under the directorship of her foster parents, and the Messianic converts had reached the   mark worldwide.

Esmeralda lay down on her bed and sobbed, while the great dog Maximus licked her hand, whining helplessly. He was trying to understand what had his mistress so upset. He blamed everyone for her sadness and allowed no one to come near her. He was always at her side.

On her way down stairs, Esmeralda overheard the family talking about Marty and Evelyn, she stopped and halted Maximus so she could hear clearly. She heard Mom ask Philip how Evelyn could not know something was wrong when Max whined and Mera grabbed hold of his neck fur, commanding him to be quiet:

"Be quiet, boy," she whispered. Then the conversation continued downstairs with Philip explaining that cancer . hardly ever cause pain until it's in the final stages."

She heard Phyllis gasp, and she put her own hand over her mouth to avoid the gasp her lips made from being heard, when she heard Phyllis say: "I can't believe it's in the final stages. My God, I watched those kids grow up, fall in love go to college, get married, and have babies. They are like my own children."

Ian agreed with Phyllis: "Marty was always the kid with the wisdom for the group. I wondered what was on his mind when he accepted Christ again last week. Did you see the way he looked at Mira and hugged her? It was like he wanted to say something or expected her to do something to help him."

Mera could feel in his quietness that Philip had looked away. There was more in his silence than worry for his friend. Could he be hiding feelings for her and was jealous of Marty? She somehow knew that he'd swallowed again, shaking the unknown thoughts from his mind and rejoined the group, by sipping his cold coffee.

"Here, let me warm up your coffee," Phyllis told her son.

Esmeralda dismissed the thoughts she held about Philip, concentrating on Marty and Evelyn...

"Did you hear that, Max? He expected me to help, and I don't know how," Mera whispered sadly. She turned and quietly headed back to her room.

In her bedroom, she threw herself on the bed and sobbed. "What good am I if I can't help my closest friend? He's done so much for me, helped Philip, and many others. Now he needs someone, and I'm useless. Who am I, anyway, God?" She shouted to the ceiling.

"You have read Psalm 89:20, the words spoken to my servant David. I now say unto you I have found you my servant, with my holy oil have I anointed you!" The unseen voice was so loud, it rattled the house and windows. Maximus barked with confusion, chasing around the room trying to sniff out the intruder.

Esmeralda heard her family screaming: "Earthquake. Esmeralda, get down here quick."

Ian said that it was fairly small, and unless there was an after shock, it would be no reason for alarm.

That very moment, an after shock rattled the house again as the booming voice spoke again to Esmeralda. Sitting erect and appearing confused, Esmeralda asked: "Who are you?"

"I Am!" the voice boomed again.

Assured that God was speaking to her, Esmeralda knelt beside her bed, her head bowed in reverence. "I've only had you visit me in dreams before, my Lord. I'm not sure how I should approach you."

"Speak the desires of your heart!"

"I know that you are God, the Creator of this universe. I know that you care about each of us and want to guide us along life's pathways. The Scriptures make it clear that You want us to be healed of our afflictions and unhappiness. You said ask and it shall be given you, knock and the doors will be opened, seek and ye shall find."

"Well!" the voice boomed in impatience.

"Oh Lord, my God. Standing humbly upon your promise, I ask that you find it within Your heart to heal Evelyn. It's not my will, but Thine be done. Amen."

"Again, your directions are documented in I Timothy 4:14. Neglect not the gift that is in thee, which was given by prophecy, with the laying on of the hands. Go, and tend to My business!" the ear shattering voice demanded.

Phyllis called Esmeralda to come downstairs to be evacuated, and together with the great dog, Mera rushed downstairs where her family stood waiting for her to get out with them. Her security rushed from the vestibule near the stairs wondering what to do in this kind of emergency.

After joining the family, Esmeralda shouted breathlessly: "Take me to the hospital. Now!"

Her family stood in unexpected surprise. Believing that Esmeralda had taken ill suddenly, Phyllis put her arms around her saying: "We are having earthquakes and must evacuate, child."

"No, take me to the hospital."

"What in heaven's name is the matter with you?"

Maximus bared his teeth in his confusion that made Phyllis back away from Esmeralda. Realizing the potential threat that Maximus could be, Esmeralda yelled:

"Heel, boy. It's all right," she said, patting the dog's head. With everyone a little calmer. Esmeralda explained: "We have to help Evelyn before it's too late."

Philip took Esmeralda's shoulders gently in his hands, spun her around to face him, and stared into her bright green eyes. He neither spoke nor released his grip on her. She looked at him for a moment, then looked away. She had always felt that people with those light bluish gray eyes were intimidating, and she wrestled to release his hold on her.

"It may already be too late, Mira. The cancer has metastasized. It's spread to many areas of her body," Philip told her.

Feeling that her only defense for the spell Philip had cast on her was to use woman's main weapon—tears and the tears rolled.

"Please take me there," she pleaded and cried convulsively.

Philip enjoyed the submissiveness he experienced in his little sister, and a warm feeling of possession flooded his thoughts. It had been years since he'd felt this way about a woman, and he suddenly wanted to hold on for all the years he'd missed. But instead, he released his hold on Mera as Rabbi Terah came into the kitchen, after the warning Maximus gave of his arrival. He was followed by security.

After greeting the family, Rabbi Terah inquired of Esmeralda why she'd been so isolated recently: "What has you so upset, girl?"

Ian spoke up quickly: "We've got to make evacuation plans due to the earthquake."

"That was no earthquake; it was the voice of God

speaking to me that shook the house. I'm fine now, Rabbi."
She threw herself in his arms. "Please take me to the hospital to see Evelyn; she's dying."

Rabbi Terah looked at Mera's family who nodded an
agreement, and he said to her: "Of course, child, we'll all
go.

                    *   *   *

The Ravin party entered the private room of Evelyn
Heller on the Medical center's oncology ward; they found
Marty sitting beside the bed, his face in his hands and Eve-
lyn asleep.

There were tubes in her arm, bladder, and an oxygen
cannular in her nostrils. Her breathing seemed labored, and
her color was pale. Evelyn was a petite woman, and the illness had caused her to lose a great deal of weight. She
looked at least twenty-years older than the last time Esmeralda saw her.

The patient groaned, and Marty jerked alert, took his
wife's hand, whispering comforting words to her. "It's OK,
baby. I'm here." Feeling the presence of someone else, he
looked around and saw Esmeralda and her party.

"What's going on? Why are you all here?" Marty
asked, appearing perplexed.

"Esmeralda wanted... No, she demanded that we bring
her to see Evelyn," Rabbi Terah said.

"Mera, you shouldn't be here," Marty said before
Rabbi Terah cut him off.

"Just listen to her son, please."

Mera took his hands in hers and whispered sympathetically. "I'm so sorry you didn't let me know."

Philip turned away when he saw the tender way Mera
held Marty's hands, his eyes filled with tears.

"Little girl, you have enough on your plate without
taking on my problems, too."

"Marty, prayer and faith are the answers," she told him.

"I have been praying, and it seems that this evil disease ravaged my lovely wife's body in spite of my calling on the Lord,"

"Why did you come to the altar during the last meeting?"

"I didn't know what else to do. I've had every oncologist in on consult, and my prayers were going unanswered. I..."

Esmeralda cut him off. "I'll always be here for you, and so will God, when you accepted Christ as your personal Savior."

"Then why doesn't He let me know He's here?" Marty snapped.

Mera squeezed his hand, and again Philip looked away. "Dear Marty, do not be conformed to this present world system. You men are powerful scientists, but God controls all. In view of His mercies, present your bodies and minds a living sacrifice, holy and acceptable to God."

"How do I do this, Mera?"

"Believing and divine guidance are essentially a matter of God applying inner peace on your mind as you seek Him. Trust in Him and He will give you the desires of your heart."

Marty took Esmeralda in his arms and wept like a small child, a deep broken spirited cry that tore at the souls of everyone present. His crying awakened Evelyn, and in her sedated awareness, she smiled a half open-mouth grin: "Hi, everybody. Are we having a pity party?"

Esmeralda sat on the side of Evelyn's bed, held her hand, and spoke softly but stern. "We don't pity you, Evelyn, for we know who holds the key to your healing."

"You don't have to try to cheer me up, just take good care of my boys. I'm sure you'll make Marty a good wife and my boys a good mother," Evelyn spoke with sarcasm flaring in her voice.

Esmeralda shook her head and both of Evelyn's hands at the same time: "Oh, ye of little faith, a powerful man once said this to his followers. Don't you know how your husband loves you? Swallow your self-pity and believe in two very important men, your husband, and your God. Believe and you can be healed," Mera said, as Evelyn wept.

Esmeralda laid her hands over Evelyn's heart and invited the rest to place their hands somewhere on her body. As the group formed a circle around the bed, Dr. Epstein, the attending physician, entered the room escorted by a nurse. Esmeralda invited them to join everyone around the bed. Reluctantly they agreed.

"Oh well, why not? We've tried everything else," Dr. Epstein said.

Esmeralda bowed her head and began to pray: "Almighty God, we love and trust in You to keep Your word as recorded in Your scriptures. You have demonstrated Your healing power so many times by using worthy servants such as we. You said to your servant this night to go in Your name, and it will be done. Heal Evelyn in the name of the Father, Son and Holy Spirit. Amen."

The fragrance of sweet smelling honeysuckles and tea roses permeated the air, and a faint bluish white fog filled the room. Evelyn coughed, and a large dark red solid substance spewed from her mouth and lower body. She coughed again, and the red matter disappeared from her person totally.

Sweat poured from Esmeralda's forehead as she released the hold she had on Evelyn, whispering softly: "Thank You, Jesus."

Philip was the first to stare at Esmeralda in shocked disbelief, but the rest of the party seemed to be mystified by the whole transaction, and they were too stunned to speak. Realizing that the healing group was too amazed to move or speak, Esmeralda smiled at them saying: "Dr. Epstein, I think you'll find her test negative for cancer. Do it soon and spread the news of God's healing miracle through His servants."

Dr. Epstein picked up the phone and ordered full laboratory tests on Evelyn.

A few days later, when Esmeralda and her party visited Evelyn again, they found her sitting up in bed, eating a regular diet. Dr. Epstein smiled when he entered and saw the party there.

"Good, I'm glad you're all here. I'm proud to tell you that my patient's tests are all negative for cancer... Of course I'll run tests every six months to be sure there is no reoccurrence of the disease."

Esmeralda hugged Evelyn, brushed her hair from her face, and kissed her tenderly, as Evelyn began to cry: "I'm so sorry for the things I said to you, Mera. You are the cutest little thing Marty has been close to since he met me," she teased.

Esmeralda declared firmly: "I'll always love and respect you and your husband, but will you get out of this hospital, and take care of your own family? I have no desire to have a second-hand man with ready-made kids!"

The group laughed, but Philip's laughter seemed more relief than jovial, as he exchanged understanding looks with Marty.

Dr. Epstein removed one of his business cards and extended it to Esmeralda: "Would you write down the address of that Temple where you teach. My colleagues and I would like to visit sometimes."

CHAPTER XIV

The middle of June, 1950, Esmeralda's eighteenth birthday had already come and gone, but a celebration was scheduled anyway, and her brother Clarence was on his way with some mysterious news.

It was a beautiful Saturday afternoon exuding the feeling of tranquility, yet some mystery. The swimming pool at the Ravin's home glistened with bluish splendor in the bright sunlight. An occasional ripple folded over the top of the pool each time the "Santa Anna winds puffed across the horizon.

The heavens were a deep blue, and only an occasional "Mare's Tail" streaked like white smoke across the sky. The beautiful wet deck, patio, and smoking barbecue pit attested to the fact that activity was about to commence.

Esmeralda exited the sliding glass door, carrying a pan of seasoned meat, and Maximus trotted along beside her. He sniffed the air, and one could not tell if the security beast was checking for potential danger or if the old cooking odors of the meat pit were tantalizing his taste buds.

Two uniformed, armed guards exited the glass door and took seats that allowed the entire perimeter to be easily observed from their vantage points.

Mera put the pan down and inspected the fire for readiness. Apparently satisfied that the charcoals were hot enough, she began placing the meat on the grill.

The oldest guard leaped to his feet to assist her: He reached for the pan: "Let me help you, Missy."

"Thank you. I have this under control, but you can help Javier fill the salad bar with ice from the ice maker and then bring all the salads out," she told him.

"My name is Dwayne. I have my men around the

property. I understand there was a serious melee here before I transferred as Security Captain of this division."

Esmeralda only stared at the young man who was obviously trying to sell his abilities to her in a very immature way. She smiled and handed him a guest list: "Your people will see that each guest's ID matches a name on this list?"

"Oh, yes, ma'am. You can be sure of that. You shouldn't be doing all this alone—"

Mera interrupted. "I am not alone; Javier and Mrs. Ravin helped. Mom had to run an errand, and the men are playing golf. That always leads to a wine feast debate afterwards. But they'll be here soon."

Mera glanced at her watch then the lowering sun, puzzled. *Clarence and the people who picked him up at the airport should also be here.* "I expect all the men will go swimming right away to avoid showering... I get it... That's why they put chlorine in pools, to bleach off the body dirt."

They laughed at this possibility, and the older guard went into the storage room to assist Javier. The guard returned with a plastic tub of crushed ice, a medium sized Hispanic man with him.

Mera returned from inside with a stack of beach towels that she fitted into shelves provided for them, and a linen tablecloth. She unfolded the tablecloth, spread it over the long banquet table, and then clamped it down to prevent the winds from kiting it away. She tilted her head in deep thought.

I wonder what is so important that Clarence had to fly out from Chicago today with no advance notice. Of course I'm always happy to see my brother; he's the only close tie I have with my real family.

Something strange has been happening to me lately. Ever since I turned eighteen. I can feel it, but can't quite understand what it is. Maybe I should see a doctor... Marty maybe; no, it's too soon after Evelyn's near death experience. How would I explain my suspicions, when nothing hurts? Just pray, and wait.

*   *   *

Sgt. Rupert Darling and a group of Yarmulke club members gathered for a secrete meeting at a darkened building in midtown. The building appeared to be unoccupied. The group of malcontents formed a circle around their leader, and all of them seemed anxious, tensed, and frustrated as their leader leaned on the lectern to speak.

"Men, our time is running out. We've got to stop Esmeralda before she tells our people about the 'Lost Laws'. She was suppose to divulge this information when she reached her eighteenth birthday; that time is two weeks past."

"What are these laws you are talking about?" a young policeman asked.

"The laws that could separate our people forever, destroying everything we've fought for centuries to keep secret."

The men looked at each other, then back to the leader, their faces showing confusion. The young policeman asked another question of the leader: "How can she know about these laws, if it's been so many centuries?"

The group waited anxiously for their leader's response and watched him grit his teeth and his jaw jerked with apparent anger. Speaking out loud, he said: "It is because she is a descendant of an old witch named Huldah who lived in the eighth century and passed these spells down. She's a witch, all right," the leader snapped, cracking his knuckles. "She confused our people then and will do it again if we don't stop her!"

"What exactly did this witch do?" the young man asked.

"She pretended to be able to interpret our Laws and confused our people, scaring them about God's punishments and what the future held for the Jews. Witch, I tell you. Nothing but a witch."

Sgt. Darling decided to add excitation to the group's fears: "You know what happens to witches."

The leader raised his hand in protest: "No one is going to harm the girl. We need her to give us the codes that open the seals to the Laws and read what it says."

"Where are these sealed Laws?" Darling asked.

"I'm not sure," the leader stated, folding is hands behind his back as he paced around the floor in circles. "We've watched her like a hawk every since we learned three years ago that she was the one with the information we need. The pieces are falling in place." He clinched his fists.

"We thought that old Jew woman in Georgia was the missing link." His pencil broke between his clinched fists, while gritting his teeth.

"What woman are we talking about?" the young talkative individual asked as they all watched the leader's restless movements...

The leader whirled around, shaking his finger at each of the men, before answering: "The one who left all her millions and property to the girl here in this area.

"We were told that together with the town's people, Miss Edna was accidentally put out of her miseries, and that every inch of her property had been searched," he shouted, "but they couldn't find the seals." He hammered his fist on the lectern top, causing everyone there to jerk in fear.

"What's our next move?" Darling asked.

"Keep a close eye on those two Rabbi's who hangs around the girl." The leader shifted his feet. "Oh, yes, I don't want problems stagnating around as long as those you had in the hospital, Sgt. Darling!"

"What about those doctor/musicians?" The young man spoke up.

"I've checked them out; they all seem clean," Darling responded.

"I have my doubts about that psychology professor," the leader said, pointing his dual index fingers, squinting suspiciously. "Bring me some good news, will ya. Oh, yeah, be careful men."

The leader walked around the circle again, looking in the faces of each man there. "That girl tore up the court building in Georgia, stopped a thirty-eight bullet with her bare hand, melted shotguns, damn near killed Darling's men at the Ravin's patio party a while back. She saved her dog's life, and her own when hit by deadly darts, healed a patient a few weeks ago of terminal cancer. I'm not sure just what we're dealing with!"

*   *   *

The evening was waning at the Ravin's home, and a great many key people had arrived to celebrate Esmeralda's eighteenth birthday.

Uncle Zech and Aunt Winnie came onto the patio full of exuberance. His first move was to pay homage to the girl Esmeralda, for he knew that this was the day that the vials containing the Laws would be opened, and the truth be revealed.

Uncle Zech greeted Mera with a hug and a kiss on her cheek, followed by the same greeting from Aunt Winnie, their son Isaiah, and Rabbi Terah.

Blushing, Esmeralda spoke softly: "Please don't patronize me, my life is hard enough as it is." She backed away from the attentive guests with her hands open and out stretched protectively.

The noise and gaiety in the pool kept most of the crowd busy, and they paid little attention to the Rabbis; homage extended to the young girl in the revealing green bathing suit.

Many of the more ravenous guests and children were eating, and the entire grounds buzzed with activity and armed security guards; the most amazing part of the security business was Maximus. He seemed to believe that he was in charge of the men in uniform, and he trotted along with them every time they moved about the yard.

Philip had a watchful eye on Mera and so did Evelyn. Theirs were like the eyes of a haunting portrait on the wall that seemed to follow wherever you moved to. Both pairs of eyes had not spent much time away from the beautiful young woman in a sparkling green bathing suit that made her bright green eyes twinkle.

Evelyn and Philip had not the only eyes that stole glances at the golden goddess as she moved about the patio attending to everyone's needs.

When Philip swam to the end of the pool where Mera was busy, he noticed his band members and the security stealing long and sinful glances at the beautiful young woman with the child-like face. It was easy to discern that Philip's gaze was one of jealousy and desire. This girl had melted the crust that covered his ironclad heart and coated it with honey.

Marty's eyes were upon his wife Evelyn who'd only recently recovered from terminal cancer. *I wonder if Evelyn is still a little jealous of Mera? Maybe she is overwhelmed in finally understanding what I've been telling her for years about this young protégé.*

Philip had gotten out of the water, but realizing that his men were drooling over his little sister, he dove into the pool again as a distraction and streaked across the water near the edge where Mera was tying a beach towel around her waist. Philip reached up, grabbed the towel, causing Mera to fall back into the water.

She screamed and decided to play a joke on Philip. *"I'll play like I'm really drowning and that'll fix him.* Mera became limp and floated to the bottom as a half dozen men and Max leaped into the water in a rescue attempt. Philip was the first to pull her up, laying her on the deck, and immediately began pumping her diaphragm to extract excess water, as Maximus licked her face.

Philip seemed frantic as he worked on the limp form of the young woman he'd become very fond of: "I'm so sorry, Mera baby. I've seen you swim before. I was only playing."

He rolled her onto her back, and was about to apply mouth to mouth resuscitation when she flexed her knees, and straightened them with her feet in Philip's chest, sending him tumbling into the pool.

Each time Philip tried to climb out, she kicked him in again. Finally, he took hold of her leg and pulled her back into the pool. Maximus joined the head dunking fun, which drew additional loud cheers and laughter. Marty's face lit up when he noticed his wife laughing at the silly water game.

Finally tired of the game they'd been playing, Mera allowed herself to be embraced by Philip, and as their wet skin suctioned together she felt a warmness that she'd never felt in any hug before. She was glad when the sliding glass door opened, exposing Domani and Clarence as they walked through.

"Clarence!" Mera screamed and swam rapidly toward the deck to greet her brother, with Max in close pursuit. After the wet greeting from his sister, Clarence greeted Rabbi Terah, Uncle Zech, and the rest of the guests whom he already had met before. He was introduced to those he never knew.

Rabbi Terah announced that the meeting would begin in the living room in about twenty minutes. "We thought it would be less conspicuous in a private setting. Javier and Maria will take the kids to watch a cartoon in the den.

*   *   *

Dressed in summer casuals, Sgt. Rupert Darling and his Yarmulke leader cruised the checkpoints in a luxury car with tinted windows.

They pulled their car behind a work truck with captions: Department of Water and Power on its sides. The truck was equipped with recording devices and speakers and parked outside the new security apartments where Zech and Winnie now lived.

"Any movement, boys?" Darling's voice was recognized filtering through the recorder.

"Nothing yet," the man with earphones on reported.

"Did you phone their apartment?" Darling asked. When he was told that the apartment had not been phoned, Sgt. Darling shouted: "Well, do it now!"

The man in the truck dialed the phone, and it rang a number of times, but no one picked up.

"You idiots. You let that old Rabbi give you the slip!"

The leader tried to calm the raging sergeant: "What's done is done. Is there anything going on at the Mandeville Temple?"

Darling dialed and a male voice answered: "Yeah."

"Nobody's here and we're just waiting on your word," the voice responded.

Sgt. Darling told his leader that he expected a slip at the airport, when he got the word that Domani would be handling the escort. "That man is as slippery as grease lightening and has a nose that can smell an intruder a mile away." From all reports, however, the San Fernando and Bay area Temple had been wired for 9:00 p.m. as well.

Sgt. Darling contacted all sites saying: "You know what to do. If this don't put the fear of God in them, they can't be stopped."

*   *   *

The Ravin's living room was lined with folding chairs, and every seat was occupied. The two Rabbis, Clarence, and Esmeralda sat at a narrow banquet table, as Clarence laid an old leather case on top.

Uncle Zech spoke first; "I have been waiting for tonight for many years. After you see what Clarence has brought, you will all understand what and who Esmeralda is. What we see here or say here must never leave this room."

Uncle Zech explained that the shape of Hebrew spelling is much different in the biblical text from what was customary at any other time in Hebrew literature. Scribes were able to read it but couldn't understand what it meant.

Special prophets or prophetess who were either descendants of Moses or of the Totem Clan were given the gifts from God to interpret these special instructions.

"First, Clarence will explain how he and his little sister play a part in this."

Clarence stood, thanked Uncle Zech, and then began to tell Esmeralda and their guests the story of how the Laws were passed down through the centuries. "Many descendants of God's chosen ones were not themselves chosen. I am a descendant of Huldah, but I was not chosen to lead as my sister has been. It is easy to tell who are, by the natural attributes they possess. Sometimes these attributes are not seen at all."

"With Esmeralda, however, she was identified at birth. She was the seventh daughter of a seventh daughter. She had green eyes when no one else in her immediate family had them, she was aware of her surroundings when she was born, looking around to familiarize herself with them.

"Again, in Mera's case, she was able to read, write, draw, do crafts by the time she was two years old. She understood the scriptures at an early age and was able to teach it to others, and her unmatched beauty made her very obvious.

"Miss Edna rode through the night when she heard of the strange birth, for she had been waiting for this very same child to be born and was told by her father before he died that the child would be born in that little farming town. She had so much concern, for she was a descendant of King Josiah and had inherited the scrolls with the Laws.

"Miss Edna knew that when you were eighteen, you'd be able to interpret the Laws, so she gave them to me for safe keeping when her health began to fail," Clarence told his sister, as he walked to her seat and placed his hands on her shoulders. I am aware that you understood the Bible, but was not thoroughly aware of what your connections were, or why you had been chosen to lead the Jews to Jesus.

She was again told that their ancestor Huldah, the woman who unveiled the future of a nation, was responsible for God choosing her to further his kingdom's work. The information about Huldah can be found in II Kings 22:14-20, and II Chronicles 34:22-33, and she brought about a revival, as you have done thus far."

"I understand that the Emerald following has reached the 20 million mark world wide."

There was a loud and long applause.

"Although there is not much known about Huldah other than she was a prophetess, a teacher, an agitator to bring about change, and the wife of Shallum, the keeper of the Royal wardrobes, and eventually a mother, she was compared to women like Deborah and Hannah among rare women of the Old Testament.

"Huldah's standing and reputation are attested to in that she was consulted rather than Jeremiah, when the lost book of the Law was found, and that her word was accepted by all as a divinely revealed one.

"When Hilkiah the priest found the book in the Temple ruins, Josiah the King sent immediately for Huldah and attesting to the genuineness of the scroll, she prophesied national ruin because of disobedience to the commands of God. Her prophetic message and the public reading of the Law brought about a revival that resulted in the reforms carried out by Josiah. With a renewed spiritual life king and people vowed to follow the God of their fathers more faithfully.

"When men recover the lost truths of Scriptures and apply them to life and morals, what great and mighty changes take place."

After the group had finished hearing about Huldah, he concluded his presentation by adding: "As a prophetess in the reign of King Josiah, she could be found sitting in the central part of the city ready to revive and council any who wished to inquire of Jehovah."

Philip's curiosity had gotten the best of him, and he asked: "If Mera is just a prophetess, how is it that she is able to accomplish so many things both physically and intellectually?"

Clarence gestured to Uncle Zech. "Rabbi Zech, would you explain please," and then he sat down.

Uncle Zech began to talk in his usual raspy voice that seemed to gain more clarity as he came more involved with the new work that he loved.

"I am an old man and would like to sit. Please excuse me. I have been told in dreams that this child would be coming. I'm pleased to be a part of this great miracle. In response to your question, Philip, Esmeralda is like David who went to battle with Goliath and the Philistines, with a single slingshot. Or Moses who crossed the Red Sea after it parted. God stepped in to assist his servants."

"Just as you've heard in the track that Clarence read to you, you can see that Huldah was a special chosen servant of God's. She was an agitator to stir up and produce change for good. She was a ruler, a leader, a warrior, a poetess, a writer, and a builder. Haven't we seen all these attributes in Esmeralda?"

"The wife and mother is missing," Pam heckled, as Joel stared at her in disgust.

Impatient, Uncle Zech answered: "She is not much more than a child. When God feels that the time is right, the rest will come."

"I want to take you back to the dreams that I've had about Huldah in the days in which she lived before Christ. God has allowed me to see her life back then, and I'd like to take you vicariously back to that time also."

The time was converted in the minds of the guests through centuries to the reign of King Josiah a son of David in Jerusalem. The hills were rolling and primitive, bustling with livestock and attending shepherds. In the market place were men and women frolicking together with skins of wine being passed around for the drinking.

The dress was typical for that century, and the odor of incense and other items of idol worshipping were all around. Some people were wearing medallions that were inscribed with symbols of Baal.

There was a statue of a goat-like figure standing on its hind legs, and a crown of gold encircled its horns. Many people kneeled before the statue to worship it, and then continued frolicking to the rhythm of the music played on animal horns and skin-drawn drums.

In the far ground, a lone woman sat holding the Torah as a few people approached to inquire of her knowledge of Jehovah.

"What is your name, girl?" a soldier asked the young woman who was dressed in brown, her black braids wrapped with ribbons, and her green eyes sparkled in the bright sunlight.

The soldier appeared impatient and threatening as he stood over the small young woman, but she seemed fearless and answered him without faltering; "I am Huldah the prophetess, my Lord, with good news from God."

"Just make sure that you and your God stay out of

trouble," the soldier growled.

Seeing the soldier harassing Huldah, several of the dancing women decided to add to the heckling and sauntered up to Huldab, mocking her.

"Tell me, Prophetess, will I marry a rich man soon and have beautiful babies?" She laughed at the woman Huldah.

With sadness and pity, Huldah replied: "You will not marry a rich man, but evil will befall you very soon, and you will walk with a wooden leg for several months. The child you carry in your belly by another woman's husband will be born dead."

"Silly witch. I am not with child and who ever heard of a wooden leg? Be gone with you witch!" she laughed.

The heckling woman twirled and spun her way around, dancing with intoxication of too much wine and did not see the large stone in her path. She tumbled over it, and a loud crack was heard; she fell and was unable to stand. It was not possible to understand which hurt more: her broken leg, or her abdomen from the abortion she had caused by her fall.

As sounds of the woman's screams brought many to help her, they were unable to get the woman to her feet for she was experiencing too much pain. "Kill the witch; she has cast a spell on us," the injured woman yelled to the soldiers.

Several men and soldiers rushed toward Huldah, but fell down as though hitting an invisible wall. Surprised, they reached out to feel for the wall but found nothing there.

Running away in fear, they picked up the injured, screaming woman and disappeared behind a crude wooden door.

*   *   *

Huldah entered her home and kissed her husband

Shallum who was busy sewing and hanging royal robes. His face was pale from insistent hard work, and he was shabbily dressed, sporting a long beard and skullcap.

"Were you able to show many the way today, my love?" Shallum asked.

"Only a few, but each one is a victory won. There is so much sin and disobedience in Jerusalem. Are you hungry, my lord?" she asked.

"I guess I could eat as soon as I finish this last robe."

"It is the last of the mutton stew. Will that please you, my lord?"

"I will be more pleased when Jehovah gives us a child; but food, I eat to live, not live to eat."

"The signs tells me that Jehovah will grant your desires for a child soon," she told him teasing.

Shallum put the robe down and rushed to his wife, kissing her and holding her tightly. "Tell me again. My heart is racing with joy and praises to Jehovah God."

As the shadows began to fall over the Palace of King Josiah, the palace guards were patrolling the gates of the high walls along the grounds. There were hammock-like beds on top the roof for the benefit of those who wished to sleep outside where it might've been cooler.

Within the dimly lit crude stone structure, there were partitions of stone separating rooms and quarters. The throne room was sectioned by fine silk and velvet drapes.

King Josiah was in a meeting with his chief priest and scribes. The king was a medium sized young man appearing to be in his late twenties, wearing a red velvet cloth draped around his shoulders and white satin dress down to his ankles on each side.

The Chief Priest was older and dressed accordingly, with a vee neck vest to his hips; and it was trimmed in gold threads and beads. Several servants were fanning the King and his Chamber Members with large straw fans.

It was obviously summer time in the desert town, and

that heat was taking its toll.

"What is the news of the wars?" King Josiah asked his Chief Priest.

The Chief Priest stood and paced around for a moment appearing saddened: "The land to the East has been lost to the aggressors. There is hardly anyone left to fight in the neighboring kingdom. All has been lost."

King Josiah appeared as though he was going to cry. "What is our next move?" he inquired of his Chief Priest.

During his response, the priest told King Josiah that he felt the Temple where the lost book of Laws was found should be rebuilt. "We had the Scribe read the laws, but he was not able to understand its meaning," the priest told him.

Josiah sadly said that these Laws had been buried because the people of Jerusalem did not want to follow the Laws given to them by the Lord God Jehovah; this allowed them to justify their sins.

"Go seek out a prophet who may be able to interpret the laws," King Josiah instructed the priest.

The priest stood to his feet, raised his hand to the soldiers who kept watch, and said: "I'll send for the prophet Jeremiah immediately."

"No. Go to the Prophetess Huldah who teaches in the market place. I've heard news of her forecasting. I believe she will be able to tell us what the Laws say," King Josiah ordered.

*   *   *

Huldah sat assisting her husband with the sewing when she suddenly stopped, stared at the lamp, then back to her husband.

"What is the matter, my love?" Shallum asked his wife. "Is it the child?"

"The child is alright, but a royal carriage cometh. I will

be summoned to go the palace of King Josiah."

"Are you sure these people will not do you harm?" Shallum asked with a great deal of concern.

"I believe it is a good mission I must take. We will pray about it." Huldah reached for her husband's hand, and they began to pray.

*   *   *

In King Josiah's palace, Huldah was treated with respect and curiosity as she sat near the light of a torch reading the fragile pages of the Laws that had been buried for such a long time. The king and his court stood anxiously by, awaiting her translations.

When Huldah had read several pages, she shook her head, and sadness enshrouded her gentle face, for she hated to tell the good king what the Lord had planned for Jerusalem.

"Speak, woman," King Josiah demanded.

"It is with great sadness that I must tell you what is in these Laws. God has promised ruins for Jerusalem and all the lands given to Moses as the promised lands, if idol worship and disobedience continue. Every country will be about war and taking away the lands that were once given to the Israelites. We must bring about a change immediately, or all will be lost and the Jews will be reduced to servants.

*   *   *

Clarence stood again and thanked Rabbi Zech for his dream of Huldah's life and prophecy.

"I tried to keep secret much that Miss Edna told me, so that you'd have the chance to grow up as normal as possible. Your mental abilities advanced so rapidly, that it scared people; our mother, in particular, who was, and still

238

believes in voodoo and magic. Then your other powers developed."

Miss Edna had told Clarence how he could find Rabbi Terah and that Esmeralda would find Rabbi Zech. She had given Clarence the case which concealed the Laws to keep until Esmeralda's eighteenth birthday, at which time she was to read the instructions from God.

No one except Esmeralda could open the seals, for they had been encapsulated by God after Huldab read them those centuries ago. Rabbi Terah opened the leather case which housed the encapsulated canisters.

"They look like golden totems," Ian said.

"You're right," Clarence replied. "Our ancestors belonged to Objibwa, an Afro-Indian tribe. The Ojibwa Indians settled in Indiana, USA, but it is not known how they came to the new world. They were later sold into slavery."

Evelyn raised her hand and was recognized, as Marty proudly massaged her shoulders: "Clarence, you said Esmeralda will be able to open the first seal; who will open the other one?"

"It will be Esmeralda's first born," he responded.

"Her first born?" Philip asked. "You mean she will have children?"

Uncle Zech quickly responded: "As a matter of fact, yes. She is physically and emotionally like all young women, just being used by God to fulfill his promise. As ministers are. She told you before that God will give her four children."

A cloud fell over Esmeralda's face and she stiffened with fear.

"What is it child?" Uncle Zech asked.

"I fear trouble in several of our sites, and I can see Sgt. Darling as the instigator of the problems. He must be stopped!" She excused herself to use the phone.

*   *   *

239

An eerie silence befell the area surrounding the Mandeville Temple. Traffic was moving along in a processional stream when a loud explosion caused several cars to run off the road at 9 p.m. Bit and pieces of building material sprayed throughout the community.

Momentarily, emergency vehicles with sirens wailing pierced the air, and smoke coiling high above the rooftops could be seen for miles as flames leaped hungrily towards the sky.

The Temple had been bombed and securing activity of curiosity seekers and emergency people filled the nearby streets.

Sgt. Darling and his leader sat listening to the news bulletins about the Mandeville bombing and the extortion of the Bay area and San Fernando Temples as well. The passengers in Darling's car suddenly felt their car being lowered as air from all tires was expelled. Surprised, he looked ahead and saw the DWP truck being commandeered.

As Sgt. Darling and his leader attempted to leave the car they were occupying, they realized that they would be stepping onto live wires all round them... Domani and his martial arts team had brought plain clothes FBI members who immediately placed the brains of the Southern California cell under arrest.

The Bay area bad several tourists just finishing their inspection and photographing of the New Temple's housing, and shopping center.

Just as the last of the visitors entered their car and started out of the center when the light began to fade indicating closing time, a loud explosion was heard and the visitors looked back while driving out and saw a flash of light and pieces of building material flying through the air. The time was 9:03 p.m.

At the San Fernando Valley Temple had ended its

meeting by one half hour, but a few people were milling around visiting with each other; the sound came, knocked several people down, broke windshields, and injured a few seriously. The asphalt spewed forth like an erupting volcano under the intense heat.

*   *   *

Esmeralda had just opened the seals and removed the Laws to everyone's amazement. Ian's concern told him that they should go to the Temple to see if anything could be done. He was told by Mera that the most important thing had been done already. She said that Domani had notified the FBI, and the Yarmulke cell in Southern California had been placed under arrest.

Esmeralda's reading of the Laws was no different than when Huldah had read those centuries ago. The Jews' continued insistence that Jesus the Christ was not their Messiah, continuing in their sinful ways and had stuck by their beliefs that they were God's chosen people, believing that He would always protect them.

Esmeralda read that God had especially stipulated the commandments that they must obey in order to receive His blessings. Again, He had placed extreme emphasis on the Ten Commandments of Moses. He warned that the lands left to the Israelites would be taken away. Even a strip of land which they will settle, called The Gaza Strip, they would be asked to vacate due to their complacency.

There would be much talk and fear about the peoples of the Middle Eastern lands where the Ishmaelite have settled. This oil rich land is the key to their strangulation on the world. So many oil-consuming mechanisms will be built out of a desire for monetary gain that will fill the land, sea and skies.

The escape for the world's people is to reduce the need for the commodity that the Middle Eastern lords are holding temptingly in their faces. "Until my people are willing to give up their false gods and return to Me, there will be continued unrest."

Many thousands will migrate away from their homelands seeking peace, but thousands will die at the hands of aggressors, becoming Nomads tossed about as leaves on rushing currents. Their search for a home will become endless and weary.

"Repent ye therefore, and be converted that your sins may be blotted out, when the times of refreshing shall come from the presence of the Lord." (*Acts* 3:19-14)

"And He shall send Jesus Christ which before was preached unto you; whom the heaven must receive until the times of restitution of all things, which God hath spoken by the mouth of all his holy prophets since the world began.

"For Moses truly said unto the fathers: 'A prophet shall the Lord your God raise up unto you, and it shall come to pass, that soul, which will not hear that prophet, shall be destroyed from among the people'.

"Yea, and all the prophets from Samuel and those that follow after, as many as have spoken, have likewise foretold of these days, for there will be more to keep the Middle East in the forefront of every discussion; it is the birthplace of the world's three great monotheistic religions: Judaism, Christianity and Islam.

"Too often this land has not been just their birthplace, but their battlefield, with adherents warning against each other for control of territory they consider holy.

"Nowhere are these conflicts more obvious than in Israel, and Jerusalem, the lands of my chosen people, who themselves chose to disobey, and be cut off from my blessings. Nowhere is there so much history of religious culture lying in literal heaps than at the Temple Mount, flash point for many conflicts over the centuries past.

"In the centuries to come, Muslims will be praying at the Dome of the Rock atop the Temple Mount, Jews praying at the Western Wall barely a stone's throw below and Christians praying along the Via Dolorosa and at the Church of the Holy Sepulcher, a few hundred cubits to the north and west. All around one can see the rubble of the centuries of conflict over this holy place. Yet they wonder who will inherit this troubled city.

"Hear me my children, the history of this place has been written in the final chapters of the Bible centuries ago. Ominously, they mesh remarkably well with the news headlines of current history news about the destruction of the old world."

"Now all these things happened to them for examples, and they are written for our admonition, upon whom the end of the ages are come." (*I Cor.* 10: 11-12)."

Wherefore, let him that thinketh he standeth take heed lest he fall."

Esmeralda broke off as she looked up into the eyes of the guests around the large table. She didn't know if she saw shock on their faces or if she was the target of their consternation. They were all suddenly speechless, and the reading was over. Phyllis buried her head in her hands and wept. It was the first time that Mera had seen her foster mother cry.

No one would say more for a long time. Esmeralda found herself without the ability to continue. She wanted to hug Phyllis or expected one of the Rabbis to say something, but not a sound came from within the group around the tale. It was the constant ringing that caused a stir within the group... The caller told of an important news flash that was on the radio and urged them to listen to it.

Since Philip had answered the phone, he was the one who dialed the radio to the news station. The announcer was hurriedly and excitedly describing the damage to the Temples caused by the bomb blasts.

According to the announcer, the most shocking news of all was when the perpetrators were apprehended by the

FBI; they captured an old and dear friend of the Ravins. Judge Harold Craven, who had been passing as Daniel Brooks, was indeed the organizer and leader of the insidious cell of Yarmulke terrorist. Together with police Sgt. Rupert Darling, they were responsible for the deaths of the three prisoners in the Los Angeles County Hospital jail ward.

Philip looked at Esmeralda in surprise and admiration: "You knew, didn't you?" Clarence quickly urged that no one ask his sister questions about what had happened to the Temples. Pamela Markowitz had much more to say on the subject though, her face more pale than Mera had noticed before as she demanded answers.

Suddenly, after loosing his patience with his wife, Joel took Pam by the arm and forcibly dragged her out of the room, and stern murmurs could be heard as an argument ensued between Dr. Markowitz and his wife.

Ian seemed terribly disturbed by the reading and the recent news of bombing, and he declared that it was important that they go to the Temple to survey the damage, and try to asset what needed to be done.

Esmeralda stared at Clarence and the two Rabbis and wondered if they too were more concerned with the demolished buildings, than they were the readings of warnings by the Lord God Jehovah. She reached for the second canister of Laws but was told by Clarence that only her first-born would be able to open that seal. After an assured amount of time, she excused herself, easing between hers and Philip's chairs. Their hands touched, and suddenly their eyes were locked on each other. *What was he trying to say to her, she wondered.*

In her own room, Mera dropped the seal onto her bed and stood at the window shivering. Maximus joined her at the window following his inspection of the canister she had just dropped on the bed... As Mera glanced down at the flagstone yard below, Max followed her gaze from her face to the yard, and then they both focused on a security guard, climbing a tall ladder that leaned against the garage.

The man was engaged in searching for intruders; she watched him for a moment, turned away to stare down the driveway, and then back to the seals that she had just read.

What is the code that I have just translated? It was not in any language known to man. Those predictions had been written after the seventh century B.C., warning of dangers to come in the twentieth, and twentieth first centuries, and beyond.

How is it possible for people to deny these inscriptions were written by God? Can't they see that he has also written directions for man's escape from destruction? He has always offered this way to escape from every disaster, if only they would have faith and repent for their sins.

What are their thoughts of me now? Will I be the object of their hatred, the butt of their humor? Please God, tell me what I should do now that the truth has been told.

At that moment, Maximus began to growl apprehensively, and a faint fog filled the room. Mera watched as a white robed character materialized from within the fog; Esmeralda looked at the ghost-like figure that spoke softly: "The words that you have just translated are from the language of the Gods. Only those prophets chosen by the Lord will ever translate it.

"I have a message for you from the Lord. 'Well done my good and faithful servant'."

Mera stared at the ghostly figure uncomprehendingly, and it turned and spoke more slowly as if explaining an obvious fact to a child: "Go out and meet with the throngs who will come to your assistance. They will be waiting for your directions at the Mandeville Temple."

The ghost-like figure faded from within the room, as Mera begged it to stay and explain more of what it was talking about, but only Maximus remained there with her.

A gentle knock on her bedroom door caused her to turn

and stare at it, wondering if the ghost-like figure had decided to return. "No way would it knock. It would just appear. Maybe I'd better answer right, Max?"

Before she had a chance to answer the door, she recognized a familiar voice outside. Philip had come to be sure she was all right. "Mera. Are you OK? Please open the door; we're all worried about you.

Like a frightened, captured bird, Mera slowly crept to the door, opened it, and then reached back to take the scrolls with the Laws.

Philip reached out his hand and offered to assist her down the stairs. She thanked him graciously, but assured him that she would be alright, and together the three of them walked down to join the remaining guests.

She felt that at long last, Philip was behaving in a normal and reasonably manner. She was feeling too that he might not be the inhuman monster she had pictured. His hand upon the dogs head as they walked, and Maximus licked his palm, had shown her a new side of him. He might just be a sad, lonely and embittered man who needed to know someone cared.

CHAPTER XV

A large gathering had assembled in the sanctuary of the Temple Beth Israel in the north central Los Angeles County area... At least a dozen Rabbis and other Jewish leaders had gathered for an urgent and important meeting.

Rabbi Leo Abraham called the meeting to order. He was a rather tall gentleman whose likeness was strikingly like the artist renditions of President Abraham Lincoln. He spoke with a sense of urgency, deep concern and much wisdom.

"Gentlemen, I have called this meeting of our people because I am horribly ashamed that I call myself a Jew. To say that a judge with such high education and character reference could be a part of a group we loathe. An Adolph Hitler in sheep's disguise, masquerading in our congregation as a true Jewish believer.

"I am sure the world will be focusing their attention on us and wig wagging their condescending fingers in our directions with shame. Although we do not embrace the theory taught by that young girl Esmeralda, we would not be a part of a terrorist cell such as the Yarmulkes for Jewish purity."

"One important way we may vindicate ourselves from that outlaw group is to show our sympathy for the Emerald Corporation's losses by going in force to help clean up those three sites and assist with their rebuilding. Stand if you agree."

Everyone in attendance was instantly in a vertical position, with loud applause echoing throughout the building...

*   *   *

In Atlanta, Georgia, a large gathering of the group called Southern Baptist was meeting with the very same theme in mind: help the new converted Christian groups rebuild their Temples. The vote was unanimous, and large cells of volunteers from all disciplines of construction had signed their names and were ready to go.

Missionary and Second Baptist, as well as the Church of God in Christ and Methodist had gathered a large amount of volunteers, and they were also on their way to assist wherever they were needed.

*   *   *

At three o'clock p.m., the Emerald Corporation's executives, security, and Philip met at the Mandeville Temple site to survey the damage and assess what needed to be done to repair or rebuild the building.

As they worked their way through the crowd, it was obvious that those beams that were not destroyed by the bomb blast were torn down by the Los Angeles County Fire Department. In order to snuff out all smoldering embers, it was customary for them to tear through all incendiary material to be sure there would be no latent sparks.

Esmeralda knew she had to save the Mishnah and the old Torah stored in the lectern in the back of the sanctuary. The room was well built and to withstand just such problems as had just occurred, but she could see the worried expression on the two Rabbi's faces, and she knew she had to try to get to those items.

The men were still at work sifting through the ruins, and they smiled and waved as she passed their ladders. She wandered off down the familiar aisles, then glanced back to see if she was being followed by her guards, but only Maximus was with her. She smiled to herself at the absurdity of the thought, for who would suspect the nature of her errand.

Some had heard the panicking of old Uncle Zech, but who would credit the eccentricity of an old Rabbi like Zech raving on about the items that should be saved.

If these items were so valuable, why did he not lock them in a safe someplace rather than leave them in the Temple's stored lectern?

Mera reached the closet that stood on the back right side of the podium. The place was big, solid and windowless with a heavy creaking door, one-half the width of the podium steps. She pulled it open and stared uneasily inside.

Inside the closet was black as night and she wished uncle Zech bad advised her to bring a flash light. The door would not open far, but she pulled it as wide as possible to give her the maximum light and then moved inside. The place was cold and damp, and had a foul smell of smoke and molding wood.

Cautiously, she groped her way across the room, stumbling over some unseen object and hurting her leg. She stopped to rub her leg and to try to become accustomed to the gloom. *This errand is not going to be as easy as I had supposed.* She suddenly felt a disturbing sense of apprehension and thought she heard heavy footsteps outside.

When Maximus growled, she was sure something was going on. "Maybe I should never have promised uncle Zech that I'd retrieve the items he panicked over."

Her heart raced as she moved further into the darkness, then she leaped like a startled frog as the door slammed shut; the darkness was absolute. Regaining her composure, she felt inside the lectern drawer and there she found what felt like the precious antiquity of Jewish history that had uncle Zech so upset.

It took a moment or two for her to stumble her way back to the door where her trembling hands seized the handle and pushed with all her might. The door did not budge, and she closed her eyes and tried to sort out the thoughts that chased around her mind like frightened cockroaches.

Perhaps the door opened inward, she thought. "Max, what is it with these doors that won't open? This is the third time it's happened to me. Could it be my own fear?" She felt Max's body shaking from side to side and knew he was trying to understand her.

She tugged vigorously with Maximus biting the knob, and then she stopped as she remembered clearly opening the door towards the outside. "Dear God, Maximus was right; there was someone out there who'd locked us in. This fight is by no means over with the arrest of the evil Yarmulke leader."

Esmeralda tried to persuade herself that when she did not return; her security would be looking for her. She huddled on the floor and tried to keep her mind occupied with positive thoughts. She knew that God wanted us to use the senses he gave us in lesser predicaments and not call for divine help always, so she waited to see if someone would come.

Sifting quietly in the dark, she hugged the Torah in one hand to her chest and Maximus in the other. She had time to remember what uncle Zech had told her about the history of this particular Torah and the Mishnah. *It was the times when the Jews were in Roman Palestine and Sasanid Babalonica, and destruction of the Temple necessitated changes in religious doctrine and practice, for the Temple had been the center of the official forum of Jewish Worship.*

As Jews were driven, enslaved and killed by the Romans, most of the important books of rabbininic Judaism were written during this period. The Mishnah written by Rabbi Judan the Patriarch. This treatise is known today as "The Chapter Of The Fathers, "and contains Hilbel's famous Maxim:

"If am not myself who am I? And if I am only for myself what am I? And if not now, when?"

As she was searching her soul for some answers, she

250

heard a scrubbing sound; the huge door swung open, and Philip led the guards inside as he cried out loud:

"Mera, please don't scare us like this. I can't bear loosing you now!" He stooped and picked her up in his arms, squeezing her close to his chest...

"Are you alright, miss?" She nodded to the inquiring guard, and he continued talking. "It was a fall-out of the Yarmulke cell who put that beam against the door. We got to him just before he injected gas into the air space above the door. Your brother here was, beside himself with concern for you. The guards carried the items that Mera had salvaged, and when they reached a more lighted area, they were greeted with cheers and applause.

Esmeralda whispered to Philip: "You can put me down now." As he put her down, she kissed his cheek gently, getting smoke smudges on his face from her hands.

She was surprised to see so many people, heavy equipment, and trucks lined up against the curb for more than a block with men in work boots, jeans and hard hats.

"Dad, who are all these people?" she asked as she handed the wrapped Mishnah and Torah to uncle Zech who accepted it with exuberance.

"I knew I could depend on you, child," Zech said.

Mera smiled at the old man, patted his hand, and then looked again to her foster father for answers.

"Honey, this is Rabbi Abraham from the Temple Beret Israel. He has come to help restore this Temple and has many workers standing by at the other two temples to do the same."

"It is from your Temple that the judge came," Mera stated.

"First of all, it pleases me to meet such a youthful and lovely Joan of Arc. The news of your accomplishments has preceded our introduction and have spread far and wide."

"Why would you help us who teaches a different philosophy than you teach?"

"My wife is a Christian and even though I may never embrace it, I dearly love her. It's about people helping people. We are ashamed that the terrorist cell was a part of our Temple membership. I am sure Christians also have traitors within their members."

"Hello, young lady," said a stout, middle-aged white man with a receding hairline and crystal blue eyes. I am John Peckingpaugh from the corporate office of Southern Baptist. My men are here from all around the United States also to assist you with rebuilding your sites. Our workers are standing by the other two sites as well."

Another gentleman stepped forward, with thick brown hair and mustache. "Charlie Hackman, Pentecostal. We are here to help you also."

Before Mera had released the last hand, another hand reached out one after the other, identifying themselves and their organizations.

"David Cooper, United Methodist."

"John King, Second Baptist."

"Earl Brown, Missionary Baptist. We are all here to do what we can to help you rebuild.

Esmeralda put her hands to her cheeks, raised her face towards the sky, and began to weep with unbelievable joy. "What a Mighty God we serve."

Philip had not released the encircled embrace he held on Mera's waist until he reached for his handkerchief to dry her tears.

"Mom, Dad, please get Bret's attention," Mera requested.

When Bret, a muscular young man in his early thirties with bright red hair and a dark mustache, came forward, Mera introduced him to all the head visitors: "This is Bret Macon, Vice President of Engineering; he'll tell you what needs to be done. You've already met my Corporate CEOs Ian and Phyllis Ravin; they know where the drawings are and will see that you have what you need: lodging, food, etc.

"Bret, see if Regional Planning will accept the same plans we used for the Bay area. I'm sure Geology will accept them. Meanwhile, Rabbi's Terah, Zech and I have urgent other business."

*   *   *

The Ravin dinning room was made ready for dinner. The large slices of red salmon with special spices went into the oven. Bok Choy was sliced and ready to be steamed with slices of red and white onions and large mushrooms. The golden macaroni and cheese casserole was just being removed from the oven and covered with baking bags to keep it moist.

As the fish aroma permeated the room with its attractive smelling spices, Mera was busy cutting and buttering French rolls and placed them on a large baking sheet. The wine was in an ice bucket chilling at the head of the dining room table, and the individual salad bowls had been filled with fresh garden greens.

The first key opened the door, and to Mera's surprise it was Philip. He flipped through the mail on the hall table, looking coyishly towards the kitchen, one hand still behind his back.

When Mera went to place the salad bowls around the table, Philip crept into the dining room, put his arm around her waist, and held the bouquet of miniature roses in her face. They were beautiful soft pink buds with white baby's breath, and this took her by surprise. She reached out, took the flowers and held them close to her cheek.

Looking at Philip suspiciously she asked: "What did I do, or maybe I should ask, what you have been up to?"

Philip stood back and stared at the picture of loveliness there before him: "It's nothing special, just a gesture of appreciation for all that you've done for me and my family."

Mera smiled at Philip, thanked him for the lovely thought, and then went to the hutch to remove a large crystal vase.

"Please let me get that for you," Philip said, appearing as proud as a young schoolboy who'd just brought his teacher an apple. Mera stepped back to allow him to get the vase.

"Wait," Mera said urgently. "When was the last time you brought flowers to your mother?"

Philip stopped to contemplate the question and then replied: "I honestly can't remember when it was." He paused. "Would you believe I've never given my mother flowers?" He appeared disappointed with himself as he admitted being remiss.

"Why don't you write on the tag: for my two best girls, or for someone special and give them to her. I'll always remember the precious gesture you made for me. No one else has to know."

"But why do anything at all? I truly intended the flowers for you."

"I know that, and you know it, too, but what will it hurt to give them to your mom? Can't you remember how envious you were when you felt I'd stolen her love from you? What makes you believe she won't feel dejected, also? Mothers have feelings, too."

"The florist shop is close by; I'll call and have another bouquet of red roses sent to mom," he said anxiously.

The telephone rang just as Philip was about to call the florist, and it was his mother.

"Philip, we're just getting ready to leave the office; we were tied up here with the Medical Center's contracts and details.

"Take your time, mom. Mera has dinner ready and we were just about to select some numbers for the upcoming holiday concert. See you soon." He hung up the phone, making an OK sign with his fingers... "Perfect," he said as

254

he dialed the florist shop and ordered the red roses for immediate delivery.

When the flowers were delivered, Philip gave the delivery boy an extra amount. He and Mera had found another vase, and he went immediately to fill it with water, and then they placed the flowers in the center of the dining room table.

"Philip, please place an ice cube in the center of plastic wrap, and place one on top of each salad. That way, I won't have to put them back in the refrigerator to chill."

Mera placed the macaroni into the warmer and set the bread in the oven to melt the butter. Philip had now finished his icing the salad chore, and walked softly behind Mera, his arms around her waist, and gently kissed her neck and ear: "I love you Mera. Let me take you to emotional paradise," he said with his body pressed hard against hers.

She whirled around, her green eyes flashing in anger, and her finger pressing hard in his excited chest: "Look, buddy! Those flowers will not pay the price to smell the hook where the ham hangs. If I was a white woman, would you behave so disrespectfully?"

Surprised at the quick-tempered mood-swing of the girl he loved, Philip apologized humbly: "I meant no disrespect, Mera. I love you and want to marry you..."

"White men don't marry black women," she snapped. "They sleep with them, even have illegitimate babies with them, but take them to the wedding chapel, no way. So why don't you find a respectful white woman, and leave me alone!"

Before the disagreement could entangle further, the senior Ravins arrived home, appearing to be rushed. "Hey, kids; we're sorry to be so late," and setting their briefcases down on the hall table. "You should've gone ahead with your dinner," Phyllis told them.

Ian gently kissed Mera's cheek, shook hands with his son, and then embraced him. Philip kept his eye on Mera, hoping she would not show her anger to his parents, Instead, she kissed the cheeks of both of them and smiled as though nothing had happened.

"I don't think either of us was hungry enough to eat without you. Besides, Philip has a surprise for you, mom." She took Phyllis by the hand and led her into the dining room, spreading out her free hand in a gesture of magic, "Violà," she said, as Phyllis' eyes sparkled with delight when they fell upon the beautiful flowers in the center of the table. Phyllis reached for the tag on the pink roses, but Mera cautioned her with dual index fingers pointing. "Those belong to me; yours are the beautiful red ones."

A tear welled up in Phyllis's eye and dribbled down her cheek, as she tried to dam it up with one of her fingers. When she read the card attached: My first best girl, with lots of forgotten love. Signed; Philip.

"You'll have to forgive a blubbering old lady, but I can only remember one time when Philip brought me flowers. It was a yellow dandelion from the back lawn when he was four years old, and a bee stung his sweet little hand. He never let go of the flower until he gave it to me, but he had no use for flowers after that."

Mera held back tears as Phyllis hugged and kissed her son. This was the first outburst of sincere emotions she'd witnessed between those two since she'd lived in their home.

Ian hugged Philip for a long time, thanking him for such a thoughtful thing to do for the girls: "I can't think of two more deserving girls than you've chosen. By the way, I'm hungry. Do you suppose we could eat soon?"

Mera took the pink flowers and moved them to the hutch beside the dessert. "I'll just move the flowers over here for the time being, and while you're getting washed, Philip and I will set out the food." Philip followed Mera into the kitchen, there taking her hand, as she looked up into his eyes: "Mera, how is it that you know so much about life?"

"It's not always how much one knows, but how much love and compassion we have for our fellow humans. It comes with salvation, the greatest commandment from our Lord as documented in the book of *John*, Chapter 15: Verses 12-13: 'This is my commandment that you love one another as I have loved you. (For) Greater love hath no man than this, that a man lay down his life for his friends'."

During dinner, more compliments were sent Philip's way for the flowers and there were dinner compliments to Mera. Ian discussed light business activities as well.

"So many things are being made ready all at once. The Temples will be ready for service this Saturday. The Medical Center is nearing completion and a new television satellite will be broadcasting soon. I love being this busy and watching so many things come together. The most dramatic reward is that we had something to do with these changes and seeing them come to fruition."

"You two have been a lifesaver to the Corporation. It could not have been done without you," Mera stated. "As a matter of fact, all of the Temple's head Rabbis have asked that I speak via television this Saturday for the grand reopening of the three Temples. It will also be networked by television satellite, so that it can reach homes as well. I am so excited."

"You got the permits to air, already?" Phyllis asked.

"What is the subject of your message?" Ian asked.

"I've talked a lot about how to have an effective prayer life, so I will teach the public how it should be done instead of chanting to God alone. *John* 14:6 is where Jesus the Messiah said: 'I am the way the truth and the life: No man cometh unto the Father but by me'."

"Ian, we shouldn't miss this lecture. Remember when you told me that prayer is prayer, and there's no right or wrong way to pray?" Phyllis taunted.

Ian changed the subject by asking Philip a question.

257

"Phil, what is the date for your MD's holiday Television Extravaganza?"

"It is scheduled for the weekend following Thanksgiving. Mera has done a great job with the music and getting two celebrity guest performers."

"Who are the guest celebrities?" Phyllis asked with excitement.

"Would you believe it is Lena Horne and Dean Martin?"

"No fooling," Ian said with surprise. "You boys are coming up in the world."

Mera smiled up at Philip and said: "They're sensational. I think they are heading for a music award. Philip is such a good interpreter of what he's singing. He gets the message across to the audience. I've watched them; some appear to be about to have a heart attack as he glides about the stage, his mellow voice quelling all frustrations and fulfilling their dreams of becoming a singer or marrying this one."

Philip's mind wandered away from the current scene momentarily: *Lord, you know how much I love this girl, but I'm having problems understanding her. Does she care about me, or am I reaching for a star too far out there? Help me, God, to do the right things to please her. I know we've had a rocky beginning, but I want to change. I am changed.*

Phyllis noticed that her son was drifting mentally and wondered what was stealing his attention away: "Son, are you all right?"

"It's nothing to be concerned about," he assured her as his eyes met with Mera's, and they both quickly looked away.

*   *   *

The Emerald Engineering staff and visiting volunteer

group workers had done a splendid job on the Temple's reconstruction. Here it was the first weekend in November, and they were ready to resume usage of the Temples. Visitors were in awe as they entered the beautiful Mandeville edifice.

The entire place exuded peace and tranquility with bubbling fountains and foliage in strategic places. The beautiful gold and white dome on top of the building had a good likeness to that of the Holy Temple Mount, and the interior was decorated in heavy red velvet and mahogany with gold leaves bordering the benches, tables and altar.

This Saturday afternoon, the 1500 seat sanctuary was filled to capacity. In the west Anthrax, Mera kneeled beside the confessional with Uncle Zech and Rabbi Terah. Their heads were bowed low, and a small skullcap was fixed on the center of their heads.

The men wore red and black robes, with a rope tied around their waists, but Mera was dressed in a white satin robe, with a gold waist rope and gold lace bordering the front opening down to the full length of the robe.

The program director waved his baton, and the musicians began a solemn rendition of an old hymn. A teenaged choir filed into the choir loft followed by the Rabbis, Mera and Maximus.

Rabbi Terah and uncle Zech thanked the audience for their attendance and praised the visitors from other denominations for their assistance in reconstructing the new Temples. Uncle Zech praised God for all those who'd come from far and wide to help in any way they could with food, lodging and donations.

Rabbi Terah stood and said: "Praise God for dreams that have been realized. Today, we are broadcasting from this site to numerous sites around the country. As Jesus Christ our Messiah was so young when he began his ministry, I now give you our baby Prophetess, engineer, artist and teacher, Esmeralda Wilkins."

More than 90 percent of the audience stood to applaud the young woman who took to the podium. Their applause continued for an inexhaustible time, and finally, Mera had to wave her hand to indicate that they should settle down.

"Good evening," she began. "Thank you for coming out today. Many of you have heard what subject I will be teaching, but to those who have not heard, it is entitled: How to Pray Effectively. You may pick up a copy of this lesson from the back table on your way out if you wish.

"First, I'd like you to look at the overhead projector which shows an artist's rendition of Jesus in prayer as he kneeled in the Garden of Gethsemane. Note if you will the artist's attempt to portray the earnest, sincerity, deep contrition and petition on Jesus' face as he prayed.

"Have you always longed for a more satisfying prayer life? Are your prayers being answered? Do you sometimes believe that God doesn't care about you? If any of these questions are on your mind, then this lesson is definitely for you.

"During the time that Jesus lived on the earth and just before His crucifixion, He drew away from His disciples for a quiet retreat and rest from their arduous ministry. He took advantage of the seclusion to pray.

"Whether He prayed out loud, or not, we are not sure. But these men who served Him and were His constant companions were privileged to listen and watch Him pray. They saw his face rapt in devotion; they sensed the presence of God and were awed by it.

"When Jesus finished praying, one of His men asked. 'Lord, teach us to pray as John taught his disciples'.

"They had seen His mighty miracles, but they did not ask for powers. They had heard His matchless preaching, but they did not ask Him to teach them how to preach. It was His prayer life, His communion with His Father God they longed to know.

"Jesus at once responded to their request and proceeded to teach them to pray. If Jesus responded so promptly to the plea of His Apostles, will He be less willing to respond to our sincere desires?

"There are at least five elements that should be present in a well balanced prayer life. The five elements are as follows:

1. 'Worship, or adoration, which tells God how much we love and appreciate Him.
2. Thanksgiving, is our attempt to thank Him for all that He does for us. For health, jobs home, family, and love.
3. Confession, admits our faults. Not just to God but to those we've wronged.
4. Worship is when we take time to adore God. It is the loving ascription of praise to God for what He is. It is the bowing of the innermost spirit in deep humility and reverence before God.
5. Intercession is the unselfish aspect of prayer in order that God's glory may be secured and our prayer life richer.'

"I would advise that we revise our daily prayers and so arrange them that each element that I have just told you finds a place in our prayer life. Christ will not pray instead of us, but He will intercede in us, and thus aid us in our weakness.

"When our thoughts begin with God, love is kindled and faith is stimulated. Only in the face of Jesus Christ, and through Him, will we see the full blaze of the divine glory.

"Let us now bow our heads; repeat after me the prayer that was taught to the disciples by our Lord Jesus The Christ:

'Our Father, who art in heaven. Hallowed be Thy name, Thy kingdom come. Thy will be done on earth as it is in heaven. Give us this day our daily bread, and forgive us our debts as we forgive our debtors. And lead us not into temptation, but deliver us from evil. For Thine is the kingdom, and the power, and the glory. Forever. Amen.'

"I will never know how many of you really listened, or if you were, did you understand. We are here to help you if you want it. You may acknowledge your desires for help by calling the Temple office, or you may come to the altar now. There will be copies of today's lesson on a table out back as you leave."

Mera stopped her appeal when she saw Philip come to the altar, crying. Rabbi Terah stepped down to meet him, and the two men hugged like old friends who'd been absent from each other for a very long time. Soon the aisles were filling up with converts, and Mera stepped down to help the Rabbis with the overload as the clerical staff came with cards for the recruits to fill out.

The musical director struck up a tune entitled: There's Room at the Cross for You.

CHAPTER XVI

February 1951 was another busy month for the Ravin household. Mera was studying and taking finals for her Doctorate Degree that was to come in early May. Construction on her eleven-bedroom, twelve-bath home, nicknamed Emerald Castle was completed and being furnished by interior decorators with Mera's request.

Mera's weekly television Bible teaching had stepped up its pace. The Emerald Fashions were buzzing with excitement for its upcoming spring fashion showing. Her two head designers had done well, she thought.

Philip was busy with his medical practice, Bible lessons with Mera, and rehearsals for the MDs' spring concert.

Mom and Dad Ravin were busy with all the Emerald Corporation's expansions and staffing of the new Medical Center. Everyone had agreed that Marty Heller be offered the position as Administrator for five hundred thousand dollars and he had accepted. The center was slated to open in April.

An assistant cook and housekeeper bad been hired for the Ravin's home, for Mera was too busy to take care of it all.

For some unknown reason, Philip decided to inspect the fashion designs for the spring show that he saw on the sketching pad in Mera's office.

He really didn't mean to pry, but the light was still on at her table; he was about to turn it off when he passed by, when he saw a beautiful sketched model wearing a shimmering green chiffon gown and her arms outstretched. There was an unusual ring dressing her left ring finger.

The ring had a large 2-karat diamond in the center,

with four small emeralds on each side. He went back to his office, returned with a Polaroid camera, took several shots of the hand with the ring and returned to his office, allowing the film to dry before putting them in his desk drawer.

When Philip walked down stairs, he found Mera scoring sheet music at the piano in the living room. Against his better judgment, he decided to sit beside her.

Mera moved to the right to make room for him and smiled up at him as she did. She rested her left hand on the sheet propped on the piano, so that she could add a note, and Philip took her hand and kissed it.

"What are you doing?" she asked as she withdrew her hand.

"I'm kissing your hand," he explained.

"Why?" she asked, examining her hand as though he'd left marks of guilt there.

"Because it's soft, sweet, and it smells good."

Mera smelled her hand, starred Philip in his eyes for a moment, and then replied: "You're silly!"

"Is that your new class ring?" he asked starring at the ring on her left ring finger. "Yes, it is. I thought it would never come. I ordered it last summer."

"May I see it?" He tugged to remove the ring, and Mera helped him with it so that he could inspect its unusual detailing. He slid the ring on his left pinkie as far as it would go, and seemed satisfied with the measurement he'd just taken before replacing the ring on her finger.

"Why don't you wear it on the right hand? Most class rings are worn there."

"I don't know why I put it there. Maybe it's because my right hand is always so busy."

"Perhaps that makes sense Mera, but it seems to be out of place."

"Alright, already. If I move the cotton picking ring to the right hand, can we get on with the scoring of this song?" she asked, annoyed.

"Hey, it doesn't really matter to me where you wear it, I just thought..."

"Don't think; it's done. See" She held up her right hand so that he could see it and then quickly started playing the melody to the new song.

"My, you're testy," he said as he started to hum the new melody.

*   *   *

Dr. Philip Ravin was just arriving in his office, still in surgical scrubs, spoke casually to the office staff and went to his private office to redress. A few moments later, he emerged from his office dressed in appropriate clothing to meet his patients. Before he began his circulation of examination rooms, he stopped at the nurses' station, handed his private nurse a slip of paper, making an urgent request.

"Melba, would you please call everyone on this list and ask them to meet me at the Calorie Counter at seven thirty this evening for dinner and an urgent meeting."

"I'll take care of it immediately, doctor," Melba replied. The brown haired, brown eyed petite nurse quickly entered the room with the label Head Nurse, closed the door, and began to make calls.

After about thirty minutes, the young woman knocked on the examining room door, poked her head in, and said: "Everyone will be there at 7:30, doctor."

"Thank you, Miss Allen."

*   *   *

At 7:30 p.m. Thursday, the ten-seat round table was already filled with Marty and Evelyn, Joel and Pamela, Uncle Zech, and aunt Winnie, and Ian and Phyllis. Everyone kept looking at their watches and searching the open aisles through the restaurant.

Evelyn was first to stop the small talk and ask questions about why they were all there for an urgent meeting that Philip had called. "He's been acting different since he was baptized, like a new person. Not at all like the old Philip."

"Isn't that what salvation is all about?" Uncle Zech asked. "We put aside the old ways, and accept new ones."

"I don't know, uncle Zech; this is different. Mom, Dad, do you have any idea why Philip called this urgent meeting?"

Phyllis spoke up. "Ian thinks he has the answer, but in the words of Mera's jargon, I wouldn't want to pimp his hand."

"By the way, where is Mera? Wasn't she invited?" Pam asked.

"We're in the dark about that, too. I got the phone call from Melba, and she knew nothing either," Phyllis said.

"Uncle Zech, do you know anything?" Joel asked

"Like Ian, I have my own suspicions," the old revived man replied.

Marty checked his watch again and appeared nervous. "It's almost eight o'clock. Where the heck is that guy?"

Aunt Winnie raised her hands in praise. "Speak of the devil; here comes the golden boy now."

"Good evening, everyone," Philip said as he took a seat, spread his napkin as though preparing to eat, and then he looked slowly around the table as eight pair of eyes stared at him without moving. Philip seemed nervous and asked: "Did you order yet?"

"Does it look like we've ordered?" Marty asked.

Philip tapped his water glass with his spoon. "Well, let's get someone over here; it's getting late, and I'm hungry."

"Tell me about it," Joel said.

Two waiters hurried up to the table, and the group began to make their individual requests.

266

Evelyn tapped her fork on her coffee cup in a gesture of impatience. "OK, Mr. Urgent. Let's have the reason we're all here, and I want to know now!"

Philip sipped his wine and then leaned back in his chair before speaking. "I'm in love, and I want to marry the young lady."

"So what's so difficult about that?" Evelyn asked.

"I didn't know you were dating anyone," Joel said.

The salads came, and soup for uncle Zech and Winnie, which caused a slight delay in conversation.

"Let me see how I should answer your questions or statements." Everyone was eating, but all the while watching Philip.

"To answer you, Joe. I'm not dating anyone, just wishing I could, and Evelyn wants to know what's so difficult about getting married. I think it is customary for both parties to agree."

"You haven't asked her?" Evelyn asked.

"Yes I have, but she won't believe that I'm serious. She said white men don't marry black women."

Evelyn, Joel and Pamela all said at the same time: "It's got to be Mera."

"It is, and she runs away from me. She let me hold her once, but I guess I got too excited after being celibate for so long; now she really thinks my intensions are dishonorable. I think she wanted to trust me at first. I feel the signs of love and caring in her, but I haven't the slightest idea how I can expose her real feelings."

In the midst of his soup slurping, Uncle Zech advised: "Stay persistent, son; this union is meant to be. It is God's choice that you, too, be wed."

Aunt Winnie smiled at her husband, repositioned his napkin in the neck of his shirt, and then patted his shoulder in agreement to what he had just said.

"Dad, is this what you suspected?" Evelyn asked.

"We live with them, and I'm not too old to recognize

the signs of love when I see it. Phyllis thinks they are be-having like real brother and sister disagreements, but not me; I recognize more than that," Ian declared.

Marty had stopped eating and was searching through the pockets of his wallet, when everyone turned to see what he was doing. "I thought I kept that paper she wrote on in my class room a couple of years ago," Marty said.

Evelyn looked at Marty piling little slips of paper on the table and asked: "What are you doing, Marty?"

"Somewhere in here I'm sure I stored the note."

"What note? Maybe I should help you sort them out; I could find some incriminating information there."

"This is the note that Mera was absently scribbling on, and when I called her attention to the fact that she was not paying attention, she balled the paper up and threw it in the trash can on her way out. I naturally dug it up, smoothed it out, and...Ah ha. Here it is."

He unfolded the wrinkled, faded note and began to read it.: "Mrs. Esmeralda Ravin, Theresa Ianna Ravin, Ter-rence Ian Ravin, Kent Tracy Ravin, and Starlyn Kelly Ravin. Now I think she said that her angel told her she'd have four children, and the first two would be twins, con-ceived on her wedding night. Theresa and Terrence sure sounds like twins to me. Here's your proof."

Philip reached for the note. "Let me see that," he said. After reading the note, he stated that he needed their help.

"I want to get her out in a crowd like this, so she won't think I'm trying to sexually assault her. Maybe I can corner her to admit she cares."

Evelyn volunteered to arrange the meeting. "Let me handle this. We'll do it this Saturday evening. She doesn't know about this dinner, so we'll plan an appreciation din-ner for her for she's done so much for all of us.

"Winnie and I don't need to be here, but want her to have my book of Haggadan, the traditional reading for the Passover ceremony."

"We can get the Star of David and have it wrapped professionally," Pam said.

"I have an old Chalice of Israel that was given to me by my grandmother. I'm sure Mera will take good care of it and pass it on to my grand daughters," Phyllis testified.

"Marty and I will pick up a genuine Seder plate for food served during Passover. We're going to make a Jew out of Mera yet."

"Remember to say Israelite to her; Jew is a religion or a way of life according to her," Aunt Winnie said.

"When we get her here, the rest is up to you Philip. Same time Saturday evening," Evelyn reminded everyone.

*   *   *

Friday morning early, Mera was getting ready to let the security escorts know she was ready to leave for school, when her private phone rang.

"Mera, here," she answered.

"Evelyn, here," the voice on the other end of the line stated.

"What is it, Evelyn?" Mera asked.

"I don't like calling at the last moment, but Marty and I were thinking of throwing a small appreciation dinner party for you tomorrow evening at 7:30. We hope you don't have anything planned."

"I don't have anything planned, but you don't have to do this; I'm not seeking praise."

"We know that, but it's something we want to do. You've been there for all of us. We're all millionaires because of you, and I owe my life to you."

"Not to me Evelyn, but to God; remember that."

"I know that, too, but you were instrumental in interceding on my behalf. Please let us do this. Because of security, I can't pal around with you as a girl friend, and I'd like to."

After listening for a while, Mera finally agreed. "All right, Evelyn, I'll be there and thank you for the generous thoughts."

*   *   *

On Saturday evening, the Ravins and Philip were dressed in their finest evening attire and were awaiting the appearance of Mera and her guard dog Maximus. Their eyes were staring in amazement, and their mouths were agape when the lovely princess appeared at the bottom of the stairs.

Mera was wearing a lovely silk lined beige suit with matching covered buttons, a low neckline that exposed a teasing part of her cleavage, and a slit on one side exposing her golden shapely leg. The emerald earrings dangled from her ears, and a matching tennis bracelet graced her left arm. She carried a Stone Martin beige fur cape and the matching necklace to the other jewelry in her hand.

"Sorry I'm slow coming down, but Maximus couldn't fasten my necklace; it kept getting tangled in my hair, and I wanted you to see me wearing the gift you gave me for Christmas." She handed the necklace to Philip to fasten around her neck.

He excitedly brushed her wavy hair from her neck, exposing the single tendril hanging attractively down her cheek. Placing the necklace around her neck, Philip glanced at the lovely view of her exposed cleavage, taking a deep breath to calm his rushing pulse.

Aware of his anxieties, Mera quickly took charge of the situation: "Did security agree that we can go in your car, Philip?"

"They said it will be no problem to take my car."

"Good," she said, elated. "I've never ridden in a Jaguar, and this will make me feel that I'm not always being watched."

270

"And you've never looked lovelier," Philip said, spinning her around to face them all.

"Your mother and I totally agree; you are breathtakingly beautiful," Ian said.

"I think you are all embarrassing me. What do you think, Max?"

The great dog barked and licked Mera's hand that petted his head. He sat down to shake hands with her, and as she shook his paw, she told him to stay. "Stay, boy, I'll be home soon."

The dog wagged his tail and seemed to understand as Mera went to the guest bath to wash and lotion her hands.

*   *   *

In the restaurant, Mera gave a cry of delight at the sight of the beautifully decorated table. The flowers were breathtakingly beautiful, and the cart which contained gifts was decorated with a lace table cover and long stemmed roses in a crystal center vase.

Philip made sure he slid back a chair that would put Mera to his right and then greeted the already waiting guests; he sat down next to Mera.

Ian and Phyllis sat on the next two seats available, and a hush fell upon the party as the new arrivals settled down; everyone paused in their wine sipping exercises to stare at Mera.

Mera thought she saw a hint of resentment in Pamela's gaze, and she used the menu to cover her suspicions. Fortunately, the waiter started with her, and she was able to forget the tell-tail resentment in Pamela's eyes.

"I'll have a large Cesar salad with grilled chicken strips, a bowl of vegetable soup, buttered French rolls and iced tea," Mera said.

Philip ordered prime rib roast, baked potato with butter, sour cream and chives, green beans and a small dinner salad.

When the food orders circled around the table and finally came to Evelyn, she asked: "Mera you're almost a vegetarian, aren't you?"

"I like meat. Some meats have too much fat. I can't stand grease, and I eat beef only once a week maybe. It is too difficult to digest, and I feel so heavy after eating it. I guess I don't produce enough digestive enzymes."

Philip spoke up in defense of Mera's rejection of beef. "The heart association recommends limiting beef in our diets. It takes longer to clear through the digestive track, clinging to the lining of the arteries, causing blocks stroke and heart disease. We used to blame it on pork.

"You just ordered prime rib," Pam criticized.

"Much of the time, we all do things that we all know is not good for us. The best things in life are either sinful deadly or fattening."

Following the food ordering, Evelyn said with a great deal of excitement: "Mera, as you already know, this celebration is for you. There's nothing we can buy that can express our love and appreciation for you and all that you do for us without even a thought."

"Here! Here!" the group shouted, agreeing with Evelyn.

Phyllis removed her gift from the table and extended it to Mera. It was a beautifully wrapped box that had a stamped sign reading fragile on it. Mera opened the card, and it said that it was from the Ravin family. As she opened the box and removed a lacy stemmed glass with detailed etchings, Phyllis told her the history of the glass cup.

"This is a Chalice of Israel; the cup holds a promise of courage, hope, honor and praise. It was given to me by my mother when I finished college, and now we want you to have it."

Mera held the precious cup to her face and kissed it; "I'll always take good care of it."

Mera opened a small jewelry box, and read the card from Joel, and Pamela. It was a gold star of David necklace. I know this one lights up your way when you are in darkness. I love it. Thank you both."

She opened the flat gift and saw that it read from Uncle Zech and aunt Winnie. It was a Haggadah. "Uncle Zech said that this is read during the Passover ceremony," Ian said.

"Oh, how sweet. It must've cost a fortune..."

"This one is from Philip. It is the Ram's horn. The people of Israel used it to notify each other of trouble or good times," Ian said.

"This is so special." She leaned over and kissed Philip's cheek.

And no Passover is complete without the Seder plate," Evelyn said. "All meals are served on this plate during the celebration of the Passover."

"How beautiful this is. Does everyone get a Seder Plate, or is the food placed on it and everyone takes turns tasting a little dabs of it?" Mera asked.

"How do I know? No one ever served Passover at our house. Marty, do you know?"

"Well, I think..."

"I think everyone takes a little dab," Ian said. "The food particles have a significant meaning, and each type of food in placed in a particular position on the plate which represents something important."

At that moment, the food arrived, and everyone began to eat except Mera. "I don't know how to thank you all for your generosity, respect and love."

Philip found a moment to bring up his special subject of love and said to Mera. "I don't think this group knows that I love you and want you to many me."

Mera took a quick look around the table and found all eyes were fixed upon her. She stirred the salad around on her fork and spoke to Philip.

"I think you've taken leave of your senses. Don't you know that if your patients knew you were married to a black woman, you'd loose half of them."

"She got a point there, Philip," Pam said. "A white woman might be your best bet," Pam said.

Evelyn appeared irritated and spoke to Pam harshly: "Instead of playing matchmaker for your friend and Philip's ex-wife, you should pay more attention to your own marriage, before Joel tosses you out there with Annette."

Ian put his hand up and tapped on his glass with his spoon: "This is a joyous occasion that is now getting out of hand with Annette being introduced into it. I am not usually a violent man, but if that woman comes near any member of my family, I will personally have her shipped to Siberia."

Silence stilled the air around the table, and it was obvious that Joel was punishing Pam by squeezing her hand to tight; her face grimaced with the pain.

Marty decided to bring life back into the stealth scenery. "What were you saying, Philip?" he asked.

"Oh, yes. I was trying to convince Mera that I'd be a good husband to her, but she runs from me."

"I think your intentions are not honorable, Philip. That is why you should find someone you respect," Mera responded.

"I don't believe you'd ever lie to me, Mera, so why don't you just say in the presence of everyone here, that you don't love me. I can never love you."

Mera began picking at her salad, and Philip shook her shoulders. "Say it, Mera. Say you don't love me!"

"I can't."

Why can't you say it, Mera?"

"Because...I...do," she said, barely audible.

"You do love me?"

"Yes, I love you." She snapped with her eyes closed as

though shutting out the world around her.

Philip relaxed back in his chair, bit his lip, and stared at the guests around the table, breathing as though he'd been in a heavy verbal debate. "How long have you known that you loved me?"

"Forever!"

"Why didn't you let me know?"

"I would've risked being called a prick teaser again if you didn't feel the same. So I told you in most of the songs that I wrote for you."

"I need your love, God Speed your love to me. Oh, my Lord, I missed the signals."

"You're so dense, Philip. We all picked up on it. And when she ran out of our dressing room, you thought nothing of it. She was livid with envy over the women who'd gathered there," Joel proclaimed.

Marty decided to taunt Philip as well: "Read between the lines, you nerd; we discussed this possibility way back when you were visiting my office. She was just a kid then, so we all dismissed it."

Philip seemed disappointed with himself, and he breathed deeply before continuing his pursuit of Mera. He knew it had to be tonight, or he might never again get this chance to get her to say she'd marry him. "Can you show me how much you love me?"

"How do I do that?" Mera asked, confused.

"Kiss me."

"Here?"

"Yes, here."

"I don't know how to kiss you the way you want to be kissed."

"How do you think I want to be kissed?"

"Spit Swapping kisses?"

"May I kiss you then?"

"Now?" she asked, shrinking away from him.

"Yes, now. I want to show everyone that we're in

love," Philip stated.

No one was eating, but all eyes were upon the young couple. Philip excited and Mera extremely embarrassed, they engaged in a long French kiss. After several moments, Mera had to pull away to catch her breath.

"What's wrong?" Philip asked her.

"You took my breath away," she replied, shaking all over.

Evelyn slapped Marty's shoulder gently: "When was the last time you took my breath away, dude?"

"Don't be silly, girl. You know it was just before we got dressed to come here," Marty teased.

Pamela came alive again and cut an icy insult. "I think we're making too much of this. If you've loved him forever, you should've just gone ahead and gotten it on. Take the man out of his misery."

Mera was terribly insulted and began to cry. "You're not my friend. You're no different than the serpent in the Garden of Eden that temped Eve." She pushed her chair back and stood to leave as Philip tried to calm her rage...

"Please, angel, sit down. Pay no attention to that kind of talk."

"I've got to get some air, Philip. The stench of mendacity is stifling me," Mera said as she raced for the patio with her security not far behind.

Philip stood to go after her and so did Ian, but Marty waved them to sit. "I think she'll hear me out; let me go talk to her."

Mera stood on the patio with her back to the door, her arms folded, as she leaned on the railing, tears trailing down her cheeks.

Marty came up behind her, gently took her shoulders, and turned her around to face him. "Mera, please don't judge all of us by the behavior Pam displayed. There's serious trouble brewing in that union, and she's fighting back the only way she understands."

"Why are you here and not Philip?"

"He was on his feet to come and so was Dad, but I asked them to allow me to talk to you first. There is a serious situation here that you perhaps have not thought about."

"Dr. Heller. What is it I need to understand? Sin and evil are easily recognized. Why buy the cow when the milk is free?"

"Mera, where on earth do you find these cute sayings?"

"I'm a country girl with a lot of naughty brothers, I guess."

"OK, but no amount of clever speech or defensive methods will keep you as safe as being the wife of someone who truly loves you. So you know that most aggressive men will back off respectfully when they see a wedding band.

"Are you saying that I'm still in another kind of danger?"

"I don't have to remind you that you've been fighting all of your life to keep men from taking advantage of you."

"That's true," she agreed.

"Mera, the truth is you need someone to protect you, and Philip needs your love. What happened when he held you was unavoidable. Being in love and wanting to make love goes hand in hand. Some men learn to suppress those feelings, but Philip is coming alive again, thanks to you, and he couldn't control his nerve reactions."

"Marry him, Mera, and make it soon. I know you love him, and he sure as the dickens loves you."

"I will marry him, if he'll marry me in the church."

"How much time do you need to prepare for the wedding?"

Shrugging her shoulders, she smiled up at Marty; "Three weeks sounds like a good enough time," she said.

"That's good. I'll send him out here right away,"

Marty promised

Mera watched Marty walk away, and then she turned to look over the balcony at the clear night's sky. There was a quarter moon rocking slowly across the sky, and Mera blew it a kiss.

She felt familiar hands on her waist, and soft familiar masculine cologne floated hypnotically around her nostrils.

The evening was getting a bit chilly, and it felt good having Philip's arms around her, his face nestled on her neck as he brushed her hair aside. She absorbed this warmth without saying anything, and then turned to face him, smiling joyfully up at him.

"Take care of me, Philip. The only baby years I've had are those Clarence and Miss Edna had time to give. As a child, I was always left to make my own decisions. Let me be your baby, your little girl, your wife, and the mother of your children."

"Mera, you are saying that you'll marry me?"

"Yes, Philip, I will be proud to be your wife."

He took a small jewelry box from his pocket and re- moved a ring that housed a 2 karat diamond in the center, and four emeralds on each side: "I prayed that you'd say yes, so I had this ring made from one of your sketched model's hand. It looked like you."

They were both so excited that it took both of them to slide the ring onto her finger.

*   *   *

Pamela appeared nervous and declared: "Where are they? Their food is cold, and it's time to pick up JJ."

"JJ is spending the night with my parents, remember?" Joel reminded her.

"They're coming now," Phyllis said, and her face lit up with anticipation along with the rest of the group, as the love birds took their seats at the table again. Evelyn was too

278

excited to wait for the announcements and asked them: "Well, don't keep us waiting."

Philip kissed Mera passionately, as he lifted her left hand for everyone to see her ring: "Mera has consented to become my wife." He had to pause momentarily for the applause and then he told them: "Three weeks from today, at twelve o'clock, we will exchange our wedding vows with uncle Zech officiating."

"Mera's biological father will give her away. Of course, we'll go to Pittsburgh this Friday to convince him" He nudged Mera to fill in the rest. "Speak up, sweetheart."

"I'm sure that Clarence will meet us in Pittsburgh for he has a great deal of influence over dad. My mother will go along if dad insists, but it will take some talking to get them to come out. I realize that my sister can't stand me, but I'd like to ask her to be my matron of honor. If she refuses I'd like to ask Mom to do it since she's now my best girl friend."

"I'd be delighted to do it," Phyllis replied.

"I would also like two other brides maids, and hope you two ladies will consent to do it." Evelyn seemed delighted that she'd been asked and consented immediately, but Pam was an if, or maybe.

"I understand if you don't want to do it," Mera told her.

Pam looked at Joel and then bit her lip to hold back team. "I'm not sure I'll be around in three weeks, or haven't you heard that Joel and I are possibly getting a divorce..."

Mera appeared to be in shock for a moment and then she spoke directly to Pam: "You know, Pam, that the life we live today is a reflection of the choices we made earlier. I apologize for my impatience with you, but I feel that the statements you make sometimes are immature. Instead of showing my impatience, I, of all people, should've recognized your cries for help."

"You married a doctor, but you wanted him to be your 'boy toy'. Pull him out of the toy box when you're ready to play. Life doesn't work that way. But that is not entirely your fault. Your parents and grand parents made you think you were a Jewish princess."

"Doctors are people, too. They need to be praised and loved by their wives. Can you imagine how depressing it must be to your husband to look at those whining females all day who resent loosing their attractiveness, some rejected by their lovers and need to cry on their doctor's shoulder."

"Can't you imagine how much he needs to loose all that tension in the arms of an understanding wife who will sooth all his stress away. Tell him you love him and appreciate him instead of pouting like an immature spoiled brat. Use the brains God gave you and not the bitter bigotry taught to you by your senior family members."

"Dr. Markowitz loved you once, and I'm sure the embers of that love can be rekindled with the proper fuel. We all love you. Remember that the choice you make today will be the consequences you'll live with tomorrow."

"I will make a three o'clock appointment for fittings at Emerald Fashions cutting room. I'd like to believe that you'll be there, Pam."

Mera got up, went to Pam's chair and hugged her tightly as Pam wiped the overflow of tears from her eyes and cheeks, and then Mera took Joel's arm and placed it around Pam's shoulder, before walking back to her seat.

"Why don't we forget the dessert, we're all too fat and sleepy anyway, and I have to put together a guest list."

Philip agreed, but before getting up, he asked the guys: "Joel, you're my best man, right?'

"I wouldn't have it any other way," Joel said.

"Marty, you'll be a groomsman with Mera's brother Clarence?"

"Absolutely," Marty said.

"Thank you all for the lovely and unusual gifts, and for the Abraham and Isaac Sacrifice celebration," Mera teased. They all laughed as they walked out.

"Dad, take the claim check and take us home. I want to sit in back with my angel," Philip said.

"When we get home, I'd like to ask a favor of you two over coffee please," Mera announced.

*   *   *

The Ravins and Mera sat in the breakfast room, stirring their coffee to the taste they all preferred before Mera took a sheet of paper from her purse.

"Mom, Dad, I'd like you to sell the Emerald Castle," Mera requested.

"The decorators are not even through decorating it yet, and you want to sell that beautiful place..." Phyllis appeared shocked.

"Yes, ma'am. Men don't appreciate women being the forerunners in their married lives, especially with large entities such as homes, so I'd like to sell the Castle to Philip for two and a half million dollars. Maybe he'll let me live there with him."

Philip seemed shocked that he'd have to spend that much money so soon: "Two and a half million. Money doesn't grow on trees, you know."

"Philip, I'm skinning this cat, and I haven't asked you to hold his tail. We'll sign the papers Monday and the closing papers just after the wedding, that way it will by California law become community property, and he'll let me live there with him."

Ian looked at Philip for approval, but Mera had just the right words to change that idea.

"Philip is not the boss of me. He won't get that honor for three weeks. So here are the names I'd like you to deposit the money into trust accounts for. With Philip and my

281

name, of course. These are our four children."

"But they are not born yet," Phyllis complained.

"So, who will know the difference? The bank doesn't ask for ages in a trust of this sort, and don't forget that the Emerald Corporation owns the bank. So deposit one half million in each child's account, and we'll add to them annually. By the time they are ready for college, they can pay their own way or buy their first home."

"What do we do with the half million that is left?" Ian asked.

"Pay yourselves for the real estate transaction, of course."

"We wouldn't do that," Ian declared with determination.

"Then find a piece of property that is large enough for an elementary school, a Junior High and a senior high school, and we'll use the extra money to buy the property and build schools for exceptional children. We'll talk more on this subject when the wedding is done. By the way, you are going to live with us, aren't you?"

Phyllis spoke up first: "No, sweetheart. You've remodeled our home and made everything here so attractive that we will just really enjoy the beauty and tranquility here."

"What will we do with so many bedrooms?"

"I'm sure with the kind of friends you have, there will always be someone staying over. Especially those entertainers who snoop around seeking newly arranged music.

Ian counted on his fingers. "From where I sit, I can see five of the bedrooms permanently occupied at all times. I really like the private school idea. Advanced kids always have a hard time, not just with their peers, but the teachers are impatient because they have to always be on guard. Philip graduated from high school at sixteen. Joe and Marty are two years older than he is. And you are just eighteen and will be receiving a Doctorate Degree within a few months."

"Then you think it is a good idea?"

"Absolutely, we have four grandchildren who will probably need the school if they come out like their parents," Ian agreed.

Mera stood up and hugged her foster parents, thanking them for all that they'd done to make her life bearable, for loving her, and having faith in her. And most of all, for taking the reins of her company when it was about to overpower her. "Thank you, too, Philip, for the obvious changes you made through sacrificing, for loving me, and wanting me to be a permanent part of your life." She kissed him the way he liked to be kissed.

*   *   *

At seven a.m. on the day of Mera's wedding, four lovely women were sitting in the waiting room of Dr. Markowitz's office. The ladies were Mera, her mother and sister and Phyllis.

Momentarily. Dr. Markowitz and his nurse came into the room. The doctor had a rolled up chart in his hand.

"Good morning, ladies."

All of the ladies spoke to the doctor and his nurse with bewilderment on their faces.

"For the two of you who don't know me, I am Dr. Joel Markowitz. I don't suppose Mera has told you why you are here."

Mera's sister spoke up in a know everything manner: "It has something to do with the wedding, I think."

"Carol, would you take Mera in and get her ready." The doctor waited until Mera and his nurse disappeared, and then he began to explain.

"Yes, your being here has something to do with the wedding. Mera has told me how she's has had to fight off sick sex offenders everywhere she's lived before. Some of these ignorant bastards wanted to get even because she rejected their advances, so they tried to defame her by spreading filthy gossip that she was sexually active.

"Do you all understand what I am saying?" The three women bowed their heads affirmatively.

"Mera wants to give her new husband a signed and witnessed affidavit verifying that she has never been with a man. I have here a chart I'd like you ladies to inspect. The one on the left shows a woman who's sexually active, probably married, but the one on the right is the virgin. This small balloon-like membrane is the hymen, which is always broken on sexual penetration. You've probably heard it called the cherry. Now if you will all follow me, we will examine Mera for the truth of her purity."

*   *   *

"Mera is getting dressed, but I want you three ladies to look at these illustrations and make up your minds which one most nearly look like our little Prophetess."

"I never doubted that she was a virgin," Phyllis said, and she signed the top witness line.

Mera's sister signed next. "I hope she will forgive me. It's not easy trying to care for a teenager and work."

Mera's mother signed last; but before she did, she prayed to God: "God, you know I have a lot of years to make up. Help me in my ignorance. I don't know the difference between a Prophetess and something evil, I was so afraid of my own beautiful baby." And then she signed with tears running down her face.

*   *   *

The Mandeville Temple was buzzing with guests and security guards. The sanctuary was decorated with white mums, red roses and green fern. A gold carpet embraced the center aisle.

The grooms ushered Mera's mother and Philip's mother down the aisle to their seats, and then they escorted aunt Winnie, Mera's grandmother, and a number of female special guest relatives on both sides.

Philip and Joel appeared from the West anthrax, behind uncle Zech, and took a center place down front facing the audience. Soon, and as a solemn march was played on the piano by Mera's uncle, Clarence came down the aisle escorting Evelyn, and Marty and Pam followed close behind. They parted at the front and each went to the proper side catering to the bride or the groom.

The organ began to play the wedding march, and the audience stood; a vision of loveliness appeared in the doorway of the center aisle on the arm of her father. Mera's father was a medium height man, appearing to be about five feet eleven inches; his brown, almost red complexion was capped by a partial head of semi-curly hair.

When the couple reached the last bench before going down front, Mera's father stopped as uncle Zech asked: "Who gives this woman's hand in marriage?"

Mera's father spoke up: "Her mother and I do." He then raised her veil; Philip stepped forward to meet them and took Mera's arm, leading her back to face uncle Zech. The entire wedding party turned to face the podium.

The lovely couple sang their vows to each other in a rendition of "Endless Love."

Rabbi Zech continued reading the laws of marriage and the part that the Lord told Adam and Eve to be fruitful and multiply. He then asked if they had tokens to give to each other to seal their vows, and they both answered yes.

They heard the audience laughing, but the wedding party remained still for they knew what was going on that caused the laughter.

Down the center aisle Maximus strolled slowly, a small porcelain basket's handle between his teeth. The basket was white with pink roses painted on its sides, and a pink satin cushion on the bottom of the basket with two rings pinned to the cushion. There was a pink bow on the handle just below Maximum's mouth, and he turned his head from side to side as though allowing the audience to see what he was carrying.

People stood to get a good look at the dog, dressed in a white shirt with a black bow tie, and a black tuxedo vest. When he reached the wedding party, he went straight to Joel who removed the basket, and the rings, passing the one with women's diamonds and emeralds to Mera's sister.

Maximus sat down with his head held high, watching the rest of the ceremony.

*   *   *

The reception was so beautiful, and the MDs played for the entertainment; Mera's uncle had catered the after party, and the food was magnificent.

Mera and Philip danced with a number of people, but they finally lost themselves in each other's arms, and everyone knew instinctively that they were to be left alone.

Pamela appeared to be more at ease, and Joel danced with her a couple of times, their eyes glancing at each other in a newly found understanding.

Then came the bridal couple's getaway for their honeymoon, and the security whisked them out under cover, without allowing them to say their farewells.

*   *   *

December 1, 1951, at eight p.m., Mera told Philip that she was having pains fairly close together. Excited, Philip dialed Joel's number and waited for him to answer.

"Dr. Markowitz, here," Philip heard the familiar voice say over the phone.

"I hate to do this to you, Joe, but Mera is having contractions," Philip told him.

"Darn! I had planned to deliver her next week. Get her to the hospital. I'll call ahead and have everything set up for her. I'll see you there in about forty minutes."

Philip then called for an ambulance and notified the security team that it would be arriving soon. He then called his parents, and when the familiar voice answered, he told his mother that Mera was in labor.

"Good Lord, we'll be on our way as soon as we get dressed," he heard Phyllis say excitedly.

*   *   *

Mera saw a lot of lights and medical equipment as she looked around the snow white room. There were medical personnel rushing around dressed in green or blue, with a white gown covering their bodies, a facemask, and a matching cap covering their heads.

Nurses were scrubbing her with a solution that smelled kind of antiseptic, and then they painted her abdomen red and dressed her in a warm white gown, cap, and booties.

An intravenous fluid was started in the vein of one arm, and the arm tied to a splint so that she could not disrupt it.

Where is Philip, or Dr. Markowitz? Another pain came that took her breath away, and her mind was temporarily on her babies and not the men who had not shown up yet. The babies had not been doing their usual gymnastics, and this made her worry.

Philip entered about that time, his brow wrinkled with concern. "Are you OK, baby?" he asked.

"I am now that you're here. Where is my doctor?"

"He's scrubbing. He'll be here any moment now," Philip told her.

"Are you helping him?" Mera asked.

"No, I'm not allowed; Dr. Seymour is assisting, but I

have to wear these scrubs to keep down infections."

"The babies are not tap dancing."

"That's because they are naturally lining up to make their exit through the birth canal," Dr. Markowitz responded to Mera's question; he and Dr. Seymour had just entered, and the nurses were helping them put on their surgical gloves. He removed the sterile stethoscope and checked Mera's abdomen for signs of fetal heartbeats.

"There they are, hammering away," he said. He then opened the sterile C-section tray, removed a sharp instrument, and gently pricked Mera's abdomen with it. "Do you feel this, Mera?"

"No, I don't feel anything."

"Good. I think we are ready to get those little angels out here. Somebody told me that the whole gang is here awaiting this event. You are a very popular little mama. Phil, are you going to handle this?"

"No problem, it's an almost everyday occurrence."

"Those times are not your own wife. Bail out if it gets too heavy."

For the next thirty minutes, there was low murmuring amongst the operating team only. Mera understood some of what was being said: "Mop that, clamp that bleeder, number 6, and suction, please."

Finally, Mera heard Dr. Markowitz say: "Look at that, will you. Girl baby is actually pushing boy baby out of her way so she can come first. Time, please"

"10:15 p.m." Someone suctioned the girl baby, and then she cried loudly as though she was angry for what they had done to her.

Dr. Markowitz had to retrieve the second baby, for he was determined to exit through the birth canal and was heading away from the C-section opening.

"Whoa, little buddy, this is the way out," Joel said, and Mera heard another loud cry as the doctor asked for a time recording of 10:18 p.m.

The nurses took the babies to an area to be cleaned up and suctioned well. They then wrapped them in a light blanket and brought the screaming babies to their parents, while Drs. Markowitz and Seymour were stitching the birth exit on Mera's abdomen.

Upon a thorough examination of her babies, Mera smiled with delight: "Ianna has light brown hair and green eyes, and Terry has dark curly hair and blue eyes. What a mixed up assortment of you and me, Philip."

"They are so beautiful; thank you, angel, for my babies," Philip said as he watched the tiny bundles snuggle close to their mother, and the crying ceased.

But all tranquility must come to an end, for the nurses took the boy baby away when Mera was stitched and cleaned. According to Jewish custom, the boy had to be circumcised, and the screaming started all over again.

"Take him to his mother please, and he'll forget that he hurts." The nurse laid the screaming baby in the arms of his mother, and he soon quieted down after Mera kissed him and whispered sweet words to him.

Dr. Markowitz put his arms around Philip, who strained to keep back tears: "Congratulations, buddy. I believe they are the most beautiful babies I've ever delivered... Nurse, would you help that mob in the waiting room dress to come see the babies."

Ian and Phyllis, Marty and Evelyn, Uncle Zech and Winnie, and Pam all gathered around the new mother and babies, making all kind of cooing noises.

Philip proudly told them how the girl had pushed the boy out of the way so that she could be born first.

Uncle Zech looked at the girl baby: "You gave them names, didn't you?"

"Yes, Uncle Zech. She is Theresa Ianna, and he is Terrence Ian," Mera told him.

In his gaveled voice, and eyes twinkling as they do when he has just witnessed a miracle, Uncle Zech said:

"See how she looks at me with those bright green eyes. She's already trying to figure out where she is. That is why she had to be born first. She's the one who was foretold to interpret the second scroll given to the Prophetess Huldah by the Lord God Himself."

THE END